Angry Sins. Copyright ©2019 by Charles E reserved. No part of this book may be used o manner or format without written permission of the author, except in the case of brief excerpts for review.

If you wish to see other books you can visit my website at www.cenelsonbooks.com or my author page on Amazon. I hope you enjoy Angry Sins.

BONUS FREE STORY! Get a FREE COPY of THE WORST DETECTIVE STORY EVER WRITTEN by submitting your email in the pop-up on my website, www.cenelsonbooks.com.

ISBN: 9798868342127

Cover by Dusan Arsenic

~ANGRY SINS~

CHAPTER 1

A churning dust cloud chased the dented F-150 down the gravel road. The driver felt as conspicuous as the crop duster working the bean fields far to the south, but there was little he could do about it. It was early July, but the rain had been scarce, none in nearly two weeks, forcing farmers to unleash the sprinkling monsters that patrolled the flat fields.

He could see nothing out of the back window and not much in the side-view mirror. Someone could be right behind him. Like a cop. But he didn't think so. The land around Morris, Minnesota, was flat for miles, like much of the southwestern corner of the state. Nothing to stop the wind from marching an army of tumbleweeds across the land every day in the fall. He'd looked in all directions for a long minute before turning off the tarred county road onto the gravel. No one. Then again, it was early Sunday morning, not a time when he'd expect to see too many folks out and about, unless they were on their way to church.

And that was why he was moving along the gravel road at a good clip this morning, fishtailing on a couple of turns. He wasn't going to church, hadn't been except at Christmas last year. His mission was one of observation, at least to begin with. The couple that worked the farm half a mile to the north were regulars at First Lutheran in town. He had little doubt they would be going to the service this morning, but he wanted to be sure.

As he approached the white mailbox of the farm across the road and just south of his destination, he slowed. Glancing in his side-view mirror, he could see the dust cloud begin to envelop him. He cursed. Should have been here ten minutes ago. The night before had been a long one. A six-pack had not been enough to calm him so he had a few more, finally passing out. His phone had woken him—a call from a spammer. He had slammed down four aspirin and a glass of water, but there had been no time for a shower or coffee. His mouth was as dry as the roadbed, and his head roared like the tires on the gravel.

Pulling into the driveway with the white mailbox, he stopped after twenty feet, between overgrown lilac hedges, the trailing dust storm moving past. He cursed again. He was certain his truck would not be visible to someone coming out of the next driveway, but the dust he had kicked up would be easy to see. Hopping out of the truck, he hustled behind the hedge to the north.

A set of weathered outbuildings and what was left of a modular home stood at the end of the driveway behind him. Most of the windows had been broken long ago, the roof on the barn looking as if some giant creature had sat on one end. The modular home had been burned, the charred screen door still hanging from a hinge. He'd smoked dope there with friends, and had heard rumors of more than one couple using the dirty mattress in the bedroom. But the land was rented out now, and the buildings hadn't been used in years.

He peered through the lilacs at the driveway across the road as the last of his dust cloud settled. Pulling his phone from his pocket, he looked at the time. They should have left by now. He was thinking he must have missed them, or they weren't going, when the black Silverado nosed out from behind the steel storage building with the curved roof. The sun reflected off the windshield as it reached the end of the driveway. He couldn't see the driver of the truck, but he could make out the woman in the passenger seat. Sharon Rose.

Sharon Rose taught third grade at Jefferson Elementary in Morris. Fifty-six, she had been a teacher for thirty-four years. She had let her short brown hair go gray this year and had put on a few pounds after cutting back on her exercising. She felt a little bad about it, like she was letting herself go, but her husband hadn't said a word. Sharon had been a third-grade teacher for four years, moving to elementary school from the middle school. She reasoned the smaller children would be easier to handle than the swearing brats in the middle school, and they were, but her enthusiasm for teaching had not returned. Sharon planned to retire after the next school year.

John Rose was her husband. A big man with a square face, he had grown up in the area and still worked a good portion of the farm as well as running a herd of dairy cows. It was a fair-sized property, nearly six hundred acres. John had farmed it all at one time but now let the government pay him to not farm eighty acres of swampy land south of the homestead. In addition, five years ago, he had rented out another 160 acres.

John's face was worn from the years in the sun, deep furrows in his forehead and on the back of his neck. He too had put on a few pounds in the last few years, but when he looked in the mirror he still saw the high school running back who had no problem getting a cheerleader on his arm. John had noticed the transformation of his wife, making it easier for him to justify his liaisons with the waitress at the Sidetrack Café in town.

The F-150 driver moved to the end of the hedge, watching the cloud kicked up by the Silverado diminish until it was a puff on the horizon. Time to do this. He hopped into his truck, backed out onto the road, and drove the thirty yards to the Roses' driveway. About twenty-five yards in, the driveway began a large loop that ran in front of the barn, along a white picket fence that bordered the yard in front of the house, and then began to curl back out toward the road, passing a two-car garage with a tin roof and a large Quonset hut. Where the driveway began its loop, it branched off to the right between a grain bin and the barn. Farther to the right were a small red wooden shed and a vacant pig barn. The F-150 pulled up next to the barn, out of sight of anyone in the house.

The driver parked and shut off his engine, and then reached between his legs for the pistol stored under his seat. He stared at it, thinking about the hours he had spent shooting the gun and imagining this moment. He lifted the weapon with his right hand, checking to see that it was loaded, though there was no real reason to do so. Just stalling. He had checked it a dozen times before he left. Laying the gun flat in his palm, he lifted it toward his face. It felt heavier than he remembered.

He got out of the truck and pulled on a sweatshirt, flipping the hood over his cap. Time to do this. He closed his door, took a step, and stopped. The gun was in his right hand, hanging at his side, and he wasn't sure what to do with it. Couldn't just walk across the yard with it swinging at his side. Thinking about how he had seen people on television tuck their pistols into their pants, behind their backs, he nosed the barrel of the gun under the waistband of his jeans. It was uncomfortable, the butt of the gun digging into the small of his back. He pulled his sweatshirt over the gun and moved to the corner of the barn.

Leaning forward, he peered at the two-story house. The siding was painted white, green shutters next to the windows. The asphalt roof looked new. There were two doors on the front of the house. The first, closest to him, was behind an open porch with four deck chairs. The floor of the porch was painted white like the house, the chairs in pairs on either side of the door. The second door was at the far end, a sizable vegetable garden pushing up against the yard just beyond. Two cement steps with black wrought-iron railings led up to the door. A limestone walkway with miniature rosebushes standing guard cut across the yard from the door to the gate in the picket fence. The grass in the yard was turning brown and crunchy, patches of clover with white flowers scattered about.

The driver could see he would be exposed as he crossed the yard, but there wasn't much he could do about that. The big oak in the front yard would hide him from someone looking out an upstairs window for a good portion of his approach, but it would be hard for anyone on the first floor to miss him. He surveyed the yard, looking for an alternative route to the house, but came up with nothing better. The driver took a breath and ran.

* * *

Blake Rose was the only person in the house. His room was on the second floor and faced the back, to the south. The sun was just nudging around the edges of the window shade. His mother had come up an hour ago and knocked on his door, asking if he would go to church with them. He hadn't bothered to answer.

Blake and his buddies had cruised through Marshall the night before, nearly ninety miles to the south, drinking whiskey from a bottle one of his friends had stolen from his father. There was a four-year college in Marshall, and they were looking for lonely college girls, but those girls were mostly gone for the summer. A car with high school girls caught their attention at the stoplight by the movie theater as they pulled alongside. The boys rolled down their windows, trying to get the girls to respond, showing them the whiskey bottle. The girls looked at each other and laughed before giving the boys the finger and turning right. The boys called them whores and bitches until the car behind them honked. They sped away, Blake leaning out the window to give the driver the finger. The trio finally ended up at the park, finishing the bottle, Blake getting home about one.

Blake was the quarterback for the local junior college football team. He was over six feet tall, and his frame was filling out. Blake had received a couple of DII scholarship offers after high school. He was excited about the offers, but his father was not. John Rose knew the boy would grow and that the big schools would come calling, and after that the pros. He said the boy needed to bide his time at the JC. Get better and bigger. The junior college was happy to offer him a scholarship and keep him in town. With Rose at quarterback, the school had won the conference, losing in the finals of the state playoffs. Everyone figured they would have a real shot at the national title in the fall.

Blake was unable to sleep after his mother had woken him with her knocking. At the sound of his parents leaving the house, he trudged down the hall to the bathroom where he leaned on the sink for a moment before reaching for the knob of the shower. Knocking. Someone at the front door. The doorbell began to sound. Blake cursed as he shrugged on the bathrobe hanging on the back of the bathroom door and went down the stairs.

The stairway ended at one corner of the kitchen. There was a wall there with a worn maple bench against it, pegs in the wall to the side of the bench for coats and caps. A full-length cupboard of honey-stained hickory blocked Blake's view of the kitchen as he reached the landing. He stepped out from behind it and looked toward the north end of the room.

* * *

The driver peered through the glass of the outer door into the empty kitchen. The adrenalin was flowing now, and he was perspiring heavily, the sweatshirt soaked. He was tempted to open the door and go inside searching for his target. The door would likely be open, but he thought it would be easier to bring his prey to him. The driver knocked on the door, rattling the glass, and waited a moment before doing it again. No one was coming. He pressed the doorbell button, holding it down, the buzzing inside insistent. Finally, he thought he could hear steps inside.

As Blake appeared in front of the bench, the driver took a quick look and then turned away. Blake was wearing a bathrobe, but it hung open, revealing navy boxers. His legs were toned, muscular, as was what the driver could see of the boy's chest. His neck was thick, seeming to drop directly from the hinges of his jaws to his shoulders.

The driver tensed as Blake approached, perspiration

beading on his forehead. Something told him to go, to turn and run, but he did neither. His right hand moved to the back of his pants, feeling for his pistol.

* * *

The sweatshirt had been a mistake. Sweat was running down his nose, in his eyes, stinging. What a stupid thing to wear on a hot day – with a cap. Stupid. And the driver was thinking that Blake had the same thought as he had stopped coming toward the door. What kind of an idiot wears a sweatshirt on a day like today? The driver took his hand off the pistol and turned away from the door. He lifted his sunglasses so he could reach under with his sleeve to wipe away the sweat. Pushed his glasses back on, reaching for the pistol as he turned toward the door.

Blake pushed open the screen door. "Yeah?"

The driver grabbed the door by the edge and pulled it all the way open, stepping around it, the gun in his right hand coming up as he did. Rose's eyes went from sleepy to wide awake at the sight of the weapon, and he raised his hands, backing away. Then he looked up and dropped his hands.

"What is this?"

The man didn't do or say anything for a moment, like he was thinking. And then a weird crooked smile spread across his face. He lifted the barrel so the gun was pointed at Blake's forehead and fired.

The driver was startled by how much louder the boom of the gun was in the house. Blake fell backward, the top of his head hitting the side of the stove, leaving his head cocked at a weird angle. The driver walked forward, standing over Blake. Blake's mouth was open, his breaths short and raspy. His eyes were wild as his mind tried to catch up with what was happening. The driver knew this was not enough. On the counter next to the oven was a butcher-block stand holding a set of knives. He tucked the gun back into his pants, stepped over Blake, and pulled a carving knife from the stand. Bending over, he looked into the boy's lifeless eyes.

"This is for her." He drove the knife into Blake's groin.

The driver straightened up, looking down at Blake. The blood running down his face, the knife protruding from his groin. He'd thought he would feel elation at this point. He'd dreamed about it, imagined it. But though there was relief, and some sense of satisfaction, of justice served, there was no elation. The driver dampened a dishtowel by the sink and wiped down the knife handle, leaving the knife in place. He wiped off the edge of the door and the door handle as he left, carrying the towel with him. As he was wiping the railing, he heard a sound. A vehicle approaching.

* * *

The nose of the black Silverado appeared on the road from behind the feed bin, the dust following and then moving past as the truck turned into the driveway. John Rose slowed at the sight of the truck parked by the barn. He thought he had seen the truck before, but he wasn't certain.

The church service had been run by middle school students as part of a confirmation project. They were handling everything from ushering to singing to the sermon. John had moaned when he looked at the bulletin after he sat down before the service. He wasn't crazy about going to church in the first place, and he'd sat through a student-run service before. When the opening song by the student choir was nearly over, he turned to his wife and told her he could not sit through any more. They needed to leave.

John pulled up in front of the garage. A man was walking toward them. He was in jeans and a sweatshirt and was carrying what looked like a towel. He wondered if the guy was here selling drugs to Blake. Ball cap with a flat brim, sunglasses, sweatshirt hood pulled up. He'd shouted at his son after he found some pills and dope in his room. How Blake would ruin his chance for any big-time scholarship. How he could kiss the pros goodbye. But the kid thought he knew it all. John climbed out and walked around the back of the truck. The man came directly up to John, stopping a few feet away.

"Who the hell are you?" John asked.

The man, his head down so John was looking at the bill of his cap, shook his head slightly. John was staring at the man, eyes narrowing, head back, when the man pulled a gun from behind his back. Frozen, John watched the gun rise to eye level. The man's head came up, and he shot John in the forehead.

Sharon had watched from her seat. She pushed her door open and swung her legs out, but that was as far as she got. Flinching at the sound of the shot, her head snapped back. Her eyes followed her husband's body as it disappeared behind the truck and then she looked up to see the gun in her face.

CHAPTER 2

The phone on the nightstand by his head was buzzing again. Peter "Doc" Hunter was lying on his back, naked, his lower half covered by a teal cotton sheet. He pushed himself up to a sitting position, his bare legs swinging out from under the sheet. Elbows on his knees, he covered his eyes with his hands, trying to block out the light creeping in around the shade. The phone had stopped for a moment, and he hoped it was a telemarketing call, or maybe his mother, but then it started again. Had to be Trask.

Don Trask was the lead agent for the Minnesota Bureau of Criminal Apprehension (BCA). At forty-seven and a solid 210 pounds, he was fifteen years Doc Hunter's senior, but Doc was likely the only agent in the BCA that Trask couldn't take in a wrestling match, although Trask would never have admitted that. Trask's office was in St. Paul. As head of the BCA, he handed out assignments for the agents.

"Hunter."

"Doc? You up yet?"

Doc looked over his shoulder at the shape of the hips under the sheet. "A while ago."

"I probably don't want to know," said Trask.

"Probably not. What time is it?"

"Almost noon."

"Shit. I got a tee time in an hour. I got to get going."

"The only place you're going is to Benton. You know where that is?"

"Hell, no. Don, it's my day off. I got a tee time at the Legacy. You know how hard that is to get in the summer?"

"The Legacy? Isn't that in Brainerd?"

"Yeah."

"And you're at home?"

Doc lived in a townhouse just west of St. Cloud. The townhouse was nothing special, but it had a spare bedroom where he stored his golf equipment and a tuck-under two-car garage where he could keep his Acura and pickup. The garage was heated, which was nice in the winter. The townhouse was part of an association that took care of snow shoveling and lawn mowing, which was a big plus.

"Yeah, I'm at home."

"That's got to be over seventy-five miles from you, Doc. You'd never make your tee time now, anyway."

"Hell I wouldn't."

Trask had ridden with Doc once. Once had been enough. The guy probably could make it. "Doesn't matter. You're going to Benton. It's south of Morris a little way. I'll text you the address. It's a farm. Three dead."

"A farm. Crap. Have they got pigs? I hate the smell of those damn pigs."

"I don't know if they have pigs, but what they do have is a mess, and cops who don't know what the hell to do."

"Who's on it? Morris?"

"The county sheriff."

"The sheriff? That's got to be Stevens County. Is it Stevens County?"

"Stop your whining. I told them you'd be there by two. Get moving."

Doc was going to whine some more, but Trask had disconnected. "Piss."

"What is it?" said a sleepy female voice.

Leaning back, Doc stroked the nicely shaped posterior under the sheet. The woman released a soft moan that made him wonder if there was time for something else before he left. "You need to leave," said Doc. "I've got to go to work."

He padded naked across the carpeted bedroom floor to the attached bathroom. He showered and shaved and walked out of the bath with a towel wrapped around his waist. He was thinking that maybe he could get a little dirty again before he left, but his companion was gone. Wearing khaki shorts and a red polo with a Nike logo and no socks, he made his way to the kitchen, where he heated the remains of yesterday's coffee in the microwave and quickly blended a spinach and mixed-fruit smoothie. Doc gulped the smoothie before pouring the coffee into a travel mug.

Doc slid on sunglasses and took a sip of coffee as he headed west out of St. Cloud. His big hands lay on top of the steering wheel of his Acura as he wiggled his back and shoulders just a bit. Getting comfortable. The rest of Doc was big like his hands. He stood six foot four, with broad shoulders. His legs and arms were muscular and toned, reflecting his regular workouts and tae kwon do sessions. Doc's face was hairless and gentle, except for a nose that had been broken more than once. The thick sandy-brown hair above his broad brow had crept down over his ears and collar in the last half year. His barber had told him longer hair was the style now, and it did seem to attract a little more attention from the ladies, but he wasn't yet convinced it was worth the hassle. It was turning blonder as the summer rolled on, and getting a little wavy. The blond was OK, but he wasn't sure he cared for the wavy. Doc had sleepy blue eyes that had people constantly asking if he was tired.

The terrain flattened as he drove west, the trees thinning at the same time. Hills and streams and lakes disappeared as the farmland ate them up. County Road 28 out of Sauk Centre had that shimmering mirage-type look, and the people on the sidewalks in Glenwood were all moving slowly, heads down, like they were walking into a wind. The temperature gauge on his dash said it was ninety-two. Hot. In Morris he went southeast on 9 and then did a quick right so he was going south on 59. After eight miles his GPS was telling him he should turn off to the right, but he never trusted the damn thing, and there wasn't a place to turn. A block farther on he saw a gravel road, slowed nearly to a stop, and looked at the map. Had to be it.

In a minute he was moving west, listening to the gravel sandblast the underside of his car, watching the dust in his rearview mirror, knowing the car wash he had spent twelve bucks on the day before had been a waste of money. The road made a slow curve to the south. He glanced at the map again to see if he was going the right way; the GPS woman hadn't yelled at him since he turned off. Then he saw the flashing lights, maybe half a mile up ahead.

A Stevens County cop car was at an angle across the

road. An officer opened his door and stepped out as Doc approached, lifting his arm in the air like he was a Nazi, which Doc didn't doubt, knowing the sheriff. Doc stopped, leaving the car running, and waited for the cop to stroll up. He rolled down his window. The cop had only been outside for a minute, but he looked hot already, perspiration forming on his forehead. A name tag pinned just above his shirt pocket said Deputy Jones.

"I'm sorry, sir, but you'll have to go back."

The heat outside was making no secret that it wanted into Doc's car. "Doc Hunter, BCA." Doc handed the cop his ID. Jones looked at it, said, "Just a minute," and walked back to his vehicle while Doc rolled his window back up. Jones sat in the driver's seat with his legs out the side, talked on the radio for a minute, and then returned and handed Doc his ID.

"Go ahead, Agent."

Doc was going to ask the cop what was ahead, but the man was already making his way back to the air-conditioned interior of his vehicle. He drove past the cop car, a little too fast, dust kicking up behind. He watched the cop in his mirror trying to wave away the cloud and chuckled.

After a little over a quarter mile, Doc could see cars parked on either side of the road. He pulled in behind a maroon highway-patrol car and looked to his right. There were two cops standing in the driveway of the farm. Doc didn't know either of them. They looked hot. One was highway patrol, holding his big-brimmed maroon hat in his hand. Stupid hats, thought Doc. The brim might have helped keep the sun away on a day like today, but they were too damn hot to wear. Totally useless as far as Doc could figure, but that was the highway patrol for you.

Doc stepped out onto the gravel and crunched his way to the end of the driveway, walking in the grass around the end of the yellow tape tied between the mailbox and an empty flowerpot. The cops stopped talking and watched him approach.

"The Beach Boys playing here this afternoon?" said the patrolman with a grin. The man's shirt was stained with sweat.

Doc smiled. "Sure are. You must be here to set up the satellites. Try to keep them clean, would you?" The man lost his grin, but the county cop next to him snickered. Doc turned to the county cop and said, "Where can I find the sheriff?" The cop turned and pointed to the two men standing in the shade of the barn.

As Doc walked down the drive toward the barn, he glanced to his left at the pickup parked in front of the garage. There was a body on the ground behind it, and as he went a little farther, another—a woman in a dress. Took a few more steps to get a better look at the woman.

"Hunter, come over here, out of the sun," ordered Stevens County sheriff Larry Pickus. Pickus was in his early fifties, shorter than average, his average build turning puffy. His blue eyes were round and open wide, like he was always surprised. Doc had worked with Pickus a few times and found the man too strict for his tastes, and he guessed most of Pickus's staff felt the same. Even today, over ninety and on a Sunday, they were all in full uniforms. Long-sleeved shirts and sweating like the proverbial pig.

"Howdy, Sheriff."

"Hunter, this is Ben Kuck," said Pickus, nodding to the tall, thin man next to him. "He's the lead investigator on this."

Doc eyed the man, who looked about to wilt like the crops Doc had seen on the way. He had a beagle nose and tired blue eyes in a long face. His brown hair was thinning and sticking to the top of his head like he might have just gotten out of the shower. "Call me Doc," said Hunter as he extended his hand. Pickus refused to call Doc by his nickname and did not approve of the request of his investigator now.

"You've had a look, I take it?" Doc asked.

Kuck turned to look at the truck and said, "Yeah. The two out here are John and Sharon Rose. Their boy, Blake, is the one inside. He's in the kitchen. Just inside the second door." Kuck pointed toward the house and they turned. "They were all shot close range. The boy was stabbed, too."

"Anyone else here?"

"Nope. Blake was their only kid. He went to the JC in Morris. This would have been his second year."

"Weapons?"

Kuck took a breath and wiped the moisture from his forehead with his shirt sleeve. "The knife is still there. No sign of the gun."

"Who found them?"

"A woman from their church, Fran Hansen. She had borrowed a couple of books from Sharon and was going to return them at church, but the Roses took off early. She drove over after the service," said Pickus. The sheriff had a full head of blonde hair, short on the sides and longer on top, with bangs on his high forehead. He ran his hand back over the top of his head now, his sweat-damp hair sticking up afterward.

"OK. I need to talk to her. Where does she live?"

"In town," said Pickus. "Here's her information." He removed a small notebook from his back pocket and ripped out a sheet, handing it to Doc.

Doc looked at the sheet. He put it in his pocket, and then looked toward the house and back to the bodies by the truck. "What do you think happened here, Ben?"

"I'm guessing the killer took out the boy, was leaving, and maybe was surprised by the Roses coming home."

That sounded right to Doc, but he said, "Why do you say that?"

"I go to the same church the Roses do. They left only about ten minutes into the service."

"Why'd they leave?"

"Don't know. The kids were running the service and some people just don't like that. Kind of feel like they're getting cheated if the pastor isn't there to give the sermon. I know John didn't especially like going, anyway."

"Hmm. So, you're thinking whoever killed the kid planned to do it when his parents were gone and got surprised by them? The killer knew the parents would be away?" All three men were looking at the bodies by the truck now.

"That would be my guess."

Doc turned to look at Pickus. "That sounds pretty reasonable to me, Sheriff. You got anything to add?"

"The county ME has come and gone, but said he'd like to get these bodies out of the heat as soon as he can. He's only ten minutes away."

"Sure. Why don't you give me fifteen minutes and then you give him a call to come back," said Doc. "He say anything?"

"Looks like a small-caliber weapon. Close-range deal like Kuck said."

"He give you an estimate on time of death?"

Pickus opened his mouth to answer, but Kuck spoke up. "They left church about a quarter to eleven. Ten minutes to get here, so I figure about eleven."

Doc caught a look from Pickus like he wasn't happy Kuck had cut him off, and Kuck saw it too, his gaze going to the ground.

"When will the crime-scene guys be here?" said Pickus.

"Should be soon," said Doc.

Pickus was antsy, like he had places to be. "What do you want us to do?"

"Give me a quick minute for a look, Sheriff, while I think about that, and I'll be right back." In other words, "wait here until I tell you." Pickus didn't look happy with Doc's reply, and Doc didn't blame him. It was hot, even in the shade, and not a breath of wind. Long-sleeved shirts, long pants. Not fun.

Doc walked to the truck and looked at the back tires. Tried to follow the tire tracks backward from the truck, but the dry ground made it nearly impossible. Looked at the way the wheels were turned and then tried to plot a line. The truck had come in straight on but stopped in front of the open garage door. John Rose must have seen something or someone as he was driving in.

Doc thought about that for a minute and then started toward the house. The windows of the house were closed, he guessed to keep the hot air out; shades drawn on most but not all. He paused under the big oak in front, looking back at the Roses' truck. Easy to see someone crossing the yard from the driveway. The limestone path cut across the yard, grass growing between the stones. Doc walked it until it branched off toward the covered porch. Stopped for a moment looking at the door there, and then at the door ahead. He didn't think the porch door was the most-used entry to the house, but he didn't know. He wondered if the killer did. Doc walked on.

The screen door to the next door was closed, and Doc took a look through the glass. Someone standing here could see pretty clearly into the kitchen. He pulled latex shoe covers and gloves from his front pocket, put them on, and stepped inside, taking a moment to let his eyes adjust to the darker interior. Blake Rose was directly ahead, his head tilted to the side, eyes looking at nothing. There was a neat hole in the center of his forehead. Someone had been a good shot. Not easy to place one like that, even if you're close.

Doc crouched next to the body. The kid was wearing boxers and a ratty robe, the robe open, arms to his side. The knife was sticking out of his boxers like some weird kind of phallic symbol. Doc wondered if that wasn't part of it. He looked up at the stove behind the body and then stood, surveying the counter. Found the block where the knives were kept, with two empty slots. Looked at the handles of the knives still there and then back to the one protruding from Blake's crotch. Looked like they were from the same set. He took a stroll around the house. Went through the parents' bedroom on the main floor but discovered nothing of interest. Found Blake's room upstairs facing the backyard. The room was easy to identify. Unmade bed, as many clothes on the floor as in the drawers. Doc found a little pot in his closet, a couple of condoms in his nightstand.

There were two other bedrooms upstairs, one with a queen bed and an old dresser, the other used for storage. The shades on the windows in both rooms were closed. Doc walked back to Blake's door and wondered if he had heard the killer in the house from up here. Maybe came down the stairs and surprised him. Or had Blake been in the kitchen? Doc walked back downstairs and looked at the kitchen counter, walking over to the coffee maker. There was cold coffee in the carafe but no sign of a cup on the counter or table. There were half a dozen coffee cups in the dishwasher along with other dishes, but the counters were clear.

Doc went back outside, flipped his sunglasses back down, and walked toward where the sheriff and Kuck stood, pretty much where he had left them. Stopped halfway to the barn when he saw the BCA crime-scene van come down the driveway and walked to the back of the Roses' truck, standing next to John Rose's body. A short, skinny guy with going-everywhere black hair got out of the truck and walked up to him.

"Hey, Doc."

"Hey yourself, Carl." Carl Miranda looked about fifteen, but Doc figured he was somewhere in his mid-thirties. He wore black-framed glasses with thick lenses that made his eyes look twice their size. If the guy had an ounce of fat on him he hid it under his Minnesota Vikings T-shirt and cargo shorts.

"What's new?"

"Got a few dead people. Two out here and one in the house, second door. I'd appreciate it if you'd process them first before you go over the crime scenes. The ME wants to get them out of the sun."

"They getting a little ripe?" said Miranda with a small grin. "No problem."

Doc walked over to Pickus and Kuck. Pickus said, "The ME should be back any minute," and Doc replied, "I told the crime-scene guys to process the bodies right away. ME should be able to have them soon."

Pickus nodded. "So, what do you think?"

"I think Ben's got it right. The guy drove in after the parents had left, took care of the kid, and ran into the parents when he came out."

"You think it's one guy?"

"Or woman, yeah. Blake have a girlfriend or boyfriend?"

"Blake wasn't gay," said Pickus, like he'd been offended.

"Kid was the quarterback of the football team. A star player. He was likely going big."

Doc rubbed at the moisture on the back of his neck. He followed football, especially college ball, but he hadn't heard of Blake Rose. "OK. So, how about a girlfriend?"

Pickus looked at Kuck like he was warning the investigator not to say anything and replied, "No one steady that we know offhand, but we can check that out."

"Good. We need a list of friends and enemies of Blake and his parents. Anyone who could tell us about them."

"John Rose lived around this area his whole life. He knew a lot of people."

"OK. We'll need to look at his financial records, too."

"Financial records?" said Pickus. "I thought you said this was about someone killing the boy."

"I said the order of things seemed right. My guess is somebody wanted Blake dead, especially with the message of the knife in his groin, but we don't know. They could have come to kill John and were pissed he wasn't here. Threatened the kid with the knife to find out where his dad was. Or maybe Sharon was cheating at bridge and one of her bridge ladies didn't like it." Doc looked at Kuck. "It didn't look to me like anyone had gone through the place looking for valuables. The kid's wallet was on his dresser with a few bucks in it. Some jewelry that looked real to me in a case in the parents' bedroom."

"Yeah, I thought the same thing. Not a robbery."

Pickus frowned at Kuck. "OK, we'll start digging," he said. "Anything else?"

"Yeah. If the killer was waiting for the parents to leave before he or she went after Blake, then the killer was close by, in a vehicle or close to one. He drove in here, and he drove out.

Check out the driveways and ditches that have a concealed view of the Roses' driveway. Some place he could watch them leave."

"You think the killer knew them, knew their habits?" said Pickus.

"Yeah. Knew the parents went to church, and the kid didn't. Who would know that?"

Pickus was looking at Kuck again. "Kuck, it's your church. Why don't you start there? I'll get some guys looking for where the killer might have been watching, and I'll head into town, put together a list of people who knew John."

Pickus had a squinched-up look, and Doc said, "What?"

"John Rose was not well-liked. Rubbed people the wrong way. He's likely to have a lot longer list of people who didn't like him than anyone who was a friend."

"Why was that?"

"John was a bully. Almost like he wanted to piss people off. I know the Morris police had to break up a bar fight involving John Rose more than once."

"Hmm. I guess we better talk to the Morris police too."

"I can do that," volunteered Pickus. "What are you going to do, Hunter?"

"Anyone going to be at the junior college on a summer Sunday?" said Doc.

"Library is open pretty much year-round, and I think there might even be a few summer classes on Sundays," said Pickus. "I know my wife took one a year or two ago."

"OK. I need to make a call, and then I'll go talk to the Hansen woman. I'll head to the college after that. Here's my card." Doc gave Kuck one and Pickus several. "You can give these to your men. Have them call me if they find anything at all. You guys, too." Pickus and Kuck looked at Doc's card for a moment and then started to walk away. "Oh, Sheriff," Doc called. Pickus turned. "You might want to get these guys some water. It's damn hot out here."

Pickus looked at Doc, nodded, and walked away. Doc pulled his phone from his pocket.

"What hole you on?" said Trask.

"You mean golf?"

"Oh jeez. What have you got?"

"Three dead, shot at close range, each in the forehead. Pistol, small caliber. John Rose and his wife, Sharon, were ambushed beside their truck when they came home early from church. The kid, Blake, was some kind of hotshot football player for the JC in Morris, and someone did not like him. Shot him and put a carving knife in his groin."

"Someone was watching the place so they could get the kid alone?"

"That's what I think." Doc paused a moment and then added, "Could have been someone come to kill John Rose, found him gone, killed the kid and stabbed him in frustration, and then got John Rose when he came home."

"But you don't think so?"

"Not really."

"OK. You need any help?"

"I got the sheriff and his guys helping right now. I'll let you know."

"Hmm. You must be playing nice with the locals," said Trask. "OK, Sunday is my day off so don't call me anymore unless you think you might be about to get killed."

"You know, Trask, I'm supposed to be under the cool pines of the Legacy in Brainerd and not in some fucking hot dust bowl in the middle of the flatlands." There was no response.

Doc looked at his phone to see that Trask had disconnected. "Asshole." Doc was looking out at the green fields around the farm, imagining they were fairways, thinking if he could win a few golf tournaments, like the Minnesota Open, he could quit this job. A car went by the end of the driveway—the sheriff's car. Doc watched the cloud trailing behind. There was something Pickus wasn't telling him. Something important.

CHAPTER 3

Fran Hansen lived in a neat white rambler with a single-car garage attached by a breezeway. Her home was inside the V formed by Highway 59 and County 9 on the south end of Morris. The house was less than four blocks from First Lutheran, where she and the Roses went to church. Doc parked on the street and walked up the pansy-lined sidewalk to the front door. He pushed the button next to the door and chimes sounded inside.

Through a screen door with a glass panel, Doc could see an interior door painted a deep-water blue. He heard a latch being removed and then a deadbolt slide back. A small woman with short silver hair and reading glasses peered around the edge of the door.

"Fran Hansen? I'm BCA Agent Hunter. I'd like to talk to you about the Roses."

A grandmother's voice said, "Do you have some identification?"

Doc retrieved his ID from his wallet and tried to open the screen door to hand it to her but found the door locked.

"Just press it against the glass, young man. I can see perfectly fine."

Doc did as he was told. The woman opened the inner door enough so her head could poke through. She gave the identification a good review and then unlocked the outer door, pushing it open for Doc to enter. She closed and locked the door after him and then led him down a short hall with open shelves filled with small animal figurines. They ended up in a living room that faced the street. The area was L-shaped, with a gold floral-pattern couch and matching recliner, along with two beige side chairs and a coffee-table in the larger section. A dining table with drop-down ends, dark mahogany and polished to death with six matching chairs in the dining area. Doc was pretty sure every seventy-year-old lady in Minnesota had the same furniture.

"Why don't you have a seat? Would you like some water, young man? Or perhaps a beer?"

"A beer would be terrific."

"I'll be right back."

Doc could hear the refrigerator in the kitchen opening and closing, glasses rattling, and paper crunching. In a few moments, Hansen returned with a tray and set it on the coffee-table. On the tray were two glasses filled with dark beer, foamy, along with some crackers and spreadable cheese. Doc had been sitting in the lounger, loving the air-conditioning, but he stood when Hansen entered. She handed him a glass.

"I hope you like porter. A local brewery makes this, and I just fell in love with it. Help yourself to the crackers."

Doc took a sip of the beer. "This is very good."

"I know. They've got a good IPA too. We can try that next."

Doc smiled. "You're not trying to get me drunk are you, Miss Hansen?"

Hansen giggled, a little-girl giggle, putting her hand to her mouth. "Heavens, no. At least not yet anyway. And you can call me Fran."

Doc sat at the other end of the couch from Hansen and filled a plate with cheese and crackers. He didn't realize how hungry he was until he noticed his crackers and half the beer was gone. "So, Fran, as nice as this is, I'm afraid we need to talk about when you found the Roses today. Is that OK?"

Hansen took a long draw on her beer and looked out the front window before looking back at Doc. "Yes. It's so sad. I just wanted to return the books I borrowed from Sharon, and there they were. I thought John might have fallen or something at first, but when I got out of my car and walked up to him, I could tell he was dead. I walked around him and saw Sharon. I'm afraid it gave me a good fright. I got out of there as fast as I could."

"You didn't go in the house?"

"Heavens, no."

"You called the police when you got home?"

"Yes."

"What time was it when you found them?"

"Well, let's see. I had coffee and a cookie after the service. Talked to Delores Peterson for as long as I could stand it, picked up one more cookie for my walk, and left."

"You walked from church?"

"Certainly. No need to put more pollutants in the air, is there?"

"So, what time do you think you got back here?"

"It was ten past eleven. I remember because I decided to drive out there before lunch, and I looked at my watch so I'd be sure I wasn't disturbing her during their lunch."

"And how long a drive?"

"A little less than fifteen minutes, I'd say, although I'm sure my drive back was quicker."

Doc was about to ask a follow-up question but sensed the woman was thinking about saying something more.

"It's such a shame," she went on. "I mean, Sharon was such a good person. She was always helping at the church or at school. There wasn't anything she wouldn't volunteer for. Her husband was a real asshole, though. I'm not sure how she put up with him."

Doc almost laughed. "How was he an asshole?"

"Oh, you know. He just thought he was better than everybody else. Yelled at anybody who did anything he didn't like. I remember Sharon got him to help put up the Christmas tree at church one year, and he put the tree up crooked. One of the boys was trying to fix it and John yelled at the boy about it. The boy tried to explain that the tree could fall over. John swore at him and called the boy several names before calling us all idiots and stomping out. His boy's the same way."

"Blake was like that?"

"The apple didn't fall far from the tree, from what I heard." Hansen finished her beer and looked over at Doc, who still had a quarter of his left. "You want to try that IPA now?"

"Um, well, Fran, I'm kind of on duty."

"I've got chocolate cookies I made just yesterday."

Doc's tongue peeked out between his lips. "Oh man, you had me at IPA."

After another beer and several cookies, consumed at the kitchen table, Doc thanked her and stood to leave.

Hansen looked up at the man. "You're a big guy. Did you play football?"

"A little. I mostly golf now." Doc had started playing golf when he was five, putting and hitting balls on the range at his father's club. He caddied there when he was in middle school, golfing in the evening, and then played on the high school team. It sucks playing spring sports in Minnesota because it never really warms up until school is out and half the events get canceled because of snow. Doc was shooting par by the time he graduated, but he was a better football player, so he went to college on a football scholarship. Golf took a back seat in college, but after he finished his undergraduate degree, he started to get serious about it.

"What's your handicap?"

Doc looked at the small woman still seated at the table. From his experience, it was a pretty serious golfer who would ask about your handicap. "I'm a scratch golfer."

"My, I bet you hit them a long way. Eight was the best I ever did before I hurt my back."

The woman was a foot shorter than Doc and he figured he could blow her over with a big breath. "Wow! An eight. When was that?" Doc expected her to talk about when she was in college or high school, but she said, "Two years ago. Took up the game when someone asked me to join the church league about eight years ago. I liked the fact that I could drink beer and play at the same time, but the ladies didn't approve, so I joined the club in town. I was just getting into it when I hurt my back."

"Sorry to hear that," replied Doc. "So, what's the best course around here?"

She thought about that for a minute. "Well, they're all pretty flat, as you might imagine. I guess Wildwoods southwest of town is about the best. Not much in the way of woods but the rough is plenty wild. It's long, and the greens are small, but there's not much sand or water." She went to the refrigerator and removed another beer while she talked. "Sure you won't stay for just one more?"

Doc thought that if the woman was forty years younger, he'd be thinking about marrying her, or at least doing other things. He was afraid that if he had another beer it would lead to another, and then . . . He shook his head, grinning.

* * *

The community college was close, less than a mile north of Fran Hansen's house as the crow flies. But it had a big ag program, so it was surrounded by all kinds of farm fields in addition to the usual fields for recreation, so it was over two miles by road. The main building on campus was two stories and red brick, like just about every other school Doc had seen. It was shaped like an L, the short, single-story wing pointing north. The longer two-story wing went west. The parking lot was inside the L, with only about twenty vehicles present, most parked as close as possible to where the wings converged. That was where the main entrance to the college was, so Doc parked by the other vehicles and walked inside.

The cool air inside the building was welcoming, even after the short walk from the parking lot. He pushed his sunglasses up after he entered, letting his eyes adjust. Doc's shoes clicked on the shiny tan linoleum floor as he wandered, looking for someone or something to give him an idea of where to go. He saw no one, the hum of the air-conditioning the only sound, but did find a sign with an arrow. The sign said "Administration," and it pointed down the hallway that bisected the short wing of the building. He didn't really expect to find anyone there on a Sunday, but the door with the Administration placard on the wall next to it was open, and he walked in.

Immediately in front of Doc was a laminate counter, brochures about the school and various programs stacked neatly in racks on top. The counter was about at Doc's waist, a desk behind it. A stunning blonde who Doc guessed was maybe nineteen was sitting at the desk, looking at the phone in her hands. Her thick hair was parted in the middle, cascading over her shoulders like she was ready for a shampoo commercial. Her white, stretchy tank top was working hard, cleavage visible. Doc was thinking he should sign up for a quick class.

"Can I help you?" She looked up at Doc with bright blue eyes as she said it and put the inflection on *you*.

Doc pulled out his ID, holding it out for her to see, and said, "I'd like to see whoever is in charge."

"Um, I guess that would be Doctor Lester." The girl had put her phone up on the desk and it buzzed, but she didn't seem to notice.

Doc was thinking he could have some fun with this girl, and that she maybe wanted to, but said, "You think you could go get her for me?"

"Who?"

"Doctor Lester."

"OK." The girl pushed away from the desk, stood, and turned, walking down a corridor between some cubicles. She was wearing pink shorts that seemed to be doing a fine job as Doc watched her go. The girl disappeared around a corner, returning in less than a minute with a middle-aged woman in white slacks and a shimmery sleeveless navy blouse.

"Can I help you?" the woman said.

Doc held out his identification again. "I need to speak to someone about a student at the college. Would that be you?"

"I suppose so. I'm the assistant dean. Why don't you come with me?"

The woman turned. Doc stepped around the edge of the counter, gave a wink to the blonde, who was taking him in as he went past, and followed Lester to her office. She rolled her chair up to her faux-oak desk and leaned her forearms on the edge, folding her hands like she was going to pray. Doc sat in front of her desk in a red fabric chair with faux-oak arms matching the desk. He felt like he was ten years old and back in the principal's office for trying to see if the girl in front of him in class was wearing a bra, and if she was, if she really needed one.

"How can I help you, Mr. Hunter?"

"What is it exactly you do here, Mrs. Lester?" He surveyed the wall behind the woman, noting the pictures of her shaking hands with the governor and the prior governor and other people he didn't know but who looked important. There were a couple of framed degrees but no pictures that seemed to be family.

"I run the college academics. And it is Doctor Lester."

"Thanks, Doctor Lester. Do you always work on Sundays?"

"Not always. The administrators switch off. We like to have someone here when the school is accessible." She seemed a little put out and said, "Now, what is this about?"

"I'd like some information about one of the students here, a Blake Rose. Do you know him?"

"We have a student here with that name. What do you want to know?"

The woman was a frustrated bureaucrat, probably thought she should be dean or, more likely, running a four-year school somewhere. Couldn't get the job she wanted so she was going to show anybody she talked to how important she was. Doc could read the look on her face and the body language and knew a roadblock was coming, so he dived right in. "Blake Rose is dead and so are his parents. Murdered. I've got a killer running around loose here, and I need to know everything I can about Blake as soon as possible."

Lester's right hand combed her tight, curly black hair, her unfocussed brown eyes dropping to her desk. Um, OK." She turned to her computer and started typing. "Blake is, was, going into his second year. He didn't have a declared line of study. His grades last year were below average but that didn't really matter."

"Why is that?"

"He was the quarterback of the football team. Big stud here. The team is doing well, so he's not likely to have any issue with his grades." Lester leaned back in her chair and said, "This is going to be a big blow to that team. They were thinking about being national champions." She said it like she was almost happy about it.

"OK, well, I'd like to talk to any of his professors or staff that knew him. Would any of them be in today?"

Lester looked at the computer screen again. "I doubt it, but you might want to try the athletics area. The football coach is probably here. I think summer practice starts soon."

Doc leaned forward and said, "Did you know Blake? Know who any of his friends were?"

The woman hesitated, just for a second, and then said, "I did not know Mr. Rose."

"OK. Who did he hang with?"

"I have no idea."

She was back in her shell, and she was lying. "All right. Can you print me off a copy of his class schedule from last year, with his professors?"

The woman did not answer, but moved her mouse and hit a few keys. "The girl at the front desk will have it for you. Now, if that is all, Mr. Hunter..."

Doc looked at her for a moment, thought about pressing her, decided to come back if he needed to. He stood and said, "Here's my card. Please call me if you think of anything." He reached the office door and turned back. "And it's doctor."

"Pardon me?"

"Doctor Hunter. Thanks for your help."

Doc was a doctor—a doctor of divinity. He'd gotten his advanced degree at Luther College in Iowa after getting his undergraduate degree at the University of Minnesota. It was why he was called Doc, but not many people knew that. Trask and a few others. He realized before he started work on his thesis that he would never use his degree. He considered quitting the program at that point, but his father had always told him he should finish what he started, and his dad was a smart man. Hunter walked to the reception desk and said, "Do you have something for me?"

The tip of the girl's tongue poked between her lips, just a tiny bit, like she was thinking something naughty. She picked up the printout on her desk and handed it to Doc, who said, "Thanks."

"Cheryl," she said before he could leave. "I get off at six."

Doc said, "Uh, thanks, Cheryl. I'll remember that," and walked away.

CHAPTER 4

Doc thought about asking Cheryl if she could show him where the athletics department was but decided that might not be a good idea. He wandered through the building until, with the help of a couple of students and a janitor, he found it. It turned out that the school was actually three stories in back of the long wing, the athletic and farm fields spread out beyond. The athletic department offices, as well as the gymnasium, some weight rooms, locker rooms, and other offices, were on the ground level.

The sign on the door said "Coach Edwards." The opaque glass to the right of the door had several posters about football at the school as well as a printed sheet with the summer football practice schedule. Doc walked in to deliver the bad news.

A man in his late forties, with a shaved head and a crooked nose, looked up from his desk. He was wearing a faded gray T-shirt that said "Morris Football."

Doc introduced himself, showing his ID and sitting in one of the three chairs in front of the brown metal desk. The desk had several dents on Doc's side, like it had been kicked more than once. The desk had a chalky white laminate top with papers scattered across it, a wire inbox overflowing. The walls of the office were concrete block, painted a faint shade of gold, masking taped with Morris Football posters and white drawing-board sheets with lots of writing in red marker. A shoulder-level brown credenza had a trophy proclaiming Morris as the conference champions for 2018. He put his ID away and said, "Are you the head football coach?"

Coach Edwards had been writing something on one of the many sheets of paper on his desk when Doc entered, but now he sat back, twirling a pencil. Edwards had broad shoulders above a body that said he still exercised once in a while but that wasn't going to last much longer. "Yeah."

Doc waited for the man to go on before he said, "I'd like to know about one of your players. Blake Rose."

"Has he done something?" asked the coach, a twinge of panic in his voice.

"Um, sorry to tell you this, Coach, but he's dead."

Edwards's face went blank, and the pencil fell from his hands. "You're shitting me."

"Nope. Sorry, but I'm not shitting you."

"Jesus H. Christ. Well, that's about the end of our whole fucking season." He was staring down at his lap, but now he looked at Doc again and said, "He's dead?"

"Yeah. Murdered. And I need to track down the killer as soon as I can. I realize this is a shock, but I could use your help,

Coach."

Edwards shook his head, muttered a curse, and said, "What do you want to know?"

"Tell me about Blake."

"He's the damn quarterback. He's the whole team, dammit. He doesn't have a cannon for an arm, but he can put the ball where it needs to be. And the kid can run, too. He's fast. He was going to take us to the national championship this year."

"OK, so, he could play football. Good kid?"

The coach looked at Doc again. "Hell, no. The kid was a prima donna. Thought he was the king and expected everyone to bow down." Doc waited for more. Edwards leaned back and said, "Look, the kid was a local boy. He could have gone off to a four-year school on a scholarship, but he chose to stay here. He was a special player."

"Did he get treated special?"

"I suppose. He wasn't the brightest bulb, but a national championship would have meant a hell of a lot to the school. Everybody knew that."

Doc had been a football player at the University of Minnesota, and a good one. He knew what kinds of favors players could receive. He leaned forward and said, "That didn't really answer my question, Coach. I assume he got some help with his studies. Was there more?"

The coach tilted his head sideways and gave Doc a funny look. "Hey, I know you. You're that Pete Hunter, aren't you? The All-American receiver at the U. Sure-thing first-round NFL pick. What the hell happened to you?"

"The NFL wasn't going to let me carry a gun, so I decided to be a cop. Now, about Blake."

"He had some issues with a girl this spring."

"What kind of issues?"

Edwards's foot found his pencil, and he ducked down under the desk to retrieve it before he said, "I don't know exactly. It was handled by administration."

"Come on, Coach. This is a murder investigation. You don't want to be withholding evidence. That would be really bad."

Edwards was twiddling the pencil in his lap again. "There was discussion that Blake might have raped a girl."

"Oh, jeez," said Doc. He wondered if there had been a charge made by the girl to the police. He wondered if Pickus knew. The charges would have likely been filed with the Morris police but still, Pickus would likely have known. In a small town like this, he probably would have known even if no charges were filed. "Might have raped a girl? OK, I need to know the girl's name."

"I don't know. I swear. Administration handled the whole thing."

"Were charges ever filed?"

"I don't know."

Doc stared at Edwards, seeing the three monkeys with their hands over their mouth, eyes, and ears, but decided the guy was probably telling the truth. He said, "How about friends?"

"Luke Ritter, he's a receiver on the team, and Zean Thomas, our halfback."

"They local too?"

"Yeah. All in the same class."

"Must have been a pretty good team at Morris."

"Blake wasn't that big yet, he grew a lot last year, but he was still good. Got upset by Willmar or they would have gone to state."

Doc held his forehead in his hand. The beers had made him sleepy and now he knew he needed some supper because he had a headache coming on. "OK, Coach. I'm going to have to have to talk to the whole team from last year. I'm going to need contact information."

Edwards reached into a side drawer and pulled out a sheet from a hanging folder and said, "Half these guys were second-year students last year, so I don't know if their information is any good."

The sheet contained addresses and phone numbers. "Are these addresses their folks' places?"

"Yeah, their home addresses," said Edwards. "The football players who aren't local stay in the subsidized housing across the street during the school year. We haven't assigned those places yet."

Doc stood. The room was closing in on him, and the gym smell wasn't helping. "Call me if you think of anything else, Coach." Doc walked to the door, turning to see the coach staring at him with the expression of Humpty Dumpty after his fall. He was going to wish the man good luck with the season but took pity on him and left without a comment.

* * *

Cheryl wasn't at her desk when Doc returned. He was a little disappointed but continued past the desk, walking into Dr. Lester's office and sitting where he had been earlier.

"What is the meaning of this?" said Lester as she removed her reading glasses from her nose.

Doc was in no mood to put up with this woman any more. Besides, he was tired, a little hungry, and he got cranky when he was that way. "This means you lied to me, Doctor. You knew about the rape allegation against Blake Rose, and you did not tell me. You have now broken the law and charges will probably be filed against you, which I guess will not look good on your record." The woman had fallen back in her chair. "You can tell me about it now and possibly avoid those charges, or I will be back with a subpoena and an officer who will place you under arrest."

Lester's head swung side to side, looking at the carpet on either side of her desk like there might be some escape hatch there. "I should probably talk to legal first," she said.

Doc put his hands on the edge of her desk and said, "You probably should, but I can assure you that if you waste any more of my time by doing that you will be going to jail."

Lester took a deep breath and released it before spoke. "All right. The girl's name is Linda Knudson. She's from Benson. The college paid her a cash settlement and provided tuition for her to attend Southwest State University in Marshall in exchange for her not pressing charges against them."

"Them?"

"Blake Rose, Zean Thomas, and Luke Ritter."

Doc slouched back, hands falling to his thighs, and said, "You've got to be shitting me."

Lester was sucking on one stem of her glasses like it was a pacifier. She pulled it from her mouth and said, "I was hardly involved. It was mostly Dean Phillips who made the arrangement."

"I don't really give a rat's ass, Doctor. You're the one who lied to me. You get me Linda Knudson's contact information right now."

Lester was immediately punching keys on her computer. She wrote the girl's address and phone number and email on a piece of paper and handed it to Doc. "I can't guarantee any of this is still current."

Doc stood and said, "And I can't guarantee you aren't going to be behind bars very soon, Doctor. You're in a shitload of trouble."

* * *

The heat and sun hit him with a one-two punch when he stepped off the curb into the parking lot. Squeezing his eyes tight while he slid his sunglasses down his forehead, he walked to his car. With the door open and his legs outside, he pulled out his phone.

"Doc, are you going to get killed?" answered Trask.

"No, but I'm about to kill a few people." He told Trask what he knew, and that he was going to need some help with the interviews.

"Can't the Morris police and the sheriff's people handle that?"

"Probably, but I'm not sure I can trust them, and there's going to be a lot of people to interview. I got Pickus and his investigator talking to people who knew John Rose, but Pickus definitely had to know about the rape, and I'm guessing the Morris cops are in on it too." Doc paused and said, "And I was thinking about something else, too."

"What's that?"

"Whoever took the Roses out was a good shot. Real good. Maybe a pro."

"A hired hit? You haven't found some of that wild weed they have growing in the ditches out there, have you?" said Trask.

"Just a thought."

"OK, it's a thought, but just hang on to that for now. I'll find someone to get out there and help. I'll let you know who," said Trask. "You talk to the crime-scene guys or the ME?"

"Next call."

"OK. See you."

CHAPTER 5

Doc dialed Miranda's number and got him on the first ring. "Carl, it's Doc. What do you know?"

"Not a lot, really. We've just finished up with the truck and now we're headed inside. Only prints on the truck were from the deceased, and not too many of those. It was pretty clean."

"The ME have the bodies?"

"Yeah. He said you could call him in the morning. Had some fundraiser thing he had to go to."

Doc said, "We got three murders here."

Miranda replied, "That's what I told him, but he seemed pretty set on going to this thing. Wife was the chairperson or something."

"Good grief. OK, anything else?"

"They were all shot pretty close up, but even then, I'd say whoever did it was a pretty good shot. Right in the middle of the forehead, every one. Bingo."

"Yeah, that's what I thought. OK, call me when you're done in the house." Miranda said he would and disconnected. Doc called Pickus.

"This is Doc. What do you know?"

"My men found what could have been tire tracks, probably from a truck, in a driveway just down the road and across from the Roses' place. Bushes by the driveway, so it would have been a good place to watch. Nothing else."

"So, it could have just been someone turning around in the driveway?"

"Could have been. The tread was kind of worn, but yeah, could be nothing." Pickus paused, then said, "I talked to Bill Palmer, chief at Morris. He said they've got nothing in the file on John Rose. There were a couple of fights but no arrests or charges."

"He say who Rose was fighting?"

"Both times it was Ed Salo," said Pickus. "Salo runs the co-op."

"OK, we need to talk to him."

"I know where he lives. I was going to go over there."

"Hold off on that. I'd like to go with you, but there's something more pressing, and I got to get something to eat first." Pickus asked where he was, and Doc said at the college. Pickus said The Windmill was a good diner, on the corner of Sixth and Main. He'd meet him there in ten minutes.

* * *

Doc couldn't have missed The Windmill if he'd wanted to. There was a big, old-fashioned windmill on top of the building, the big blades turning in the summer-evening breeze. He went in the back door, which was at the end of a narrow hallway with the restrooms, and the smell was less than pleasant. As he emerged from the hallway, however, the odors of grilled hamburgers and fries and some kind of Italian dish dominated. Doc found a booth, red Naugahyde seats with a worn Formica-topped table, and slid in. He ordered two waters and a beer. The waitress was just turning away when Pickus appeared, and he ordered a whiskey sour.

Doc looked at the man like he'd like to strangle him, but Pickus didn't notice as he dumped his silverware out of the napkin. He set the napkin in his lap and said, "So, I told you what I know. What have you been up to?"

Doc was about to read him the riot act when the waitress returned with the sheriff's drink and Doc's beer. They both ordered the special—a patty melt with fries and a salad. Doc watched her leave and then turned to Pickus and said, "I had an interesting visit with a few people over at the college. They told me Blake Rose had been accused of rape by a girl there. You know anything about it?"

Pickus took a sip of his cocktail and said, "I'd heard about it."

"Oh, bullshit. In a town this size you knew all about it. What the fuck, Pickus? Don't you think that was something I should know?"

Two women at the table to their left were staring at them. "Keep it down, Hunter. This is a family place." Pickus took another drink, smiling at the women and raising his glass to them before turning back to Doc. "OK, I'm sorry."

"Sorry isn't going to do it, Pickus. We've got a killer running around." Doc raised his bottle to his lips. "Now, tell me what you know."

Pickus sipped his drink. "The girl made a complaint to the college. The college claimed there wasn't enough to go on, and the girl threatened to take it to the police. The college offered her a deal to stay quiet."

"Leave the school, with free tuition at another—"

"Right, but the girl went to the cops in Morris anyway, who told her essentially the same thing that the college did. So, the girl went back to the college and took the offer."

"And I take it that the lack of evidence in the case and the refusal to let the girl file a complaint had something to do with Blake Rose being star quarterback?"

The waitress came by, saw the sheriff's empty glass, and asked if he'd like another. He said he would, and Doc ordered another beer. "You got to understand, Hunter. This team, with this kid, had a strong possibility of bringing a national championship to the area. That's big money, Hunter. And not just short term."

"I've heard that story already. And what about the other two?"

"You mean . . . ?"

"The boys. Ritter and Thomas."

"Yeah, well, they didn't take part in the rape, but they were there. They were part of the deal. Nothing would be said."

The drinks arrived. Doc drained what was left of his first beer, handed the waitress the bottle, and took a sip of his second. "We need to see the girl and her family, and we need to get hold of those boys, pronto."

"You think they could be in danger?"

"Hell, yes. Don't you?"

The women looked over again, and Doc gave them the

finger.

"That wasn't necessary."

"Well, I'm a little ticked off here, Sheriff, in case you couldn't guess." Doc expected the man to say something, but instead he leaned back and put down about half of his second whiskey. Doc said, "Ah shit. There's more, isn't there?"

"There was another incident last year," said Pickus.

Doc sipped his beer, silent.

"Another girl lodged a complaint with the police."

Doc just shook his head. "All three again?"

"Yeah. Well, only Rose was accused of the rape. Thomas and Ritter supposedly just watched."

"Supposedly?"

"Nothing was ever proven. The county attorney refused to prosecute."

"Let me guess. The county attorney is a big football fan."

Pickus looked away. "His kid was on the team."

The waitress came with their food. Doc didn't feel like eating by then, but he did, and he felt better afterward. He wanted another beer, but figured he shouldn't. It looked like it could be a long night, and he needed to stay sober. There were so many things running so many ways he wasn't sure where to start. He needed Trask to call him.

Pickus knew the girl from the incident at the high school. She had been Blake's girlfriend at the time. She hadn't finished her senior year in Morris. "They moved to Alex," said Pickus. "I'm pretty sure I have the contact info."

"What a mess. OK, as much as I don't like these other two boys, even though I don't know them, we need to at least locate them and make sure they're OK. Let them know what's going on." The waitress came with their bill but Doc told her he'd need another beer. "Then we got to talk to the girl from the college and her family, and then the girl from the high school." A thought flashed through Doc's mind, but he lost it. He was silent for a minute, and finally said, "Has Kuck turned up anything?"

"No. I talked to him just before you called. He said that he confirmed the times the Roses got to church and left. Nobody really talked to them because they got there just as the service was beginning."

"All right. Let me make a call, and then you and I will go talk to the boys. Tomorrow we're going to need to interview Blake's teachers and kids from his classes, at the college and high school. You think about how we can do that while I'm on the phone."

Doc stepped out onto the sidewalk in front of the restaurant. The sun was still up, but moving toward the horizon, and was definitely not as intense. There was a breeze now, out of the west, and it really was a pleasant evening. One he should be enjoying on the nineteenth hole in Brainerd.

When Trask connected, Doc didn't let him talk. "I need that help, bad. More stuff has come up." Doc filled him in on the incident at the high school. "There could be more, for all I know, but I don't think Pickus is holding anything back."

"Jeez, Doc. You've got a real octopus by the tail down there."

"I don't think an octopus has a tail, but, yeah, it's a mess."

"Gary LeBlanc should be there late tonight. You know him?"

LeBlanc was fairly new to the BCA. Doc said he had met

him at a BCA meeting. "Tell him to call me when he gets here."

"Could be pretty late. He just finished something up in I-Falls."

"International Falls? You couldn't find someone farther away?" said Doc. "Whatever. I got to go."

"Right. Don't get shot."

Doc said, "Thanks, Dad," and hung up. "Crap."

Doc followed Pickus north out of Morris and then east about five miles. They'd pass a farm site every half mile or so, but there wasn't much else to see. Trees were pretty scarce but there was a cluster of oaks in the yard of the home where Luke Ritter lived. Pickus had said that Ritter's father, Ted, was a mechanic with his own shop in town, and his mother, Barbara, was a teacher. Ted's parents had left the farm to him when they passed, and he leased out the land. There was a barn across the yard from the single-story cedar-sided rambler, with a fence enclosing a few acres connecting to the barn. A couple of horses had their heads over the fence closest to the yard, watching them. Two more galloped in the area behind the barn.

Pickus walked up two steps to the front door of the house, and Doc trailed behind. The house was stained a grayish blue so it was hard to tell in the fading light whether it needed a paint job or was supposed to look that way. Mosquitoes were starting to arrive, Pickus slapping one that had taken a liking to his neck. A slender middle-aged woman in a light-green dress came to the door.

"Sheriff."

"Barbara. This is Agent Hunter from the Minnesota Bureau of Criminal Apprehension," said Pickus.

"Oh no. I thought this stuff was all settled."

"If you're talking about the incidents with Blake Rose

and Zean Thomas and your son at the college and the high school, Mrs. Ritter, it is, and it isn't," said Doc. That confused Pickus and the woman. "If we could just talk inside for a minute, I can explain. Is your son here?"

"Yes, he just got back from work." She backed away, holding the door for them. "Well, come on in. Ted's in the living room."

The men followed the woman through a kitchen that smelled of fried chicken to a room with an L-shaped leather sofa, a couple of upholstered chairs, and a large-screen television. Ted Ritter was sitting in one of the chairs, beer bottle in hand, and he stood when they entered.

"Sheriff. What's going on?"

Doc cut in. "Mr. Ritter, I'm Agent Hunter of the BCA. If you or your wife wouldn't mind getting your son, we'd like to talk to all of you at once."

Barbara disappeared through the kitchen.

Ted Ritter was taller than his wife, over six feet, and thin like her. His blond hair was thinning, wispy on the top, and he had a rough, tired face. He did not offer the men a drink or ask them to sit, so they all stood in awkward silence until Mrs. Ritter and her son returned. Luke Ritter was another two inches taller than his father, blond too, with long arms and large hands that Doc thought probably served him well as a receiver.

Luke looked at Pickus and then at Doc. Pickus started to introduce Doc, but Luke cut him off. "Shit. You're Pete Hunter. Wow!" He turned to his father. "Dad, that's Pete Hunter, from the U." He turned back to Doc. "Man, you were something else."

"Yeah, well, that was years ago. We've got something much more serious going on here. If you would all sit down, please."

Ted sat back in the chair he had occupied, one Doc guessed he spent just about every night in. Barbara and her son sat together on one side of the couch. Pickus didn't look like he was going to sit, so Doc pointed him to the other chair. Doc leaned on the arm of the couch.

"We've got a situation that we need to talk to you about. It's my understanding that Luke is friends with Blake Rose, and that there have been a couple of incidents in the last two years involving girls and Blake and Zean Thomas."

"That was all settled. Why are you bringing that stuff back up?" said Barbara.

She was about to say something else when Doc raised his hand and said, "Blake Rose was killed today. We have reason to believe the killer was out to get revenge on Blake. It is also possible that the killer may see some association to what happened in one of those incidents and come after Luke."

"Blake is dead?" said Luke eyebrows popping up.

His mother looked at him and said, "Luke. Didn't you hear? You could be in danger."

The boy just stared at Doc.

"This is totally supposition on our part at this time, but we wanted to be sure you were aware of the situation," said Doc. "The sheriff is willing to put a deputy here through the night if that would make you feel safer. Again, we don't know that Luke is in any danger at all."

"Does Zean know?" said Luke.

"We're going there next," said Pickus.

"What do you think, Ted? About the deputy," said Barbara.

"I don't know. Seems a little much. And I've got plenty

of guns." He looked at Pickus and said, "What do you think, Larry?"

"Couldn't hurt."

"Well, is he just going to be outside, sleeping in his car?" said Barbara. "I mean, we're just getting over this last deal. I don't want people driving by and seeing a cop car in the yard."

"He could park behind the barn," said Pickus.

"Let's just hold off for now," said Ted.

Barbara nodded and said, "Yeah, Ted's got guns."

Doc looked at Luke. "Blake have any other friends besides you and Zean?"

"Not really. He was kind of an asshole, you know."

"What about girlfriends?"

"He kind of liked to play around. Said he didn't want any girl's feelings hurt because he wasn't available."

"Big of him," said Doc. "The girls you three got in trouble for at the college and at the high school—he wasn't going out with them?"

"It wasn't Luke's fault!" said his mother. "He was just there. He tried to stop Blake."

The boy looked at his mother and then back at Doc. "Blake was going out with Jenny Wyman when we were seniors. Linda had turned him down for a date. He didn't like that."

Doc could see the boy thinking about what had happened. He stood. "OK, we need to get going. Here's my card if you think of anything more I should know. And call the sheriff if you change your mind about the deputy."

"I'm sure we'll be fine," said Ted as he stood.

Doc wasn't so sure.

CHAPTER 6

It was getting dark by the time they pulled into the driveway of Zean Thomas's home. He lived kitty-corner across the town from the Ritters, in a little subdivision built in the seventies. There were concrete curbs and streetlights, and the trees and shrubs were pretty sparse. The builder had kept his landscaping budget low. The houses were cookie-cutter split entries with attached two-car garages and aluminum siding. The Thomas home was in the middle of a block, its brown stain looking black in the fading light. The sidewalk was crumbling around the edges and bricks lining the sidewalk were at odd angles, weeds covering some entirely.

Pickus knocked, and Rod Thomas came to the door. Thomas was short like Pickus, and in his late forties. He was barefoot, in jean shorts and a washed-out red T-shirt.

"Sheriff. What's going on?" A small girl with short, curly blond hair came running up the stairs behind Thomas and grabbed his leg. He lifted her so she was sitting in the crook of his arm and she reached up, grabbing at her father's bushy dark hair. Doc figured she was a mistake.

"Zean home?"

"Yeah. Is he in trouble?"

"How about Meg? Is she here?"

"In the kitchen, I think."

"Good. You mind if we come inside and talk to all of you at once?" Thomas was staring at Doc, and Pickus turned back. "This is Agent Hunter with the BCA. Can we come in?"

Thomas didn't say anything, but backed away from the door, holding it with his free hand until they were all in the small entryway, and then pushing it shut. He made his way past Doc and Pickus, climbed the stairs, and called out to his wife, "Meg, Sheriff's here. He needs to talk to us."

The second level had a living area directly to the left, and then a dining space beyond that. Both areas were furnished with the kind of stuff you'd get at the big furniture warehouse out by the entrance to the freeway. In good shape, but certainly nothing fancy. A tired-looking woman in white shorts and a sleeveless flowered top, about the same height as her husband, appeared in the open doorway to the kitchen that was directly ahead, wiping her hands on a dishtowel. Rod put the girl down, and she scooted across the carpet to her mother, hanging on to the woman's leg. She found the top of the girl's head and ruffled her hair.

"Sheriff."

Pickus was introducing Doc to the woman when Rod came walking back into the room with his son in tow. Pickus introduced Doc to Zean and asked everyone to sit.

Zean remained standing, staring at Doc. "Hunter? Pete Hunter? You played at the U, didn't you?" said Zean, in awe of the big man in front of him. Zean wasn't much taller than his parents, but he was muscular. Doc figured he'd be tough to bring down.

"Long time ago. Anyway, we need to talk to you folks about something serious. Why don't you have a seat?" They all found places, including Pickus. The girl climbed into her mother's lap. Doc remained standing. "OK, so you know, Blake Rose was killed today."

"Blake?" said Zean, his mouth hanging open.

"Afraid so. He was shot earlier today."

"Shot? Oh my God!" said Jean.

"Yeah. So, anyway, we haven't caught whoever did it yet, but we wanted to warn you that it's possible that this person is on some kind of mission of revenge for what Blake did to the girl at the college this spring, Linda Knudson, or possibly the girl from the high school, Jenny . . ." He looked at Pickus, who said, "Wyman."

"So, what does this have to do with us?" said Rod.

"It's possible, since your boy was associated with what happened, that the killer may come after him, too. We don't know that—it's entirely supposition at this point—but we want to cover all the bases." They were all quiet, except the girl, who was pulling at her mother's ear and making noises. "So, um, the sheriff has agreed to leave a deputy outside your house tonight if that would make you feel safer."

"In the driveway?" asked Rod.

"Could be in the street if that would be better, Rod," said Pickus. "Up to you. We talked to the Ritters, and they decided not to have a deputy. For tonight, anyway. Again, up to you."

Rod looked at his wife, daughter in her lap, and said, "I

got a little girl, too. Put a guy in the street."

"OK. I'll call as soon as I leave. He should be here in less than half an hour."

"Damn! Blake is really dead?" said Zean.

"Zean! Don't talk that way in front of your sister," said Jean.

Zean looked at her and said he was sorry.

"Zean, can you think of anyone Blake may have upset, besides the Knudson and Wyman girls?" said Doc.

"Well, I know he didn't make very good friends with his professors. Didn't do his assignments and told the professors there was nothing they could do about it because he was the quarterback."

"And what about his teachers in high school? Same thing?"

"Pretty much, except for Miss Draper." Zean got a big smile on his face, and his mother told him to be quiet, that was only a rumor. Zean responded, "She left before the year even ended. She was definitely getting big."

"So, Blake was possibly having an affair with a teacher?" asked Doc, glancing over at Pickus, who shook his head to tell Doc he didn't know about it.

"Yeah," said Zean with a grin. "They did some extra studying at her place."

"OK. Anyone else?" The boy shook his head just as Doc's phone buzzed. He excused himself and walked out the front door. "Hey, Carl."

"Hey, Doc. You catch this guy yet?"

"I got it narrowed down to most of Morris and a few hundred other people. What do you know?"

"Well, you're not going to like this, but we found drugs

in the kid's room. Mostly pot and cocaine, with a few pills."

"Ah, shit. So, just using?"

"Looks that way."

"Anything else?"

"A bunch of prints, but none on the knife and no gun."

"OK. Well, thanks. Talk to you." Doc disconnected. Pickus was standing next to Doc now. "They found drugs in Blake's room. Dope and coke and a few pills. Didn't look like enough for him to be a dealer."

"So, now maybe this was about drugs?"

"Maybe, but I don't think so. A pissed-off dealer would probably have robbed the place. Still . . ." Doc looked at Pickus. "You got a handle on the dealers around here?"

"Pretty much. They've been small-time mostly, but we busted a place south of town last year. Mexicans. Lots of guns."

"Well, we can't run down that hole right now. We need to talk to those girls, Knudson and . . ." "Wyman," finished Pickus. "Right, and then we need to talk to the professors and teachers, and probably the dean at the college too. And that teacher Blake might have had an affair with. You know anything about that?"

Pickus shook his head.

"I got the contact information for the two girls," Doc went on. "And I called the principal at the high school, and she's going to call in the teachers that had Blake last year. She said a couple are out of town on vacation, but she can get most of them. I couldn't get hold of the dean or assistant dean, but I'll try again in the morning."

Pickus said he would call the principal about the teacher, too. Then he said, "How about Salo?"

Doc gave hin a puzzled look.

61

"Ed Salo. The guy John Rose got in a fight with."

Doc gazed off at the moon coming up. "I've got an agent coming in to help, tonight or early in the morning. The guy's going to need a few hours of sleep, so why don't we meet at The Windmill for breakfast, say eight, and set up a plan?"

"Works for me. Where are you staying?"

Doc hadn't thought about that.

"Try the Ramada out by the college. The motel downtown sucks."

* * *

Doc checked in to the Ramada. It seemed fairly new, built in this century anyway, and his room was clean. Trask had sent the phone number for LeBlanc. Doc got hold of him and told him the plan and where he was staying. He gave LeBlanc a rundown on what he knew and said they could meet in the lobby or at The Windmill. LeBlanc said he was a few hours out but that sounded fine, and he'd see Doc in the lobby in the morning.

Doc walked to his window and opened the curtain. He had a small balcony. He pulled the sliding glass door open and stepped outside. The night was still, the sky sparkling with a million stars. It had cooled, but he guessed the heat would return in the morning. Probably a good day for some golf. Doc walked back into his room, shut and locked the sliding door, and closed the curtain.

His golf bag was leaning on the desk, and he pulled out the putter and took a few balls from the side pocket. He dropped the balls on the floor, nudged one to the side, and stood over it. The bathroom was just inside the door to his room. From where he stood across the room, he had a line to the edge of the bathroom door frame. It would be tight. He'd have to get past a chair leg and the bed frame, and the carpet was uneven. Not an easy shot. There was a light click as the club struck the ball. The ball rolled toward the chair leg, and Doc thought it was going to hit for a second, but it curved away at the last instant. It struck the bottom of the door frame dead center, just kissed it, and ricocheted about six inches past. "Perfect." He putted for nearly an hour more, clearing his mind so he could sleep.

CHAPTER 7

Gary LeBlanc was waiting for Doc in the lobby. LeBlanc was thirty, average height, average build, with flat, dark-brown hair parted on the side. His nose was a little pudgy, but other than that, nothing about LeBlanc stood out. He'd be the guy in the room at a meeting that no one would notice. It was a good quality for an agent, but it didn't do much for his love life. LeBlanc was sitting in a chair reading the *Morris Chronicle* when Doc showed. LeBlanc stood and put out his hand. "Doc."

LeBlanc was wearing khakis, a button-down short-sleeved white cotton dress shirt, brown socks, and shiny brown loafers with tassels. There was a blue blazer in his lap. LeBlanc had read the section in the BCA manual on agent dress code. Doc had skipped that section and most of the rest. Doc had a new golf shirt on, this one with a Pebble Beach logo, and the same shorts and sockless shoes. Sunglasses on his head.

"Thanks for coming."

"Didn't know I had a choice."

"Neither of us did, I guess. I know I should be on the course."

"Killers are darn inconsiderate," said LeBlanc. "But they do keep us employed."

"There is that. So, you want to follow me over to the café? I'm pretty sure we're going to need to split up."

They made it to The Windmill at eight. Pickus was in the same booth as the day before, coffee in front of him. Doc introduced LeBlanc to Pickus, and the men shook hands over the table before Doc and LeBlanc slid in. The waitress was immediately at the table, the BCA agents both ordering coffee, all the men ordering breakfast. The men sat quietly as the waitress returned with coffee, refilling Pickus's cup.

"OK, so we got a shitload to do," said Doc. "You got anything new before we start?" he said to Pickus.

Pickus rubbed the dark stubble on his cheek. Doc hadn't shaved because he didn't like to shave, and for some reason women seemed to like a little rougher look. He had one of those beards that grew slowly, mostly blond, so he'd only shave a couple of times a week. But Doc guessed Pickus was not in the same boat. The man was likely very scheduled, shaving every morning, wanting to look his best for the public that elected him. His tired eyes also said the man hadn't gotten much sleep. "I still haven't got hold of the dean. I did get the contact information for the teacher Blake supposedly had an affair with from the principal. She wanted to know when we wanted to talk to Blake's teachers. And Kuck is starting on John Rose's financial records."

"Can Kuck help us with interviews?"

"Yes," said Pickus.

"OK, so unless you think Sharon Rose might have someone in her bridge group who wanted to kill her because they thought she was cheating..."

Pickus shook his head.

"OK, then. I think we need to focus on Blake Rose and John Rose. My inclination is to stick with Blake, but we're way too early for that."

"We're leaving the drug thing alone?" said Pickus.

Doc had thought about that as he was lying in bed the night before. He didn't think it was a high probability, but it was the most likely explanation for the possibility that there had been a professional hit man involved. "Yeah. I called Trask when I got up to see if he can find out if the DEA task force in this area has Rose on their radar, so he's going to do that, but we'll stay off it at least until I hear back." They all took a sip of coffee, strong and just a little bitter, and then Doc said, "OK. Sheriff, why don't you and Kuck start at the college. Talk to Blake's classmates and team members and his professors. We're looking for anything about anyone who might have wanted the kid dead. Maybe there was a second-string quarterback who thought he should be starting..." This assignment didn't sit well with Doc because Blake had been attending the junior college when he was murdered, so it was most likely that there would be a connection there rather than at the high school, but he didn't think he had much choice.

"We can do that," Pickus said, "but there are a lot of kids, and football players especially, who aren't from around here."

"Just start with the ones who live in the area." He handed Pickus the printout with the professors and the sheet showing the football players. "I'm guessing the professors can give you some idea if any of the kids in their classes didn't get along with Blake, but you'll need to talk to the kids, too. I assume the professors or admissions can give you those rosters. I believe the assistant dean will be happy to help with that."

Pickus looked at the sheets. "Some of the professors may not be from the area or be away for the summer."

"Call them. We need to talk to all of them."

"And what about the dean?"

Doc didn't really want Pickus talking to the dean. For all he knew the two had already talked. "Leave the dean for now."

The food came, and the men focused on eating. Doc had ordered French toast, something he considered a risky move. Often the toast would be too soggy or too dry or there would be stuff on it like nuts or berries, but he liked French toast, and he never made it for himself. Actually, he never made much for himself. He poured some maple syrup over it and took a bite. It was just as he liked it, like his mother made it, with some powdered sugar sprinkled on top. Doc went through it all in a hurry, dragging the sausages through the syrup left on the plate. After the last bite of sausage, he leaned back in the booth, finishing his orange juice. He liked a good breakfast. Made him feel like he was ready for the day. His dad always said a good breakfast was the key to a good day and so that was what Doc did. When he was up before noon.

"Gary and I are going to visit with the two girls and their families and then start with the teachers at the high school. Why don't you give me the principal's contact information? And the information for the teacher involved in the affair, um . . ."

"Draper," said Pickus.

"Yeah, and the two girls from the assault complaints."

"Draper is way down toward Spicer," said Pickus.

"Serious?"

"Yeah. I guess she's teaching there now."

"Man, that's a trip," said Doc. Doc started thinking about a course he had played south of Willmar. It was a nice course, not like some in the Cities or up north, but a challenge. It would be on the way to Spicer. Close, anyway. If there was a lull in the investigation, and there were often lulls, and Trask owed him from yesterday anyway, maybe he could get a round in. "Well, OK, we got to talk to her. I'll get hold of her."

Doc and LeBlanc stood on the sidewalk outside of The Windmill and watched Pickus get in his car and drive away. Pickus had gotten a spot in front, making Doc more certain the man had been there drinking coffee for a while before he and LeBlanc arrived.

"You don't really trust the sheriff, do you?" said LeBlanc.

"Not really. But we got to push on this thing to see if we can get some movement, and right now, you and the sheriff are all I've got."

"So, what do you want me to do?"

Doc looked up at the scattered angel-hair clouds being brushed slowly east. It was going to be a nice day. Hot, but nice. Great for a quick eighteen in the morning. "Don't suppose you can get me in at the Morris Country Club?"

"*Is* there a Morris Country Club?"

Doc looked over at LeBlanc. "I guess that's a no." He pulled his phone out of his pocket. "Let me make a few calls." Doc moved away down the sidewalk as he talked, returning to where he had left LeBlanc as he finished his last call. "OK. I got hold of the Knudsons. The mother, um, Angie, and the daughter are home. We'll go there first. The principal at the high school, Mrs. Kimball, said she would be there at ten thirty and try to have as many of Blake's teachers as she could find, so it will be tight, but I think we can make it. I'll drive."

Doc preferred to drive his own vehicle when he could. Not that he felt that strongly about driving; it was just that when you were six foot four and over two hundred pounds, it was hard to get comfortable in just any car. Doc was comfortable in his car. He'd had the driver's seat modified so it went back more than normal and was a little lower so his head wouldn't hit the roof. The leather seat had molded to his shape and the steering wheel tilted and adjusted to fit his long arms. It was comfortable.

They took County 9 southwest. It was a two-lane asphalt road, and ran diagonally across the state from Wahpeton all the way down to Willmar, so it carried a fair amount of traffic, including a number of semis. Doc passed a few, but by the time they pulled into the farmyard of the Knudson home it was after nine thirty. There was a woman of average height standing on the front step of the white two-story home to their right as they pulled onto the gravel drive. She was wearing navy shorts, a puffy white blouse, and a red apron tied around her waist. She brushed a strand of brown hair from her face as they pulled to a stop.

The agents got out of the car, and were about to introduce themselves and show their identification when they caught the woman looking over their shoulder. The men turned at the sound of a barn door shutting behind them. A man in dirty jeans, work boots, and an orange T-shirt walked across the driveway and stood next to the woman. He wiped his palms on the front of his jeans and held a hand out to Doc.

"I'm Rusty Knudson. This is my wife, Angie. I guess you're the BCA agents."

Doc and LeBlanc showed their IDs.

Mr. Knudson looked at the IDs and handed them back. "What's this all about? We're not real excited to be talking about what happened to Linda again."

"We understand that, sir," said Doc. "But we've had a murder, and we kind of want to catch the killer."

"Should be giving whoever did it a medal, if you ask me," said Angie.

The murders must have been on the morning news. "Yeah, well, we still got to do our jobs, so we'd really appreciate any help you can give us." The Knudsons stared at Doc. Angry stares. This wouldn't be easy. "Can we talk to your daughter?"

"Do you really need to do that?" said the woman. "She's had more than her share."

"Yeah, we understand that, and we'll be as brief as we can, but we do need to talk to her."

The Knudsons looked at each other. Angie said, "I'll get her," and disappeared into the house.

The men waited on the front steps. Doc looking out at the farmstead. Rusty's brown eyes stared hard at Doc and he said, "You're the Pete Hunter that played for the U, aren't you?" Doc turned back and gave a tight-lipped smile but didn't say anything. "I saw you play once, against Iowa. Man, you smoked 'em. At least five or six catches and two touchdowns."

He was about to say something more, but the screen door behind him opened and Angie and Linda walked out. The girl was taller than her mother by an inch or two, with her father's dirty red hair tucked behind her ears and running over her shoulders. She was attractive—the kind of girl who would get noticed.

Doc introduced himself and LeBlanc and asked if they could ask her a few questions. The girl's defiant blue eyes turned to her mother, who gave a terse nod. "All right. Why don't we go get out of the sun?" Linda led them to a picnic table in the front yard under an old willow. She took the middle of the bench, her parents on either side, Doc and LeBlanc on the other side of the table.

"So, as I guess you know, Blake Rose and his parents were killed yesterday at their farm. We're trying to get any information we can that can lead us to their killer or killers. We are talking to you because it may be possible that their deaths had something to do with the incident you had with Blake," said Doc.

"What? Like some kind of revenge thing?" said Linda.

"It's possible," said Doc.

"So, you think one of us killed them?" said Rusty.

Doc could see the color rising in the man's face. "Not at all, Mr. Knudson. I mean, if you did kill them it would be good for you to tell us."

"I was on the south forty all morning, and the girls went to church," said Rusty.

"I didn't go," said his daughter.

"What?"

"I said I didn't go. I told mom I didn't want to go, and she went without me. I just stayed in my room."

The girl and her father were exchanging angry glances when Doc said, "Um, Linda, did you have any boyfriends at school other than Blake?"

"Blake wasn't her boyfriend," said her mother. "He was a rapist!"

Doc ignored her. "So, Linda, any boyfriends?"

"I had a few dates, but nothing more than that. Nobody steady or anything."

"How about in high school?" said LeBlanc.

"Well, I dated Mark for a while my senior year, but we kind of broke up when he went to Mankato last year."

"Mark who?" said LeBlanc.

"Church," she said.

LeBlanc said, "Have you seen him this summer?" The girl said she hadn't. LeBlanc asked if she had a number for him, and she pulled out her phone and found his number.

Doc looked at the parents and then at their daughter. "So, I know this is hard, but I have to ask. When Blake raped you, we understand there were two other boys there, Zean Thomas and Luke Ritter. Is that correct?"

"Yes."

"And what part did these boys have in the incident?"

Linda clasped her hands in her lap. "They didn't do anything to me, but they didn't stop Blake either." She looked off for a minute, and then added, "Well, that's not exactly right. I remember one of them yelling at Blake to stop, but that's all."

"Can you think of anybody who would want to harm Blake Rose and his parents?" said Doc.

Linda's blue eyes narrowed. "I don't know anybody who liked that creep. But I don't know about his parents. What do you mean by anybody?"

"Just that. Anyone who knew him at all. Students, professors, anyone. Anyone who hated him enough to kill him," said Doc.

The girl gazed down at the table in front of her and shook her head.

Doc looked at her a moment, and then at LeBlanc. "OK. Well, thanks for your time." He extracted his legs from under the table and stood. Fishing a card out of his pocket, he placed it on the table. "Please call if you think of anything." He took a step toward his car and stopped, turning to look back at Rusty Knudson. "Good hunting around here, Mr. Knudson?"

"Not bad. Got an eight-pointer last fall."

Doc smiled. "Nice. Well, you folks have a good day now."

When they were in the car, LeBlanc said, "You a hunter?"

"Naw. Just wanted to see if he was."

CHAPTER 8

Doc dropped LeBlanc at his car, and they both made it to the high school by ten thirty. There were a dozen cars in the staff lot in front of the building, and about the same number in the student lot to the north. The administration offices were just to the right of the main entry to the red-brick building. They walked into a reception area to find an empty desk in front of them, a boy in shorts sitting in a molded plastic chair against the glass wall to their right. The boy was focused on his phone, looking up only when Doc said, "Hello. You happen to know where the principal's office is?"

The pointed to his left, and said, "Down there."

LeBlanc followed Doc down a tight hallway with tiled walls to an open door with "Principal Kimball" on the nameplate. Doc looked inside to see a dark-haired woman with reading glasses on her nose sitting behind a large wooden desk. Doc knocked on the open door and stepped inside, LeBlanc close behind. "Principal Kimball?"

The woman stood and came around the front of her desk to greet them. Even with her hair teased, she was a couple of inches under five feet, and in the tailored blue slacks and cream top she wore, it was easy to see she was thin as well. She removed her reading glasses and extended her hand.

"Debbie Kimball. And you are Hunter and LeBlanc of the BCA?"

"Uh, yes ma'am."

"All right. Why don't you gentlemen have a seat and we can get started." Kimball returned to her chair, and the men sat in matching upholstered office chairs. She scooted her chair up to the desk. "I have assembled the teachers that had Blake Rose as a pupil in the conference room. I am afraid only seven of the ten are available, but I'm certain that should be more than sufficient."

"And why is that?" said Doc.

"As far as I can tell, the teachers of Blake Rose are all in agreement about the boy." She looked at her watch. "Now, how do you want to proceed?"

"Well..."

"Perhaps it would be best if you ask me the questions you have first, and then you can talk to the teachers."

"Uh, sure," said Doc. "What can you tell us about Blake?"

"Blake Rose was a conceited, entitled ass. As his football skills increased, so did his belligerent attitude. He was verbally abusive to other students, especially those smaller in stature and in lower grades. He bullied and cheated on his studies and was disruptive to the school. I was happy to see him go."

"Did you know the girl who filed a complaint against

him, Jenny Wyman?"

Kimball was visibly upset at the mention of the girl. She removed her glasses and rubbed the bridge of her nose. "Yes. She was a very nice girl. It was a horrible thing that Blake Rose did to her."

"And you know Blake Rose did it?"

"Everyone did."

Doc looked at LeBlanc, who was taking notes, his nose down, avoiding Principal Kimball's glare. "OK. Were any other complaints filed against him?"

"None."

"None?"

"Rose and his two henchmen threatened anyone who they thought may have any inclination to complain. One boy was beaten."

"By Rose?"

"No doubt, but the boy refused to say anything."

"I see. So, you wouldn't happen to know the names of the kids that he bullied?" said LeBlanc.

"I have asked our district legal counsel if I can supply that information. As I have no first-hand knowledge of the abuse, they have advised that I not provide any names."

Doc had been so captured by the persona of this woman that only now did he notice the pictures of the woman on the credenza behind her. In each picture Kimball was holding a gun, either a rifle or a handgun. There was a ribbon around her neck in each picture, and in most she was shaking hands with someone. Doc now noticed the plaques on the wall behind the credenza. The woman was a shooting champion, state, regional, and national. "You like to shoot, Mrs. Kimball?"

She did not follow his gaze. "Shooting is very exacting

and rewarding. I am quite good at it." Doc waited for more, but she had finished. "Shall I take you to the teachers now?" she said as she stood.

"Just a minute," said Doc, holding up his hand. "Any of the students or staff here shoot with you?"

"No. It's something I do on my own to relax," said Kimball. "Anything more?"

"Um, what about the teacher that Blake had an affair with? Miss Draper."

Kimball looked down at her desk top. "I'm sorry. I don't have any details on that. Miss Draper is no longer a teacher in the district. I believe the sheriff has the last contact information we have for her. Now, shall we?"

The agents looked at each other. Kimball had obviously been advised not to discuss the affair. They followed her out of the office, down the hall, and into the entryway. She was marching them across the building when Doc's phone rang.

"Hello?" He listened for a moment, said, "No problem," and disconnected. "OK, I need to make a run to Alex." He looked at the principal and said, "Agent LeBlanc will be conducting the interviews with the teachers," and then to LeBlanc, "Gary, I'll call you when I'm on my way back."

* * *

The Wymans lived between Holmes City and Alexandria, about a mile off 27. They were on a small lake, one of many in the area, in a tiny single-story rambler that looked like it had been or was part of a small resort, the homes on either side nearly identical. There was no driveway or garage. Prodigious oaks towered over the house, the yard below turned to moss. Doc pulled up in front of the home at noon. His stomach was grumbling as he turned off the car, getting him thinking he maybe should have gone on to Alex to get some lunch first. He knocked on the glass portion of the screen door.

"Yeah?" A woman's voice, rough, and then a cough. Doc could smell the cigarette before she reached the door. "Who are you?"

"Agent Hunter, BCA." Doc held his ID up. "I talked to you about an hour ago."

She pushed the screen, the door opening about six inches. "Yeah, yeah. Come on in."

The woman turned away, and Doc just got his fingers in the door before it shut. The woman, who was stooped and wore a ratty pink housecoat and slippers, walked down a short hall with a wood floor and into a small kitchen. She sat in a scarred maple chair with a torn seat cushion in front of a wood-laminate table. She stubbed out her cigarette and took a sip from a tumbler of gold liquid next to the ashtray. She waved her hand in front of her face and said, "You don't smoke, do you?"

"Nope."

"You want a drink?" She raised her glass to her lips again.

"Think I'll pass. Thanks."

The woman's hair was cut short, more salt than pepper, and had a look like she'd just gotten up, kind of flat on one side. Doc thought she was somewhere close to fifty, but it was hard to tell. He remained standing.

Eloise Wyman watched the smoke coming from the ashtray for a while, and then looked up at Doc. Her eyes were bloodshot blue, with the red nose of a drinker, her pale cheeks sagging like the skin under her exposed arms. "You're a big one, aren't you?" She coughed, making no move to cover her mouth.

"I was wondering if I could talk to your daughter, Mrs. Wyman."

"Not happening. She's long gone."

"Where has she gone?"

"Not where. She's dead. Killed herself, the little shit. Meth."

"I'm sorry. When was this?"

"I have no fucking idea." Wyman took another drink. "She took off five or six months ago. They found her in some ditch."

"Did she leave with anyone?"

"That piece-of-shit kid from over by Hoffman. Kid was bad news, but she wouldn't listen to me." Wyman finished her drink, looking into the glass like there might have been a leak.

"Do you have a name for the boy?"

"Lee someone." She was thinking about it. "Jackson or Johnson. Green hair and a shower ring in his nose. So many tattoos you couldn't tell what color he was. Drove a fancy black Mustang."

Doc looked around the place while she rambled. Dishes piled in the stained sink, one cupboard door hanging on by a single hinge. And now another smell overriding the cigarettes. Doc looked at the refrigerator. He didn't want to know.

"How about your husband? Is he around?"

Her deep, throaty laugh turned into a cough. "The only thing he's around is anyone who can get him high."

"And how long has he been gone?"

"Since Jenny was three or four. I don't remember exactly. He'd be gone for days at a time, and then he just didn't show up no more."

"Hmm. Mind if I take a look in your daughter's room?"

"Help yourself." She pointed to the right, the skin under her arm shaking. "Down the hall and on the right."

The girl's room looked like she could have taken off just hours ago. The single bed with a bookcase headboard was unmade, a worn blue sheet half off the bed and on the floor. Drawers on a small dresser matching the headboard were open to varying degrees, some empty, some with stray articles of clothing draped over the edge. A cross on a necklace of wooden beads hung from the frame of the mirror attached to the dresser. A couple of small dolls sat on the dresser leaning against the mirror, along with makeup, a plastic headband, a ring, and a broken bracelet. A small jewelry box, empty. A yearbook. Doc paged through it, remembering his own high school yearbook and how important it had been. He walked back to the kitchen with the yearbook and stood looking at what was left of Eloise Wyman. "OK. Well, thanks, Mrs. Wyman. I'm going to borrow this yearbook, but I'll bring it back," said Doc, holding up the book. Doc waited for a response but got nothing. He was going to ask her if her daughter had any other boyfriends in high school but decided he'd do better looking at the yearbook. "OK then. I'll let myself out." The woman still didn't seem to hear him, looking over her shoulder at the whiskey bottle on the counter. Time for a refill.

Doc walked back to his car and sat with the door open, long legs outside, feet on the ground. He pushed the number for Trask.

"Trask."

"You're in early."

"Yeah, well, I got one of my agents sapping all my resources, so I have to do some real work."

"I got a little more for you." Doc asked him if he could track down a kid near Hoffman with the name of Lee Jackson or

Lee Johnson. "He's got a black Mustang, probably pretty new. In his late teens, maybe a little older. Might have a drug arrest of some kind, but I'm only guessing about that. He ran off with the first girl Blake Rose assaulted, Jenny Wyman. I'd like to talk to him."

"LeBlanc get there?"

"Yeah. He's talking to Blake Rose's teachers."

"OK. Nothing on Rose from the DEA. I'll get back to you on the Mustang kid."

Doc had made a list of things to do on his phone the night before and he checked it now, found a note about calling the ME in Morris, and dialed the number. After a couple of transfers and a hold listening to an old Eagles song, Gus Meyer, the medical examiner for the county, picked up. "Doctor, it's Agent Hunter with the Minnesota Bureau of Criminal Apprehension. I'm wondering how you're doing on the Rose autopsies."

"Just finishing up, Agent."

"What do you know so far about their deaths?"

"All the Roses were shot with a small-caliber weapon at close range. We have recovered all the bullets."

"Is that what killed them all?"

"Yes. Blake Rose had been stabbed in the groin, but that occurred after he had been shot. I can't say for certain that he was dead before he was stabbed."

Doc clenched his teeth. "Anything else? Defensive wounds?"

"Sorry. Based on the neat placement of all three shots in the center of each of their foreheads, there's nothing to indicate any of them fought their killer, or even tried to get away."

Doc tried to put himself on the farm at the time the

Roses encountered their killer. Did they know him? Did he surprise them? A pro?

"Agent? Are you still there?"

"Yeah. Sorry, Doctor. How about the order of killing?"

"The boy, Blake, first. And then his parents—most likely Mr. Rose and then his wife."

Doc pictured the scene by the car and held his arm out, pointing his finger at John Rose, and then shifting his arm to point his finger at Sharon Rose. That felt right. But who had done it and why?

CHAPTER 9

"How you coming with the teachers?" Doc asked LeBlanc as he drove.

"Almost done," said LeBlanc.

"Anything?"

"Pretty much what the principal said. There isn't a lot of remorse."

"Any of the teachers seem like they'd like to have killed him?" asked Doc.

LeBlanc said, "Most of them."

"Great. This kid was Mr. Popular. You get any names of classmates and bullied kids?"

"Yup. Plenty," said LeBlanc. "And I got the name of the kid Blake supposedly beat up."

"Any other former girlfriends?"

"No. Maybe the kids can tell us more."

"Maybe. We should probably talk to Blake's two buddies again about that, too," said Doc. "Um, you didn't happen to get a number for that teacher, Draper, from any of them?"

LeBlanc gave the number to Doc.

"OK. Why don't you break for lunch after you finish with the teachers, and then start on the kids."

"What are you going to do?"

"I'll check in with Pickus and see if I can reach the teacher. Oh, and we should probably try to see Linda Knudson's former boyfriend, Mark Church. See if you can get contact information for him from the school and text it to me. I'll try to see him, too."

Doc was pulling out of the Wyman driveway when he realized he was hungry. He also realized he didn't have a clear idea of where he would be going next. Alexandria was five miles away, and he remembered a bar there that had good burgers and beer, so he headed that way.

* * *

The Shack was pretty much just that. There was a gravel parking area in front, enough for eight vehicles if they squeezed close together. Treated pine steps led up to a covered porch, the four-by-four poles holding up the sagging roof, the roof tilted noticeably to the north. The spaces between the weathered and stained cedar floorboards were easily big enough in spots to grab a high heel, so there was a "No high heels allowed" sign next to the door. The door itself was what remained of a screen door, the top section of screen nearly pushed out because people had used it to open the door. The bottom half was covered by a piece of plywood on either side of the frame, both pieces carrying the scars of regular kicking.

There was a long dark bar to the right, a brass footrest running its length. Two men in their sixties, both with ball caps and wearing jeans and T-shirts, sat nursing beers at the bar, two stools between them. They turned to look at Doc as he crunched across the discolored oak floor, stopping to fill a paper tray with peanuts, and then making his way to a booth on the opposite wall. He brushed some peanut shells from the shiny oak seat and slid in. Doc looked out the window at the sparkling blue water of Oxbow Lake. The Shack sat on a steep shoreline of the lake, a deck jutting out over the lake. There was no furniture on the deck; it had been closed several years ago after the railing had given way under a patron leaning on it as he enjoyed the view.

The bartender plopped a glass of water in front of Doc and said, "You know what you want?" The man was bald with a large red blemish almost like a lightning bolt on top of his head. Maybe a relative of Harry Potter, thought Doc. He wore a spotted green T-shirt with "The Shack" across the front, and a stained white apron over faded jeans.

"Yup. California, medium, and fries. Not those sweet potato fries, the regular ones. And a beer. Dark."

"I got a Summit IPA on tap."

"Let's do that. And thanks for the water."

When the man returned with Doc's beer, he'd gone through half of the glass of water. Doc did this for three reasons. One, he was thirsty. Two, his time in the Wyman house had left him with a bad taste in his mouth. The third reason was that drinking lots of water before he started on the beer tended to fill him up, and he didn't find himself too drunk or tired to keep working. Doc took a sip of his beer, thinking he should maybe have more water, and pulled out his phone.

"Pickus. It's Hunter. What do you know?"

"Just leaving the college. Talked to four of Blake's professors. None of them were too impressed with the boy when he bothered to show, which didn't seem to be too often. He either slept through class or was talking and obnoxious. One professor tossed him from a session. Said he was sure Blake was drunk. That was a morning class."

"So how did he pass?"

"Apparently his assignments were always turned in and he showed up for tests. Football players get tutoring and extra help, I guess."

Doc didn't have to guess. He knew. When he'd been gone for away games or missed a class for "social" reasons as a freshman, his papers and assignments were magically done. He didn't like it at first—it made him feel like he was cheating—but by his senior year he had no problem drinking or smoking enough that those feelings had disappeared. Somewhere along the way, he had been convinced to trade in his premed major for a more manageable degree in physical education. That bothered him for a while, too, especially when his father found out, but he was on a full ride so he didn't feel too guilty about that either. "So, where are you off to now?"

"Interviewing classmates and team members."

"You talk to the dean?"

"I thought you said you were going to do that."

"Yeah, that's right. I forgot." Doc hadn't forgotten, he just wanted to be sure Pickus remembered.

"Well, don't bother trying to catch him at the college if you do. The assistant dean said he wasn't in."

"OK, good to know. LeBlanc is talking to students too, and I just finished with the Wyman girl's mother." Before Pickus could ask, Doc added. "Apparently Jenny Wyman ran off with some kid up that way a while ago, and now she's dead."

"Dead?"

"Meth, I guess."

"She kind of freaked after the assault from what I heard. Turned into one of those goth kids."

"Yeah, well, if someone had taken her seriously maybe that wouldn't have happened. And maybe we wouldn't be here today."

"I did what I could. The DA—"

"Ah, bullshit!" Doc cut in. "You and everybody else that had anything to say put football ahead of doing the right thing."

Pickus was silent.

"OK, so I'm going to try to get hold of that teacher Blake had an affair with. And the dean. Oh, Trask said there's nothing on Rose with the DEA, so hopefully we can just kind of put that to the side until we run out of other rabbits to chase. I'll talk to you later."

Doc called the number he had for the dean, but there was no answer so he left a message. He tried Hailey Draper with the same result, leaving a message asking that she return his call. His burger and fries came as he disconnected. The fries were out of a bag but the burger was homemade by the looks of it, hanging out beyond the edges of the sesame seed bun, and done just right. He wolfed the burger down, dragging the fries through a pile of ketchup until he found they had disappeared too. The rest of his beer went down after the last fry, Doc pushing his plate and glass to the center of the table. His phone buzzed.

"Agent Hunter," answered Doc, wiping ketchup off his bottom lip.

"Agent. This is Hailey Draper."

"Thanks for returning my call. I'm calling about—"

"How do I know you are who you say you are?"

"Hmm. Well, I suppose you could call the BCA office in St. Paul and ask, but maybe it's enough to tell you that I'm calling about Blake Rose." The line was silent. "Miss Draper?"

"I saw the news last night. I was afraid this might happen."

"Afraid of what?" The woman was silent for a while, and Doc said, "Miss Draper?"

"Yes, all right. I guess we can meet."

"OK. Um, can you text me your address?"

"Yes. When do you think you'll be here? I'm about a mile west of Spicer."

"Just a minute." Doc pulled up Google Maps on his phone. "OK, looks like a little more than an hour. I'm coming from Alex. I'm eating a late lunch so I'll probably be there about four."

* * *

The address turned out to be a small cabin on Twin Lake, just off County 9. Twin Lake was shallow and small, under two hundred acres, like a lot of the pothole lakes in the area. It had a good population of bass and pike and panfish, but wasn't much for walleye, Minnesota's favorite eating fish. Big Green Lake just a mile to the east had a good population of walleye and had hosted the Governor's fishing opener the year before. The governor had been shut out as usual.

Doc turned into the yard, stopping his Acura in front of the single-car detached garage that stood sideways to the lake. The garage and cabin were newly painted slate gray with white trim around the windows and doors. Doc extracted himself from his car, sliding his sunglasses on top of his head as he surveyed the area. The lot for the cabin was small, maybe seventy-five feet of lakeshore and not more than a hundred feet to the gravel road. A huge Norway pine dominated the small yard, similar trees reaching up into the sky as far as he could see to the east, the yard carpeted with brown needles. There was no door on cabin, but a line of rose-colored paving stones ran from the side of the garage to the side of the cabin, and he followed those. Doc was looking out at the calm water on the lake and had just raised his hand to knock when the door opened.

"Agent Hunter?"

The woman was wearing tan shorts and a powder-blue T-shirt with sequins on the collar. She was tall, nearly six feet, with shining black hair pulled back in a ponytail and deep-blue eyes. High cheeks pulled at a dazzling smile of white teeth surrounded by full, red lips.

Doc grabbed the edge of the door and stared. "Um, yeah. Miss Draper?"

"I'd like to see your identification first."

Doc dug it out of his pocket, held it up.

"Come in, but please don't let the door slam. The baby is sleeping."

Draper turned and walked inside, Doc watching her appreciatively.

The interior was compact but nicely done, with pine paneling and oak floors. A small dining table sat against the wall directly to Doc's right. A bar with four stools separated the table from the kitchen. Immediately to the left was a living area with a couch and two upholstered chairs, the seating all facing the picture window that looked out on the lake. There was a hall beyond the kitchen, which Doc assumed would lead to a bathroom and bedroom. Draper took an open beer from the bar and lifted it to her lips, then said, "Sorry, would you like a beer? Or isn't that allowed?"

"What are you drinking?"

Draper held her bottle out to him. It was an IPA from a local brewery. Doc was picky about his beer and studied the label. "Is it good?"

"I think so."

"OK then."

Draper pulled a bottle from the refrigerator's lowest shelf, Doc observing as she bent at the waist. She opened the bottle with an opener hanging from a nail on the side of a cupboard and handed Doc the beer. He took a long sip. The beer was good.

"Why don't we go out to the lake?" she said. "It's a little warm in here. No air, I'm afraid."

Doc followed her to the lake side of the cabin, where two red-plastic lawn chairs sat under a pine facing the water, a matching table between. They sipped their beers as a duck and five ducklings swam by, the mother duck squawking, trying to hurry the young ones on.

"So, what can I tell you, Agent Hunter?"

"Doc," he said. "Call me Doc."

"OK, Doc. What would you like to know?"

She crossed her long legs and waved her painted toes in the air. Her nails matched her lips, and Doc was immediately thinking he'd like to get a closer look at that paint. "I'm looking into the death of Blake Rose and his parents, as you know. I believe you had Blake as one of your students."

She giggled, putting her free hand to her mouth. "Come on, Agent. You can do better than that. You obviously know there was something going on between Blake and me in Morris, and I already told you I have a baby here, so why don't you just ask?"

"So, I take it the baby is Blake's?"

"That wasn't so hard, was it?" Draper smiled. "Yes, it's Blake's child. I was stupid and lonely, and he was good looking, and I let him into my pants."

"He didn't force himself on you?"

"Afraid not. Like I said, I was stupid. And drunk. The kid had protection, but obviously that didn't work."

"So, you just left?"

Draper finished her beer. "I knew I couldn't stay. There was certainly no future for us as a couple and no future for a pregnant single teacher in a small town. I took a medical leave and then resigned. Took last year off, moved here, had the baby, and then applied for an opening at Spicer. I'm a math teacher and math teachers are in demand, so they hired me. I start in the fall."

"Did Blake know about the baby?"

"He knew. He was shitting bricks when I told him I was pregnant and was keeping the baby. Begged me to get an abortion so it wouldn't ruin his football career." Draper laughed and looked out at the lake. "Football career. He was in high school."

Doc finished his beer and said, "Were you upset with him?"

She turned back to him. "You mean like upset that he had ruined my life, and I wanted to kill him?"

"Maybe like that."

"Sorry. I was the one who screwed up. Along with his condom. He was just a stupid kid full of hormones, like most of them his age."

She looked back at the water, her empty bottle dangling

in her long slender fingers. Doc watched her a minute and then looked out at the lake, too. A cooling breeze came across, barely enough to move the needles on the pine, but it felt good. She shook her bottle and stood, holding out her empty hand.

"You want another?"

Doc said, "Sure," and she went inside, returning with a single beer.

"You're not having one?"

"Nursing. Not supposed to get the baby too drunk, you know."

She smiled at Doc, and he picked up maybe a little pain there. "You OK?"

"Oh yeah. It's beautiful here. Just a little lonely."

"No family?"

"My parents are from Lakeshore. You know where that is?" Doc did. His parents lived on Lake Minnetonka, west of Minneapolis. "My dad is like a muckity-muck at Cargill. They wanted me to get rid of the baby—it would be too embarrassing for them—but I told them to stick it. They said good luck and don't bother coming back."

"They may change their mind."

Her blue eyes looked a little sad. She had thought about this. "Maybe. But in the meantime, I'm on my own, and a baby is going to make it hard at work, and socially."

Doc took a long drink of his beer. He liked it. And Hailey Draper. "You have day care lined up?"

"Yup," she said. "Just last week."

"You've got no worries then. Attractive woman like you. You're probably a great teacher, too."

"You don't know me at all."

"I'm pretty good at judging people. It's kind of what I

do."

She looked at Doc for a long moment, and seemed about to say something when there was a cry from inside. "Somebody's up. Excuse me."

Doc could hear her talking inside and then the crying moving through the cabin behind him. He turned to watch Draper carrying the baby out of the house.

"This is Charlie. He's a hungry little snot, so you don't mind if I feed him, do you?"

Doc had all kinds of emotions about this. He'd seen his older sister breastfeed her babies, but that was his sister. He hardly knew this woman. And on top of that he felt a little jealous that this small baby was going to be having fun with what were some obviously very nice breasts, and he was not. "No, no problem." She started to lift her shirt, and Doc said, "I'm just going to take a quick walk down to the lake." Pushing himself up in a hurry, keeping his eyes focused on the water, he stepped away.

Doc walked to the shore and then out on the dock, sipping his beer, noticing it was almost gone again, and wondering what he was doing. He should and could just leave. There was nothing here that was going to help him find the killer. But he didn't want to go. He'd had a couple of beers, and he was relaxed, and he was enjoying his conversation with Hailey Draper. She was smart and easy to listen to, and even easier to look at. Still, there was a murderer on the loose. Doc drained the rest of his beer and turned, chancing a peek. Draper was just lowering her top, the baby quiet. He walked back and stood in front of his chair.

"He seemed to have liked that."

"Men. They're all the same." Hailey laughed. The baby

stirred but then was quiet again. "So, Doc. You have dinner plans?"

There was a little voice in the back of his head screaming, "No, no, no!" but he said, "Not really."

"I've got some steaks in the refrigerator and a bottle of cabernet. You interested? I'm not very good at grilling."

"I can give it a try."

Doc grilled the steaks, and she baked a couple of potatoes and put a premade salad in a bowl, and they ate out on the two chairs facing the lake. The baby woke for a while, and Doc held it for a bit before she laughed and said he'd better give the baby back because he was obviously uncomfortable holding a human so tiny, and Doc was grateful for that. The baby was fed again and went to sleep. They sat outside, the sun setting behind them reflecting off the windows of the homes across the lake, and finished the bottle. They talked about themselves some, she being freer about what she said, not knowing anything about Doc's football past, and he didn't mention it. And he was fine with that. Finally, the mosquitoes chased them inside, and they did dishes like an old married couple, standing at the sink. And as Doc was stretching to put a bowl in the cupboard on the other side of her, leaning over her, she turned and they both looked at each other for just a moment before he forgot about the bowl.

CHAPTER 10

There was a buzzing. Again. A sleepy voice behind Doc said, "You should probably get that. It's the third time in the last minute." Doc gave a low growl. He pushed himself to a sitting position, legs over the side of the bed, and reached for his shorts on the floor. "Yeah."

"Hunter. Where are you? I tried your room and your phone like ten times."

It took a moment for Doc to dig the voice from his memory. "Um, LeBlanc?"

"Yeah. Listen, you need to get here now."

"Where?"

"The dean's house. He's dead."

* * *

The dean of the Morris Community College was named

Dean—Dean Alcott. The board and the administrators and the professors and just about everybody else at the college had a good laugh about it when Alcott was hired five years earlier, calling him Dean Dean and Dean Squared and Double Dean and some other names made up by the students that were not as polite. Not to his face, but he had heard most of the names and jokes by the end of his first year. But he wouldn't be hearing them anymore. Dean Dean Alcott was dead.

Alcott lived about two miles south of the college in a small, secluded area of nice homes. The area was heavily wooded, the homes on two-acre lots that fronted the Pomme de Terre River. These were not the newest homes in town—those were in a subdivision west of 59—but they were definitely the largest. The first home in the area was built for David Lockwood, owner of the two Dairy Queens in Morris as well as the property where Alcott's home and the others in the area now sat. Lockwood's neighbors didn't care for the egotistical know-it-all, but he put on a big party every summer with a cooler full of ice cream treats, so they put up with him.

Alcott's home was not as grand as Lockwood's, but it was still nice. It had two stories (three in back), an attached triple garage, and a brick driveway that circled a fountain in front of the house. There were dormers across the second level and a brick chimney matching the bricks in the driveway. An oval stone patio in back of the house had a fire pit in the middle and looked out at the river.

Doc was glad to see the road in front of the house had been blocked off in each direction. He stopped short of the Stevens County squad parked across the road. Deputy Jones, the same deputy who had been at the Rose place, got out, and walked up to Doc's window.

"You must be getting pretty good at this," said Doc.

Jones looked at Doc and said, "Yeah, it's a rare skill. I'll move my car." Jones backed his squad up enough for Doc to pass and then moved it back into position.

The driveway was crowded. The sheriff's car, LeBlanc's vehicle, the ME van, a Morris police car, and a small red Prius. Doc parked behind the van and walked up to the porch, where LeBlanc met him.

"You look like shit, Doc. You wearing the same clothes as yesterday?"

"I got waylaid. What do you know?"

"What's waylaid mean?"

"Just what it sounds like. So . . ."

"Dean Alcott was found just inside the front door, single shot to the forehead. No sign of forced entry. ME is looking at him now."

"Who found him?"

"Some girl from the college. The dean was supposed to be at a meeting this morning and didn't show, so the assistant dean sent her out here to check."

"Blonde? Blue eyes? Nice looking?" said Doc. A puzzled LeBlanc said, "Who?" and Doc said, "Never mind. Where is she?"

"The girl? Inside."

"Anyone else live here besides the dean?"

"I guess not." LeBlanc looked at the house. "Big place for one guy."

Doc followed LeBlanc's gaze and said, "Yeah. Um, you got any more gloves?"

LeBlanc fished a pair out of his pocket.

Doc put them on, and said, "Let's go in."

They didn't go far. Inside the doorway at the bottom of the stairs was the body of Alcott. A man Doc assumed was the ME was bent over the body. Pickus and Police Chief Bill Palmer stood watching.

"Where have you been, Hunter?" said Pickus. "I tried to reach you last night."

Doc had seen the call but had ignored it. "I got waylaid." He looked at Palmer. "I'm Agent Doc Hunter."

"Bill Palmer." Palmer was just past fifty and about six feet tall. His thick neck was bent forward like his head was too heavy to hold up. Palmer looked up at Doc with tired eyes like he was looking over reading glasses and held out his hand.

They shook hands as the medical examiner stood up and said, "Doctor Meyer. We talked."

"Howdy. You know anything yet?" said Doc.

"I'd say dead at least twenty-four hours, maybe more. Only wound is the gunshot to the forehead. Looks identical to the ones that killed the Roses. No defensive wounds or other obvious marks."

"Jeez," said Pickus. "He killed the Roses Sunday morning and then came over here Sunday night. The guy is on a rampage."

Doc said, "It's not a rampage." They all stood looking down at the body for a second, and Doc said, "He live here alone?"

"Yeah," said Palmer. "His wife passed about five years ago. Cancer."

Doc looked around. "Big house for one guy." He looked at Palmer. His black hair was cut military style, and he had big old-man ears. "Who was here first?"

"One of my guys. Jackson. The girl had called nine-one-

one, and the dispatcher sent him over. He called it in as soon as he saw the body."

"Anybody else come in besides those two?"

"Nope, not until Pickus and I and the ME showed."

"All right. I've got a BCA crime-scene unit on the way. Be maybe an hour. Where's the girl?"

Palmer nodded to the open door behind him and said, "In there."

Doc looked that way and said, "OK," and then to Pickus, "We need to talk. I'll talk to the girl a minute and then maybe we can talk outside." Pickus nodded, and Doc broke from the group, LeBlanc at his side.

They walked through an open doorway into what was a formal dining room. There was a china cabinet with a glass top and glass shelves over a red maple sideboard to the left and a matching cabinet at the other end of the room next to another open door leading to the kitchen. An oblong maple table was in the center of the room, three chairs on each side, one on each end, with two additional chairs against the wall ahead of them. The blonde receptionist Doc had met at the college sat at the end of the table closest to them, a Morris cop sitting in one of the chairs against the wall. The cop stood.

"You can go, Officer," said Doc. The girl looked up at the sound of Doc's voice, her eyes red, a tissue clasped in her hands. Doc said, "How you doing?"

"OK," the girl said.

Doc introduced LeBlanc. "So, I didn't get your last name the other day." Doc pulled out a chair and sat to her left.

"Hoke."

The girl was wearing a pink T-shirt today, with white shorts. She must like pink, Doc thought. "So, Cheryl, why don't you tell me what happened? Take your time."

She looked down at the tissue in her hands and said, "OK. Well, Doctor Lester came up to my desk, and she said I needed to drive over here to get the dean for a meeting. She said his phone must be broken or something, and that I should call her when I got here to let her know that the dean was on his way. She was steamed."

"That's good, Cheryl," said Doc. "Do you remember what time that was?"

"Yeah. It was eight fifteen, because I looked at my phone when I got in my car."

"And you came right here?"

"Yeah."

Doc waited for a while, and then said, "OK, go on."

Hoke took a deep breath and said, "So, I walked up to the front door and rang the bell. I could hear it ringing inside, but nobody came to the door. I was going to leave, but then I decided to knock, just in case the dean didn't hear the bell, like he was in the bathroom or something. Anyway, when I knocked, the door opened a little."

"You didn't turn the knob to open the door?"

"No. It was open. So I just pushed it open a little more and leaned my head in and said, 'Hello,' but nobody answered. I was going to yell again when I saw the dean on the floor."

Doc could see the girl tensing up, breathing harder. "You're doing great. You're like a professional witness."

Her glistening eyes looked at Doc. "I am?"

"Absolutely. So, what did you do then?"

"I couldn't stop staring at him, and then I just screamed and ran for my car."

"You drove off?"

"No. I was going to, but then I called nine-one-one, and the woman told me just to stay here and stay on the line until the police showed up." The girl took a deep breath.

"You were very brave to wait. Did you see or hear anyone before the police officer showed up?"

"No. I was kind of freaking and almost left, anyway. It seemed like he took forever."

"So, how about when you drove in? Do you remember seeing or hearing anyone?" said Doc.

"Uh-uh."

Doc looked at LeBlanc and then said, "You did great, Cheryl. Thanks for your help. An officer is going to take your statement, and then you can go."

"What about Doctor Lester? She's going to be really pissed by now."

"Don't worry. I'll take care of her for you." He patted the girl on the arm and returned to Pickus and Palmer, who didn't look like they had moved. Doc was about to say something to Pickus when his phone buzzed. Trask. "Sorry, I got to take this," Doc said as he walked back outside.

"OK, I found your black Mustang kid."

"That was quick."

"Yeah, well, it wasn't that hard. He's dead."

"When?"

"Beginning of last week. Just south of Wahpeton. Killed with a single shot. Farmer found the body. Kid's name was Lee Jackson. Traced him through his car registration. They got prints off the car that weren't Jackson's, but they don't know who."

"Aw shit," said Doc. "What kind of weapon?"

"Small-caliber pistol. Shot in the head."

Doc said, "I need to get up there."

"Yeah, you do. So, where are you now?"

"Morris. The dean of the college has been shot. Looks the same as the Rose killings."

"Jesus, Doc. That's five down. You got to catch this guy."

"I'm working on it."

"Well, work a little harder. I'll send you the contact information for the Wahpeton chief."

Trask was gone. Doc thought maybe he *should* work a little harder, considering he had kind of taken the afternoon off yesterday, but then he got to thinking about yesterday and wondering if he could work out a visit to Miss Draper again in the near future. The sun was a warm hand on his cheek, and he looked up at the cloudless sky. A beautiful day for golf. And that wasn't going to happen either. "Fuck."

* * *

The killer was surprised by how easy it had been. After all of his worrying and almost backing out, there really hadn't been that much to it. Just one shot, and boom, they were gone. It was really pretty exciting, but when it came down to it, not that tough. He'd scoped things out, planned what to do and when. That was probably the most important part—the planning. Not only did it make sure that things went like they were supposed to, it kind of got him revved up.

The druggie up in North Dakota had been the first. The killer had followed Jenny when the druggie picked her up. They stopped at his place and were in there for a long time. The killer knew what they were doing in there, and he almost went in and shot them both right then, but they came out before he could make up his mind and the druggie took Jenny home. Jenny had died that week.

And that was when he started his plan. He wanted to go kill the druggie bastard right after he heard about Jenny's death, but it wasn't just the druggie's fault, was it? If they'd done something about Blake before Jenny, none of it would ever have happened. Jenny and Linda Knudson would have been fine, but they weren't, were they? They'd all had a hand in killing Jenny. All of them that protected Blake.

So, he had planned it out. He'd always been a planner. His father had taught him that. Plan things out and there won't be any surprises. Like they'd taught him in the Boy Scouts: Be prepared. And the killer had done that. He'd made a list, putting each victim in order of when they would be killed, and then planning how that would happen. And so far, it had gone according to plan. Well, almost. Blake's parents had surprised him. He really hadn't planned on them, but there wasn't much he could do about it. They had to go.

The killer figured that the druggie would be the easiest, and he had been right. He went to Lee Jackson's place and told him he was a friend of Jenny Wyman, and Wyman had told him that Jackson had some good shit. Jackson was a little skeptical at first, saying he didn't think the killer looked like a user, but the killer convinced him that was because he was in sports, and that he didn't use during the season. Jackson seemed to buy that, but remained a little leery, finally inviting the killer to follow him to Wahpeton to a place he knew where they could try some stuff together.

The killer became a little suspicious himself when Jackson led him to an abandoned farm, thinking he might try to rob him or have someone waiting to rob or kill him, but there was no other vehicle at the place that the killer could see. They stopped behind an old barn, and Jackson got out. The killer pulled a pistol from under his seat. He got out and walked up to Jackson, who was standing at the back of his car. Jackson was shining the light from his phone on the lock on his trunk, focused on getting it open.

The killer held out his gun and said, "Move away from the car."

The light was disappearing fast, but there was enough for Jackson to see the gun. He raised his hands. "Whoa, man. No need for that. I just keep the stuff in the trunk."

"I don't care," said the killer. "Move."

Jackson was chatting nervously, stopping on the gravel a few yards behind the car, and the killer guessed he was already high. "Come on, man. What do you want? Money? I keep it in the trunk with the stuff. There's not much, but you can have it. Come on."

"You killed her," said the killer. "You killed Jenny."

"Who?"

"Jenny Wyman. You killed her."

"Wait, wait, man. That goth chick? No, man, no way. She OD'd, man. It wasn't me."

"It was you." The killer stepped up to Jackson, his gun inches from his forehead, Jackson's hands up as high as he could reach. The killer wasn't sure he could do it. He'd shot animals, but never a person. Shooting a person was like walking through a door to a dark place, some place you'd never been to, and you could never leave. And the killer wasn't sure he wanted to go there, but then he looked at the face of the scumbag who had poisoned Jenny. Stared hard at him for what seemed to a long time. And then he shot him. He pulled his phone from his pocket and held the light over the druggie, Jackson's open eyes giving him a start. The killer watched for a minute, to see if Jackson would move, but there was no sign of life.

CHAPTER 11

Doc, LeBlanc, and Pickus stood in the front yard of the dean's house. Doc updated them on the Wahpeton killing, and Pickus said it was surely a rampage now. LeBlanc and Pickus gave updates about what they had done yesterday. "OK, this seems more and more about Blake Rose, but we can't forget about John Rose," said Doc.

Pickus said, "And the drug thing."

"And the drug thing. But right now we need to keep our focus on Blake and the people connected to him and these rapes."

"I think we still ought to talk to Ed Salo," said Pickus. "The guy didn't like Rose or his kid. And he didn't like the way Blake got away with the assaults."

Doc was tempted to tell Pickus to forget it, but he needed his help. "OK, set it up for late this afternoon. Don't make it too early. I don't know how long it will take in Wahpeton, and I want to talk to that Church kid today." Doc looked at the heavily treed yard, the next-door neighbor's house to the west barely visible, the one to the east not at all. "Sheriff, we need to get someone to talk to the neighbors, see if anyone saw anything. Can Kuck or someone do that?"

Pickus said he and Kuck had their hands full following up with the college kids but he would see if Palmer could do it. Doc thanked him and said he would call them both when he was on the way back from Wahpeton to let them know what he discovered. He drove back to the Ramada and showered. As he toweled off, his lack of coffee and food and sleep all hit him, and he flopped down on his back on top of the bedspread, naked. "Ten minutes," he muttered, and closed his eyes.

Twenty minutes later a knock at the door and a voice calling, "Room service," woke him up. He yelled, "Come back later," and sat up, elbows on his thighs and head in his hands.

Dressed in the same shorts, with a Pine Beach polo shirt he especially liked, Doc drove to The Windmill to grab some breakfast. He had the same waitress, and she looked at him like she was kind of afraid. He assured her he wouldn't swear or shoot anyone if she could just get him his order as fast as possible. While he ate his French toast, Doc called Wahpeton to tell them he was on the way, and then called Carl Miranda.

"You back in Morris yet?"

"Almost. You know you don't need to keep giving me work. I'm plenty busy."

"Yeah, well, I just can't help sharing the love. So, anyway, give me a call when you're done there. Please work with the ME to get the slug and compare it to the ones from the farm. There's another guy shot up in Wahpeton that I think might be related, so, if they recovered the slug, I'll have them send it to you. Or maybe I can get it today and bring the slug back with me. How long do you think you'll be?"

Miranda said he didn't know, but that he would call Doc when he was close to done.

It was a straight shot to Wahpeton from Morris on 9, but it was still over an hour. Doc made a couple more calls on the way, connecting with the parents of Mark Church, who said they would have their son call him.

After crossing the river into North Dakota, Doc went south out of Wahpeton on 127 nearly three miles before going west a half mile and then finally south again on a gravel road for a few blocks. There wasn't much to see. Level farmland for miles with an occasional farmstead or windbreak of spruce, or clumps of trees and rocks. But it was green, despite the dry spell. Rich river-basin soil that was good for growing wheat and beans and sugar beets, and just about anything else. His GPS told him to turn down a long gravel drive lined with barbed wire at that point. Doc wasn't sure if his GPS was right, but he saw a white pickup in the yard at the end of the drive with someone standing next to it, and turned in.

The pickup had "Wahpeton Police" written on the side and the man leaning on the driver's door was the chief, Andy Nichols. Nichols was tall and thick. His hands were large and strong, like he worked in the fields for a living, and he made sure Doc felt the pressure when they shook hands.

"Thanks for meeting me on such short notice," said Doc as he slid his sunglasses up.

"No problem," said Nichols. He looked Doc over. "You going golfing later?"

"I wish. If people didn't keep killing each other maybe I could get in a round, but it's becoming darn difficult. You golf?"

"On occasion. The Bois de Sioux course on the river north of town is actually pretty nice. Long, but in good shape. Nice greens. Only course I know where you can play in two states."

"Hmm. I'll think about that. So, what can you tell me about what happened out here?"

Nichols bounced off his truck, said, "Follow me," and started walking. There were three buildings on the site, a house, a silo, and a barn, all looking like they had been abandoned years ago. The barn had collapsed in on itself in the front, and Doc wondered why the "weathered barn wood" thieves hadn't made off with the boards. It was apparent from the tire tracks in the gravel that there had been a number of vehicles here, including a tractor. With the empty beer cans and other trash lying about, Doc assumed all the tracks were not from police and emergency vehicles.

Nichols stopped a little way past the barn and pointed to two sheets of corrugated steel siding on the ground. "The body was there, under the siding. Whoever killed him dragged the siding from over by the silo to cover him up. Had to be pretty strong to do that. Those sheets are heavy."

Doc walked over to the siding and squatted, looking over the area. "It hasn't rained here since the body was found, has it?"

"No. Been pretty dry. We got a few prints off the metal that are a close match to what was on the car, but that metal is so rough it's hard to get anything good off it."

Doc looked carefully at the edges of the metal sheets. They were rough, with burrs and sharp edges, and he wondered if whoever moved them might have been cut or scraped, but he couldn't see anything. "Did you have a technician take a close look at the edges of the metal, especially by where you found the prints?"

"I assumed they did that, but I don't remember for sure. Let me make a call."

"Where was the car?" Doc asked.

"In the barn," Nichols said, pointing, and then turned away and started talking to someone on the phone.

Doc stepped carefully into the barn. It looked like the rest of it could come down at any minute, and there were boards with nails on the cement floor. The floor was dirty, the cement only visible in a few spots. The tire tracks were easy to see. Doc inspected the area around the tracks, squatting again, before standing and looking around the area. He heard the flap of wings and looked up to see a couple of pigeons on the rafter above him, and he moved back toward the door.

Nichols walked up and said, "They looked. Didn't find anything."

"Thanks, Chief. I just needed to be sure."

"Anything else?"

"So, what do you think happened?"

Nichols looked at the metal sheeting and said, "I'm not sure. We have quite a few kids come out here and party, from North Dakota and Minnesota. This spot isn't any secret. I'm guessing the boy had maybe come out here to deal or use or both. He's got a record. Maybe a deal went bad. Thing is, he wasn't in the car when he was shot. As far as we can tell, he was shot where we found him."

"Hmm," said Doc. "Was he robbed?"

"We think so. Nothing in the car. Traces of meth in the trunk. No wallet or phone on him. Kids always have phones."

"Yeah. What about the guy that found him?"

"Doug Nelson," said Nichols. "Owns the property. He had been working the field on the other side of the silo and came through here on his tractor. Saw the car in the barn and stopped. Then he saw the steel panels and was going to put them back by the silo when he found the body."

"When was this?"

"Friday."

"Friday? I thought he was killed early last week."

"That's what the ME thinks. He'd been here a few days."

They stood looking at the barn and silo for a moment. Doc said, "You still have the car?"

Nichols said he did.

"I'd like to see the ME's report and look at your files. Maybe talk to Doug Nelson, but I'll have to see after I look at the file."

"That shouldn't be a problem," said Nichols. "So, what do *you* think happened?"

Doc shook his head. "I don't know yet. I've got four people dead over by Morris, and this one is kind of tied to those in a way. I'd like to take the slug pulled from this kid and have our tech guy compare it with what we have, and then I'll know better if these things are related. But right now, I have to think they are."

They were walking back toward their vehicles, Doc saying he would follow Nichols, when Doc got a call.

"Hunter."

"Um, is this the BCA agent?" said a young voice.

"Yes. Agent Peter Hunter. Who is this?"

"Mark Church. You wanted to talk to me?"

CHAPTER 12

It was well into the afternoon by the time Doc left Wahpeton. He had looked at the police reports and crime-scene photos, interview with the farmer, autopsy report and photos, and forensic reports. All of it said the person who had killed Jackson could be the same one who had killed the others. The bullet he now had should make that clear. Miranda called just before he was about to leave, letting Doc know there was no sign of anyone having robbed the Alcott home. They had taken a bunch of fingerprints off of the front door handle, but there were prints on top of prints and most would likely be useless. He said they had also gone through the dean's car and phone, but found nothing of interest there either. Doc told Miranda he'd meet him in an hour at the dean's house and give him the slug from the Wahpeton killing. Miranda said he would really like to go get something to eat. Doc told him about The Windmill and they decided to meet there.

Doc stopped at the Dairy Queen he'd seen on his way into town and ordered a burger, fries, and a Coke. He wanted a Blizzard, but he needed the nourishment and the caffeine first. He called Pickus as he ate.

"Sheriff, it's Doc. What can you tell me today?"

Pickus said he and Kuck had talked to a dozen of Blake's classmates, who all seemed to agree that the boy was a "stuck-up asshole" but none seemed to have a reason to kill him, and they didn't seem to know anyone who would.

"OK," said Doc. "Any of them know Linda Knudson?"

"A few," Pickus said, "but no one was close to her."

Doc said, "All right. Maybe you should switch to the football players now. I'm thinking those guys might have more of an axe to grind. Maybe Rose tried to horn in on one of their girlfriends, or he assaulted someone else I don't know about yet."

"OK. I have a meeting set with Ed Salo for four thirty."

"That's not going to work. I'm just leaving Wahpeton, and I'm talking to the Church kid when I get to town. How about this evening?"

"Like what time?"

"Let's say eight. We can go to his place if that makes it easier."

Pickus said he would try to reschedule and would let Doc know. "What did you find up there?"

Doc told him what he knew. "I got to think right now that it's the same person doing the killing. Shot in the head with a pistol, up close. I'm bringing the slug back to compare with what we have from the Rose and Alcott killings. This one was a little different though. The boy was shot in the back of the head."

"Maybe he was trying to run away."

"Maybe." This didn't seem to mean much to Pickus, but it had Doc thinking.

"OK, then," Pickus said. "I'll see if I can reschedule Salo and call you back."

Before Pickus could disconnect, Doc said, "How many people in the county do you think have handguns?"

Pickus laughed. "I'd say just about everyone in the county has a rifle and maybe half to a third of those have at least one handgun. And there are probably a bunch of unregistered ones out there, too."

"That's what I thought. OK, talk to you later." Doc hung up and then dialed LeBlanc.

"You waylaid again?"

"Not yet. I just finished in Wahpeton." Doc gave him a rundown and asked LeBlanc how he was coming along.

"The girls are OK to talk to, most of them anyway, but the boys all have attitudes. I can't believe their language. I pity their teachers."

"You should get married and have kids."

"What?"

"You sound like a parent, or an old person at least."

"Yeah, well, anyway, I'm still working through my list."

"No hints of Blake getting away with any other assaults?"

"No. You know something?"

"Nah. Just poking," said Doc. "So how about the kid Blake beat up? You talk to him yet?"

"No, he's still on the list."

"OK. Why don't you hold on that one until tomorrow, and I'll go with you. I'm kind of running out of prime suspects here. Lots of potential ones, but not prime."

Doc got hold of Mark Church next. Church lived with his folks in a house in town, and they agreed to meet there in about an hour.

It took Doc an hour to get to The Windmill. The place was busy. Full of people with gray or silver or blue hair, or no hair at all, so it was easy to pick out Miranda with his thick black hair. There was another technician seated across from Miranda in the booth, Dale Nervic. Nervic was about the same age as Miranda, early thirties, and nearly as thin. He had stringy blond hair, a bony face, and diamond studs in each ear.

Miranda scooted over as Doc slid in. "I thought I might be in the senior center by mistake."

"It's the Senior Tuesday special," said Miranda. "Four thirty to five thirty. Meatloaf and mashed potatoes and pie. Only five ninety-nine."

Doc glanced at their plates. "So, you two are seniors now?"

"It looked so good we just had to try it," said Miranda.

"And is it?"

Nevic nodded, his mouth too full of mashed potatoes to speak.

Doc handed Miranda a manila envelope. "Here's the slug from the killing up in Wahpeton. How soon do you think you can take a look at it?"

"Tomorrow morning," said Miranda. "You need it back?"

"It needs to go back to the Wahpeton police. There's an envelope in there for it, if you wouldn't mind." Despite the burger and fries he'd just eaten, the smell of the meatloaf was making Doc hungry, not to mention how fast the technicians were putting it away. And the blueberry pie looked awfully good. "Is it all you can eat?"

"Yup," said Nevic.

Just then the same waitress Doc had had in the morning showed up with a big smile and said, "Can I interest you in the special, sir?"

"I'm already interested, but I'm afraid I'm not old enough. I will be back, though."

Doc slid out of the booth, looked longingly at the meatloaf in front of Miranda, and said he'd talk to him in the morning.

* * *

The Church home was only about eight blocks from The Windmill. They lived in what Doc guessed was one of the original homes in town. It had a big corner lot and was two stories, painted white, with square red-brick posts on either side of the sidewalk leading from the front door, just inside where the sidewalk from the house met the sidewalk going around the block. Red-brick planters matching the posts stood on either side of the steps leading up to a covered porch in front. Doc knocked on the wooden screen door, painted a grassy green to match the trim.

A tall kid walked up to the screen door from inside. His long brown hair was turning blond from time in the sun. His attempt at a beard was not a success.

"Yeah?"

Doc held out his identification. "BCA agent Hunter. Are you Mark Church?"

Church looked through the screen for a minute at the

ID and then pushed the door open, stepping out, Doc backing out of the way. He didn't have a shirt on, the swimmer's torso v-shaped. "We can talk out here. It's too hot in there. The air isn't working." They sat in wicker chairs facing the street. "So, what's this about?"

Church didn't seem afraid. Most people, especially kids his age and younger, were a little intimidated by being questioned by a BCA agent, especially one as big as Doc. "I understand you and Linda Knudson had a relationship?"

"What do you mean?"

"In high school?"

"We dated for a while." The kid's finger was drumming on the chair handle. Impatient.

"So, nothing serious?"

"No. I dated other girls, too."

"Like Jenny Wyman?"

"Some," said Church. He stared at Doc. "You need to tell me what this is about."

"I'm investigating the murders of the Rose family. Just trying to get in touch with people who knew them. How well did you know Blake Rose?"

"Not very. We didn't have any classes together."

"You knew about him being accused of assaulting Linda and Jenny?"

"Sure. Everybody did," said Church.

"And how do you feel about that?" said Doc.

A car went by, and Church watched it pass. "The guy was a piece of shit," he replied. "He should have been locked up."

"Yeah, probably," said Doc. He could see the tension in Church's neck. "You a swimmer?"

Church turned to look at Doc. "I'm on the team."

There were groupie girls that followed the men in college sports. Doc had spent time with a few as a football player. But for some reason, the swim team always seemed to have the most. Doc figured it was because the swimmers were practically naked, their small suits leaving little to the imagination. "Nice. Those girls following the swimmers are pretty hot." Doc stood.

"Were you a swimmer?" said Church.

"No, but I always wished I was." Doc slid his sunglasses down. "How about hunting? You a hunter?"

"Deer and ducks."

"How about shooting? You have a pistol?"

"My dad does. I've shot it before."

"You a good shot?"

"OK. My dad is better."

Doc wondered if he shouldn't talk to the father, but decided to move on for now. "Thanks for your time." Doc walked back to his car and got on the phone.

"Pickus."

"Sheriff, it's Doc. How you doing?"

"Spending a lot of time on the phone. Turns out most of the players live out of town."

"Yeah, I saw that on the sheet the coach gave me. Anyone pique your interest?"

"There is one kid, a receiver. Blake was really on him about dropping a few passes. The kid did not appreciate it."

"Hmm. He know the Knudson girl?"

"Yeah. Had her in a class. Said he didn't know her that well, but . . ."

"He didn't happen to be from Morris, did he? I mean, if we tie the Wahpeton killing to the ones here, I think we're kind of looking for someone who knew Jenny Wyman."

"No, he isn't from here, but he did know Wyman," said Pickus.

"How's that?" said Doc.

"He was a second-year player. Sometimes those college boys take a look at some of the younger girls, too. He said he'd met her at a party but didn't date her."

"I should have thought of that," said Doc. "So maybe he did more than just meet her?"

"Maybe."

"OK. So, I just finished talking to a kid named Mark Church who admitted to dating Wyman and Knudson and seems to have some anger issues. If I give you the address, can you see if he or his parents have any pistols registered? And you should probably do the same for your football player and Wyman's father."

"I can do that. We still on with Salo tonight?"

"Yup. Eight. Text me the address."

Doc looked at the sky, seeing only blue. He could squeeze a bucket of balls in, but that probably meant he wouldn't get any supper until after talking to Salo, and who knew how long that would go. He called LeBlanc. "You like meatloaf?"

CHAPTER 13

Ed Salo lived north of town, off of 5, on Pike Lake, which was more of a pond than a lake and had no pike in it. In fact, there were no fish in it at all, as it froze out every winter. Pike Lake was as much a breeding ground for mosquitoes as anything, which was why Doc, Pickus, and Salo sat on deck chairs inside the screen porch behind the house as the sun moved lower.

It wouldn't be long before the bloodthirsty creatures would be buzzing, crawling on the screen, looking for a way inside. Doc hated mosquitoes, hated just the sound of them. If he could hear them, he'd start feeling them crawling on his skin, and before he knew it he'd be slapping himself all over. His mother always said it was because Doc had sweet skin; whatever the reason, if there was one mosquito in a room of fifty people, it would find Doc. Unfortunately, he also reacted spectacularly to their bites. He'd swell up, and the itching seemed to last twice as long on Doc as others. His mother had tried all kinds of lotions and sprays, but nothing worked. Doc would often end up scratching himself until he bled.

Salo was a small man with a big voice. He was bald on top, with a ponytail in back. Salo was maybe a little heavy for his size but Doc sensed he had some muscle under his button-down sport shirt. Salo was holding a gin and tonic when Pickus and Doc arrived. He offered to make one for his guests. Pickus demurred; Doc said that sounded good.

Salo sipped his drink, stirred his cubes with a finger, and said, "How can I help you gentlemen?"

"We're investigating the deaths of the Rose family," Doc began. "Trying to get to know them a little better. What was your relationship with the Roses?"

"Well, as director of the co-op, just about everybody in the area who farms knows me, and I know them. John Rose was a customer."

"How did you and Mr. Rose get along?"

"Not especially well. The guy was entitled, you know. Nothing was ever good enough for him. I think I could have given him a thousand a bushel and he still would have complained."

"You two ever come to blows?" said Doc.

Salo's dark eyes looked at the setting sun leaking through the trees in his backyard. "No, not really. We have an annual get-together in February of all the co-op members. Last year Rose had a few to many and started yelling about me cheating everyone. I told him what I thought of that, and we pushed each other, but that was it."

Doc looked in his glass and was surprised to see his drink was half gone. "You have kids, Mr. Salo?"

"Yes, a son and a daughter."

"How old are they?"

"Tom's going into his second year at the college, and Julie just graduated from high school."

"They know Blake Rose?"

"I believe he asked my daughter out." Salo poured down the rest of his drink. His tongue moved behind closed lips under a hook of a nose.

"You're not sure?" said Doc.

Salo's eyes turned black. "I'm sure."

"Is your daughter here?"

"She's out with friends."

Doc figured there was more. "What happened?"

Salo was looking deep into his glass. "It was last fall. Julie was a junior. She was all excited about going out with the quarterback. Thought they were going out for dinner and a movie and got all dolled up. Blake showed up an hour late, no apology. They took off, and he started driving west, out of town. Julie asked him where they were going, and he said that plans had changed and they were going to a party. Apparently, he was smoking dope and tried to get Julie to do it too, but she refused. Anyway, they were a couple of miles outside of town, and he pulled off into this abandoned farm and stopped. It was pretty dark by then, and Julie could see there was no one there. She asked where the party was and he said, "Right here," and reached over and grabbed her breast. She pushed him away and got out of the car. He just laughed and drove off."

"And did your boy know him too?"

"Yes." Salo shook the cubes around the inside of his glass. "The kid should have been locked up long ago."

"Did your children know Jenny Wyman and Linda Knudson?" said Doc.

"They've been to the house before."

Doc glanced at Pickus and then turned back to Salo and said, "Where were you Sunday morning, Mr. Salo?"

"Here. I got a new mount, and I was putting it up." Doc had an obviously confused look on his face, and Salo stood. "Come on, I'll show you."

Doc and the sheriff followed Salo through the kitchen and down a narrow stairway, Salo flicking on the lights as he went. Doc had to duck slightly as he got to the bottom stair to avoid the ceiling. He took two steps and stopped, Pickus almost running into him.

"Wow!" Doc said. The room was big, thirty-five feet by sixty, with dense tan Berber carpeting and oak-paneled walls. The light in the room was provided by recessed lighting and spotlights in the beamed ceiling. Each spotlight was focused on a trophy animal, either head mounts or full mounts of smaller animals, and birds on the walls or full mounts on the floor. A tiger prowled in the middle of the room, a brown bear stood in one corner. Water buffalo, wildebeest, impala, elk, deer, moose, cougar, and other large animals peered at them from the walls. Birds and smaller mammals, most Doc didn't recognize, were perched or made to look as if they were in some form of natural habitat around the bigger mounts or on shelves. Along one wall were gun racks holding trigger-locked long guns and pistols in drawers.

Doc walked over to the tiger and gently touched the teeth in the open mouth. "You shot all these animals?"

"Most. I purchased a few, mostly the birds. Many you can't hunt, but it's not illegal to have a mount." Salo walked over to an open box on the floor and lifted out a head. "A bushbuck I took last year in central Africa. This is the animal I was looking at on Sunday."

Doc looked at Salo holding the animal head but remained by the tiger, stroking its fur. The man had pistols, was obviously a good shot, and did not like the Roses, or the way Blake had been given a pass. It was personal for him.

"You were here by yourself on Sunday?"

"Yes. My wife had taken the kids clothes-shopping at the outlet mall."

Doc looked at Pickus, who was examining the claws on the bear. "OK. Thanks for your time, Mr. Salo. We better run."

Outside, Doc leaned on the door of Pickus's vehicle, holding it shut.

"Did you know about his arsenal?"

"I knew he was some kind of big-game hunter, but I'd never been inside before."

"But you knew he was a big hunter?" Doc said.

"Sure. Everybody did," said Pickus.

"Well, I didn't," said Doc, leaning close to the smaller man. "It would be nice if you would share."

"I'm the one who said we should talk to Salo. He's got a bone to pick with Rose."

"Yes, he does. And with you too, Sheriff. You might want to be careful."

Pickus thought about that for a second and said, "You think so?"

"I do." Doc glared at the smaller man. "Did you know about Salo's daughter? Blake going after her?"

The sheriff looked down. "No. Well, I guess. Salo complained to Palmer, and I eventually heard about it from someone."

"From someone? What the hell does that mean?"

"I don't remember who, all right?"

Doc was bending over now, in Pickus's face. "Others you didn't really know about?"

"Two. One in his junior year and another this year. No charges were filed."

"Reported to Palmer?"

"Yeah." Pickus turned away.

"Christ! And how many more that didn't get reported?"

"Well, I don't know that."

"Of course you don't, you—" Doc raised a hand to belt him, but instead he turned away, took two steps and a deep breath, and then came back. A mosquito buzzed, distracting him, and he slapped his neck, although he wasn't sure the bug had landed there. "Any of the dean's neighbors see or hear anything?"

"One woman, two doors down, claims she heard a car going by about midnight, but didn't see anything."

Doc waved at invisible bugs in front of his face and slapped his neck again, checking his palm for blood. There was none. "OK. Well, I got to make some calls and get some sleep. LeBlanc and I are going to interview the kid Blake bullied and then keep going on his other classmates. I assume you've got plenty of kids still to interview?" Pickus said he did. Doc slapped himself in the forehead and said, "I'll talk to you tomorrow," and went to his car. He watched Pickus drive away and then looked at his phone. It was just past nine thirty. Doc thought about making the run to Spicer but it would be close to eleven by the time he got there and he didn't want to risk falling asleep behind the wheel. He thought about calling Draper, just to talk to her, but was afraid that might be misinterpreted as something he wasn't sure he wanted to get into, so he drove back to the Ramada.

He took his second shower of the day, and then called LeBlanc, telling him he'd meet him at The Windmill at eight. Then he called home. A woman answered.

"Hi, Mom."

"Peter? Is that you?"

"Yes, Mom. How are you?"

"I'm fine, but how are you? Is something wrong?"

Doc smiled. "I'm fine, Mom. Nothing is wrong."

She pushed it. "Are you sure? You don't usually call this late."

Doc looked at the clock by the bed to see that it was after ten. Late for his parents. "Yeah, sorry. I'm fine, really. Is Dad around?"

"Have you been hurt or something? You're not getting married, are you?"

"Good grief. No, Mom. Really, I'm OK. Not getting married. Just had a question for Dad."

He could hear her release a breath. "Just a minute. I'll get him."

"Peter," came the deep voice of his father.

"Dad, it's your son, the doctor."

It was how they started nearly every conversation now. Doc had started it as kind of a dig at his father, and kind of a joke, after he had received his doctorate in divinity. Doc's father was James T. Hunter, one of the world's top neurosurgeons. He practiced at the University of Minnesota. All through Doc's high school days, his parents had assumed he would go to the U of M and study premed. Doc just figured that was what he would do. Then he got a football scholarship. Football made it more difficult to keep up grades and class schedules, especially for premed, so he switched majors. With help, he kept up his

GPA.

But then, in Doc's last season, he was blocking on a running play and laid out an Illinois safety who'd never seen him coming. The kid went down and stayed down. Doc's teammates were patting him on the back for his block, but Doc couldn't take his eyes off the kid being wheeled off the field on a stretcher. The kid never recovered from the hit, and Doc didn't either. Doc still set receiving records and had professional agents hounding him, but he was done with football. He felt lost. He finished his undergrad degree but had no desire to be a doctor and work in the same hospital where he'd visited the kid he hit, who would never walk or speak again. Doc took it that God was trying to tell him something, so he enrolled at Luther College for a master's in divinity, and then his doctorate. He knew after he began his doctoral studies that it wasn't for him, but he finished his degree, because his father said he should, and he almost always listened to his father.

"Kind of late, son. You OK?"

"Yeah, I just had a question for you. You know that neighbor of yours, Herger?"

"Pat Herges? The Mercedes dealership owner?"

Doc's parents lived in Minnetonka, a western, upscale suburb of Minneapolis. "Yeah, that guy. So, doesn't he do a lot of big-game hunting?"

"Yes. I've been to his house a few times, and he has several big-game animals mounted inside."

"OK. So, how expensive is it to do that?"

"Big-game hunting?" said his father.

"And the mounts?" said Doc.

"Well, I don't know exactly, but I did inquire about some animal he had shot in Africa one time, and I believe that he said he probably had twenty-five thousand invested in each animal. Why do you ask?"

"It's for a case I'm working," said Doc.

"You probably could get an estimate from the internet."

"Yeah, I know," said Doc. "But I hadn't talked to you or Mom for a while so I thought I'd give you a call."

"I'm sure your mother appreciates it," said his father.

"And what about you?"

"I need to be in surgery at five tomorrow morning, so I'll have to see how I feel then and let you know."

"Sorry, Dad."

His father laughed. "I thought you cops were supposed to be more perceptive than that. I'm just kidding. How's your golf game?"

They talked for a few minutes more, his mother coming back on the phone to be sure he wasn't shot or anything, and then making him promise he would be home for the Fourth of July. Doc said he would be and hung up. He checked on prices for safaris and mounts and decided his dad was probably pretty close, even a bit shy. Doc walked to his golf bag, removed his putter, dropped two balls on the floor, and began the same routine he had on the first night. He decided the towel he had around his waist was a distraction after he'd pulled two putts to the left, and he tossed it on the chair. His putts were dead-on after that, eight in a row, and he wondered if it would be possible to golf in the nude somehow, just to see if he could improve his score.

CHAPTER 14

The Fellers never locked their doors. Well, almost never. They used to when their two boys were little, but after the boys got their licenses they often came home late, so the doors were left unlocked. And now that the boys were in college, the Fellers never knew quite when they might show up, so it was just easier. Besides, in the thirty years they'd lived in their home just west of Morris there had never been an issue with anyone trying to break in. Not with them or the neighbors. And Lee Feller would know if there was. He was the county attorney.

Lee and his wife, Cindy, an accountant, usually went to bed pretty early during the work week, about nine or a little after. They'd read in bed until ten, and then the lights would go out. They used to stay up and watch the news at ten each night, going to bed after, but that had fallen by the wayside when the kids showed up, and now the early bedtime was normal. Saturday night, and sometimes Friday, they might make it past eleven if they were with friends or watching something on Netflix, but that was about as wild as they got.

Tuesday night, at just past eleven, the Fellers were both asleep when Cindy was roused by a sound from the other side of the house. The Fellers' bedroom was at the end of a hall that went past a bathroom and the family room, and into the kitchen. On the other side of the kitchen was a narrow room with a coat closet, a bench, some oak cabinets, and a sink. Beyond that was the garage. She lay there listening, eyes open, not sure she had really heard anything, when there was another sound, and the cat jumped off the bed.

Cindy sat up and pushed Lee as she leaned close to his head and whispered, "Lee. Wake up. I heard something." Her husband made a groaning noise. "Lee, there's someone in the house."

Lee rolled onto his back, eyes still closed, and said, "It's probably just the cat or one of the boys. Go to sleep."

Cindy was awake now. She couldn't imagine why one of the boys would be home so late on a Tuesday night unless something bad had happened, like maybe they had been kicked out of school. Both had taken summer jobs at their colleges, living in the dorms. She was having a hard time with the boys both away at school. Worrying about how they were eating, how they were doing at school, who they were associating with—just about anything she could think of. Cindy was a worrier.

But she knew what she had heard had not been the cat. It was quiet again. Maybe Lee was right, and it was nothing. About to close her eyes and slide back under the covers, Cindy saw the light. It wasn't one of the overhead lights. This light was moving, like someone shining a flashlight.

She bent close to her husband's face. "Lee. There's someone here. You need to go see who it is, or I'm going to get up."

Lee groaned again, opened his eyes, and looked at the black ceiling. "Fine." He threw off the covers, swung his feet out, and sat on the edge of the bed for a moment, looking at the floor. He sighed, stood, and had begun to feel his way toward the doorway when he saw the light down the hall. Lee stopped. There had been a few cases in the last year or two where he had prosecuted some drug dealers. Bad guys, not from the area, and they'd been put away. He thought about that for a second more, but he still figured it was one of the kids. He was just past the bathroom, when the light was suddenly in his eyes.

He raised his arm to shield his eyes. "Who is it?"

"Bad news for you. You should have done the right thing. Drop your arm."

Lee Feller was thinking he didn't recognize the voice. That was his last thought. The bullet entered his forehead and tumbled through his brain before resting against the back of his skull.

* * *

Cindy Feller heard her husband's voice, she couldn't quite make out what he said, and wondered who he was talking to. She was just getting out of bed when she heard the shot, incredibly loud.

"Lee? Lee? What was that?" said Cindy as she stood frozen by the side of the bed.

The Fellers slept with the windows open in the summer. Cindy liked the fresh air, leaving the shades up so they wouldn't make any noise when a breeze came through. Lee preferred not to hear the outside noises at night, and he liked it cooler when he slept. He said they made enough money to afford to run the air conditioner and close the windows, but Cindy wanted the windows open, and they were on her side of the bed, so she prevailed.

The light in the hall had gone out when she had heard the gunshot. Now, in the faint light coming in from the window behind her, she could see someone entering the bedroom.

"Lee?" The figure moved by the foot of the bed, Cindy backing away, hitting her bedside table, knocking over the lamp and nearly losing her balance. She reached for the wall to steady herself. "Lee?" Suddenly there was a light in her face. She shut her eyes, and then she was dead.

CHAPTER 15

LeBlanc was looking at an old issue of *Field & Stream* when Doc made it to the lobby in the morning.

"I thought we were meeting at The Windmill," said Doc. His shorts and shoes were the same as the prior three days, but he had gone casual with a 2017 U.S. Open T-shirt from Erin Hills, Wisconsin. He'd been to the final round and had several more shirts from the event.

"Just wanted to be sure you didn't get waylaid again."

"Nah. It got too late."

LeBlanc held up the magazine so Doc could see the article he was looking at, an article on fly-fishing for smallmouth bass, and said, "You ever fly fish?" Doc said he had, but not for several years. He said his dad was big into fly-fishing, and that they would go to New Mexico and fish for trout but that he had never fished for smallmouth with a fly rod. "We better get going," Doc said. "Might not get a booth."

The Windmill was busy again, but they found a booth and the waitress was immediately there with water for both of them. Doc hadn't seen her before. She had bronze hair and was a little chunky, but in the right places. She gave Doc a big smile and asked if he'd like a minute. He thought about saying he'd like more than a minute but instead said that would be good and she left.

"That ever get to you?" said LeBlanc.

"What?" said Doc as he looked at the menu. He figured he should have something other than the French toast and sausage again, but he didn't know what.

"The waitress. She was like ogling you."

"Ogling? Is that even a word people still use?"

"It's a good word," said LeBlanc.

"What are you having?"

"I don't know. Hopefully the waitress will notice I'm here and take my order." LeBlanc hid his face behind the menu.

"You a little touchy today, LeBlanc?"

"It's just been a while, you know?"

"Not really," said Doc with a tight smile. He was about to amend his comment when his phone buzzed. "Sheriff. What have you got?"

"Bodies," he said. "The county attorney and his wife. You better get over here. I'll text you the address."

Doc stuffed his phone back in his pocket and said, "Come on. We got to go." He was sliding out of the booth just as the waitress returned.

"Are you ready to order?"

"Sorry, we got to go, but I'll be back."

The woman smiled at him. "I'll be here."

ANGRY SINS

* * *

The Morris cop at the end of the road recognized Doc and waved him past. LeBlanc had ridden with Doc, Doc figuring the fewer vehicles the better, and he was right. There were two more cop cars at the end of the driveway. The sheriff's car and the chief's truck were both in the driveway, as well as two other vehicles and an ambulance, two men leaning against it, leaving no room on the driveway, so Doc pulled off on the yard. Doc and LeBlanc walked up to Pickus on the front step.

"Inside," said Pickus, turning for the door.

"Just a minute," said Doc. "How were they found?"

"A clerk from the county attorney's office, Brad Kloster, came over about a quarter to eight. That's his car in front of mine," said the sheriff, pointing at the blue Chevy. "He knocked and didn't get any answer. Walked around the house looking in windows but didn't see anything. He was about to leave when a gal from the company where Mrs. Feller works, Jeanie Thomas, drove up because Mrs. Feller didn't show up and wasn't answering her phone. That's her car in front of the Chevy." Pickus pointed at the CRV. "Anyway, they decided it was a little odd that both of the Fellers hadn't shown up for work and thought maybe there could be a gas leak or something, so they tried the front door. It was unlocked, and they went in."

"The door was shut?"

"Yeah, but unlocked."

"Any sign of entry anywhere else?" said Doc.

"Door to the garage and the garage door in back were both unlocked but closed," said Pickus.

"Anything taken?"

"Doesn't look like it," said Pickus. "His wallet is on the

dresser with credit cards and a little cash. Her wallet was in her purse on the kitchen counter, and had cash in it."

"What about the ambulance?"

"The dispatcher sent it. They checked out both victims when they arrived and then called the ME," said Pickus. "Thought you might want to talk to them before they left so I had them stay."

"Kloster and Thomas inside?" said Doc.

"In the dining room."

Doc and LeBlanc put on gloves and shoe covers.

Palmer was standing at the corner where the hallway turned toward the bedroom. He nodded when Doc approached. Doc stopped next to Palmer and looked down the hall at the county attorney lying on his back with a hole in his forehead.

"One shot?" said Doc.

"Yeah," said Palmer. "Same as the others."

"Where's the wife?"

"Bedroom," Palmer said, pointing. "Careful where you step."

Doc didn't move, staring at Palmer.

"What?" Palmer asked.

"I want names. I want the names of the girls that complained about Rose. The ones you didn't bother with so the goddamned football team wouldn't lose its star quarterback."

"Now, you listen here, Hunter! I—"

"No, *you* listen," said Doc, now inches from Palmer's red face. "If you'd had had the guts to do something about Blake Rose two years ago, we likely wouldn't have six people dead now. And now your precious football team is fucked, anyway. I want those names today."

Doc turned and started down the hall, LeBlanc following but not looking at Palmer as he passed. They didn't see the body at first. Doc walked past the foot of the bed, stopping at the sight of Mrs. Feller crumpled against a nightstand.

"She turned away when he shot," said LeBlanc, looking over Doc's shoulder.

"Yeah. Had no chance, though." Doc continued to look at the woman. "Why kill her? I mean, if her husband was the target, and you've got to think he was, why kill the wife?"

"Not taking any chances with a witness," said LeBlanc. "And making sure he had more time to get away."

"Maybe, but the killer came in here looking for her. I hope he's not starting to like this."

They talked to Kloster and Thomas, but learned nothing of immediate interest. The ME had arrived while they were interviewing Kloster and Thomas, and Doc asked for a call if there was anything. After walking through the rest of the house, they went out to talk to the ambulance guys. As they were finishing up, Pickus came over.

"Hunter."

"Just a minute, I need to make a call." Doc dialed Miranda.

"I was just going to call you," said Miranda.

"What do you know?"

"The Wahpeton bullet did not match the others we have. Same caliber but different gun."

Doc thought about this for a moment and then said, "OK, well, I hate to tell you this, but you need to get back out here again. I got two more."

"You're kidding me. This is getting to be a lot of driving, Doc. Can't you catch this guy?"

"Not yet. Anyway, I'll text you the address. Thanks,

Carl." Doc disconnected and was thinking about calling Trask to give him an update, but Pickus was breathing down his neck.

"Jesus, Hunter. We got to catch this guy," said the sheriff. "People hear about this and they're going to be shooting the paperboy. This is a rampage now for sure."

"Yeah. So, we better talk to all the neighbors again. Two shots. Someone had to at least have heard something this time."

"OK, I'll work with Palmer to get that covered, but this guy needs to be caught. You got any ideas who it is yet?"

"I was thinking the county attorney, but that's off the table, I guess," said Doc.

Pickus did not smile.

"LeBlanc and I are going to push hard on the kids," Doc said. "We're talking to the bullied kid today. And we'll talk to those other girls when I get the names from Palmer. We just got to keep at it."

Pickus looked up at Doc and slowly shook his head.

CHAPTER 16

The BCA agents watched the sheriff walk back to the house. Doc said to LeBlanc, "I got to call Trask."

Doc called and got Trask's assistant, Larry Stoxen.

"Larry. It's Doc. Is he ducking calls again?"

"Very perceptive of you, Agent. The superintendent is trying to schedule a budget meeting. I'll put your call through."

After a moment, Trask came on the line.

"I got two more," said Doc, "and one is the county attorney. Pickus is calling it a rampage, and I'm starting to agree with him."

"Jeez! The county attorney? That's almost as bad as shooting a cop."

"Almost."

"The media is going to be all over you now," said Trask. "So, when are you going to nail this guy?"

"I wish I knew. Someone's mighty angry about something."

"You know what that something is?"

"I'm pretty sure it was the Rose kid getting away with the rapes that triggered things, so that means parents and families of the girls, and maybe boyfriends, and I'm working my way through the list," said Doc. "But the kid may have assaulted a lot more than just the two that filed complaints. I know of at least one other girl he tried to go after, and the father was not happy about it."

"You think it's a single shooter?"

"Yeah, too neat to be more. The killings are too much alike. And it doesn't look like there have been any robberies."

"You're not still on the hitman thing, are you?" said Trask.

"Can't rule it out. The guy's a good shot."

"OK, well, I don't know what I can do except to yell at you to hurry up and catch him," said Trask.

"You can do one thing," said Doc. "I'm not sure it's related, but it may be. Can you have the fraud guys check out an Ed Salo here? He runs the co-op. He's the parent with the daughter who Blake Rose tried to go after."

"OK, but what are they looking for?"

"The guy has a zoo full of animals in his basement that he shot. I'm talking lions and tigers and bears, oh my. From what I can find, there's no way a guy running a co-op makes anywhere near enough to do that."

"Fine. But don't call me again unless it's to tell me you nailed this guy," said Trask. "I'm busy."

"I heard," said Doc, and Trask was gone. Doc turned to LeBlanc. "Let's go eat."

***

It was eleven by the time they made it back to The Windmill. The place was not as crowded as before, but still crowded. They got the same booth and the waitress brought over water.

"You still serving breakfast?" Doc asked.

"All day," she said, pen poised above her pad.

"Great. I'll have French toast and sausages and a large orange juice, please."

She wrote down the order, gave him a big smile, and was starting to turn away when LeBlanc cleared his throat. She apologized and took his order of eggs and hash browns and left.

Doc leaned back, drank half his water, and looked around. "This place is a goldmine, LeBlanc. You ought to buy it."

"I don't have anywhere near the money for it, and besides, the staff needs a lot of work."

"What do you mean?"

"Good grief, Hunter," said LeBlanc. "She was ogling you so hard she completely forgot I was here."

"She's just busy. She has a very nice disposition." Just then the waitress walked by, asking if Doc would like any more water, filled his glass, and walked away.

Doc looked at LeBlanc's glass. It was nearly empty. "She's just busy," he said again. "I got to run out to the car. I'll be right back." He returned as the food arrived, and they both dug in, eating in silence. Doc finished first, sliding his plate toward the edge of the table and putting a book on the table.

"What's that?" said LeBlanc.

"This is the yearbook of Jenny Wyman. I went through it last night and found kids who made comments that were a little more than 'Have a nice summer.' Boys who may have been interested in her. I thought we could compare it with your list to pick out candidates of higher priority."

While they worked the waitress came to take their plates and asked if they wanted anything else. Doc said, "No thanks," but LeBlanc said, "What do you recommend?"

She said the apple pie was just coming out of the oven, and LeBlanc said he'd have a piece with ice cream. The waitress smiled and said she'd be right back.

"What was that?" said Doc.

"What?"

"You don't have pie with breakfast."

"You obviously did not grow up on a farm," said LeBlanc. "We had dessert with every meal."

"Really? That just doesn't seem right."

When LeBlanc's pie came, it looked and smelled like it was just out of Doc's mother's oven. Doc called the waitress back. "A slice for me, too," he told her.

They ate pie while they worked. They narrowed down LeBlanc's list to half a dozen plus the bullied kid, Paul Nelson, and Mark Church. Doc added the Salo boy, Tom, and the football player Pickus had mentioned, saying he'd need to get the kid's contact information. Doc also told LeBlanc they'd need to add the other possible assault victims, as soon as he got the names from Palmer.

Doc leaned back in the booth and sighed.

"What?"

"We got too damn many," said Doc. "How the hell are we supposed to interview all of these people before Christmas? We need an army."

"We can only do what we can do," said LeBlanc.

"Keep shaking the tree."

They decided to stay together for the time being. While they worked the waitress, whose name tag said "TINA," came by to get their plates and asked if they'd like anything else. Doc said, "Just the bill, thanks," but LeBlanc said, "What time do you get off?" She said she was done at three and LeBlanc said he'd have to work later than that, but he'd like to call her when he got off, and she gave him her number. Doc smiled.

* * *

Rickie Kern worked at the BigValu hardware store in the strip mall on the east side of town. He said he got a lunch break at noon and could talk to them then. Doc spotted Kern standing down the sidewalk from the BigValu, in front of an empty storefront, smoking a cigarette. They pulled up in front and Doc stepped out, walking up to Kern.

"Are you Rickie?"

The boy was almost as tall as Doc, but skin and bones. He had a skeleton face under thinning brown hair, and long fingers on his bony hands. He dropped his cigarette and stamped it out. "Yeah." He wasn't interested in the ID Doc showed. "What do you want to know?"

"We understand you knew Jenny Wyman," said LeBlanc.

"She was in my class."

"Was she a friend?" said LeBlanc.

"I guess. I mean, we never really hung out much, but we were friends." Kern was running his long fingers through his hair.

"Do you know Linda Knudson?"

"Yeah. She was in my class too. I didn't hang with her at all, but I knew who she was."

"How did you feel about Blake Rose getting away with raping Jenny?" said Doc.

"It sucked, man. That jerk should have been arrested or something. Jocks always get a free ride." They were in the sun, and Kern's forehead was beginning to perspire.

"How did they get a free ride?"

"You know. They got off easy if they got in trouble. Always getting help with their grades."

Doc knew that what Kern said was true to some extent in college, but the kids participating in sports and other extracurricular activities in high school were more likely to be the students who were driven, and they just did better in class. "Did other people in your class feel the same way?"

"Yeah. A lot of kids did."

Doc glanced over at LeBlanc and then back to Kern. "Any of them upset enough to want to kill Blake?"

Kern's droopy eyelids went up. "No. You think a kid killed Blake?"

"Where were you last Sunday morning?"

"Working, like usual." Kern looked at his watch and said, "I got to go," and walked away.

Doc and LeBlanc watched him go for a second and then went back to the car. "He seemed pretty eager to get away from us," said LeBlanc.

"Yeah, but that didn't really help," said Doc as he started the car. "You better check his alibi, but I don't think he's the shooter, or knows who is. Who's next?" said Doc as he backed out.

CHAPTER 17

Next was John McDonald. He wasn't on the list of names LeBlanc had put together, but McDonald had written something in Jenny Wyman's yearbook that made Doc interested. McDonald lived in town, about two blocks from Mark Church. McDonald was working for the summer at the nursery out by the highway and had just gotten home from work when the agents arrived. He was standing in the driveway of the small two-story, looking at something in the trunk of his car, when Doc pulled in behind him. McDonald slammed the trunk shut and turned to look but couldn't see who was in the car because of the glare off the windshield.

McDonald was a little over six feet, thin, but not skinny. He had a beard going, dark, which helped to make it look a little better than it was. He watched while Doc and LeBlanc exited the car.

"Peter Hunter and Gary LeBlanc, BCA," said Doc as he

handed McDonald his ID. The skin on McDonald's tanned face had lighter streaks where the sweat had run down, and his forearms were nearly black with dirt. "We called earlier."

McDonald handed Doc his ID back, glanced over at LeBlanc but didn't bother to look at that ID, and said, "This is about Blake Rose?"

"Yeah," said Doc. "You know him?"

"I knew who he was. We'd say hi when we passed in the locker room, but that was about it."

"You were a football player in high school?"

"No, baseball," he said. "I'd see him sometimes when he worked out."

"You knew Jenny Wyman?"

"Yeah, but we never went out or anything."

"But you liked her?" said Doc.

"I guess. She was nice." The boy was looking at the ground. He'd lift his head a little to speak and then his gaze would drop again. Shy.

Doc stared at the boy through his sunglasses. "In her yearbook you wrote that you'd really miss her. Sounds like you more than liked her."

McDonald tried to wipe the dirt off his forearm but it only smeared. McDonald's green Trenton Nursery T-shirt was sweat-stained, his jeans dirty. "I said she was nice. But she was out of my league."

"Why's that?"

The kid shrugged. "She was just too good-looking, you know? And she went out with Blake."

"Did it make you angry when you found out about Blake assaulting her?" asked LeBlanc.

McDonald quickly turned his gaze in LeBlanc's direction. "Sure. The guy was a prick, and he hurt her. She left school after that."

"You try to contact her after she left?" said LeBlanc.

"No," said McDonald.

"You know she's dead, right?" LeBlanc said.

"Yeah, I heard." McDonald was scraping the ground with his foot now.

"And did you know Linda Knudson?"

"I knew who she was, but she wasn't a friend or anything," said McDonald. "We never even talked."

"But you knew about her assault?" said LeBlanc.

"Of course. I go to school there."

"Where were you on Sunday morning, John?"

"Uh, I don't know. Home, I guess. I didn't have to work."

The kid was definitely nervous. LeBlanc pressed. "Can anyone confirm that?"

"Um, I . . . no, I don't think so. My parents are gone. I was here alone."

"Where are your parents?" said Doc.

McDonald was rubbing his palms on his thighs. "They went to visit my grandparents and uncle south of Albert Lea."

"How long have they been gone?"

"Since Saturday." McDonald had been leaning on the trunk of his vehicle but now he pushed himself up. "Listen, I need a shower. I got to go."

"Big date tonight?" said Doc.

"No, I'm just really dirty," said McDonald. "Can I go?"

"Sure, John," said Doc. "And thanks for your time." Doc turned away and then quickly back. "You a shooter, John?"

"I don't hunt," said McDonald.

"How about shooting?"

The boy was looking at Doc, thinking about an answer. "Yeah. Some of us get together once in a while and do some shooting."

"With pistols?" asked LeBlanc.

"Yeah. We go down to the dump and shoot bottles and rats and raccoons."

"Who's we?"

"Just some guys from school. Larry Devers, Mark Church, Randy Estes."

"Rickie Kern or Paul Nelson?"

"Paul, sometimes. Not Rickie." McDonald had been sideways to them as he talked, his head turned in their direction. "Is that it?"

"Where's your gun, John?"

"I don't have one. I use Mark's or Paul's." McDonald said he had to go again and practically ran to the house.

The agents watched him disappear into a side door and then went to Doc's car. Doc started the car with the door open to get the air going, and then shut the door. He lifted his sunglasses and wiped the perspiration from the back of his neck and the side of his face. His shirt felt sticky against his back.

"The kid was a little too nervous," said LeBlanc. "He's holding back."

Doc looked over at LeBlanc. The guy was casual today, in a short-sleeved blue dress shirt and khakis. No tie. He'd left his sport coat in the back seat. Doc could see no effect from their time standing in the sun. "Don't you sweat?"

"You know, not too much. My mom used to think I had something wrong with me and took me to the doctor, but he said some people just don't sweat as much as others."

"I thought the body needs to sweat."

"Oh, it does, and I do, but just not that much."

"Hmm." Doc looked back at McDonald's house. "We need to find out more about John McDonald and whether he or his parents own a pistol. And I really don't want to say this, but we'd better put Devers and Estes on our list. And we'd better put some pressure on before somebody else ends up dead."

CHAPTER 18

Paul Nelson worked at the Scheeler's grocery store on Seventh. He said he could meet the agents on the side of the building after he got off work. It was only six blocks to the store from McDonald's house. Doc looked at his phone and could see no message from Palmer about the girls, and that pissed him off. They had twenty minutes before they were supposed to meet Nelson, and the police station was on the way to Scheeler's, so Doc decided to stop and see the chief.

When they turned the corner on Fourth, a block from the station, Doc pulled to the curb. LeBlanc looked up from his phone and said, "What?" and Doc said, "The circus has begun."

Four vans with satellite dishes, along with several other vehicles, were parked along the block ahead of them on either side of the street. Doc could make out the call letters of two stations from the Twin Cities as well as one from Fargo.

"We going in?" said LeBlanc.

Doc just stared ahead, the engine running. "I'm thinking. Maybe I should just try to give Palmer a call."

Just then an attractive blonde in a red jacket and skirt got out of the van closest to them and walked to the back of the van. The woman was average height, but had on heels that made her look tall.

"Aw, shit," said Doc.

LeBlanc said, "What?" and Doc said, "Gloria. G-L-O-R-I-A. Gloria."

"The blonde?"

"Yeah."

"She's hot."

"Yeah, too hot for me. I'm not supposed to be anywhere near her."

"Why's that?"

The blonde was joined by a shorter man at the back of the van. They had opened the doors in back and were looking for something.

Doc kept staring straight ahead. "Um, it's kind of a long story. I gave her a little information one time I thought would help a case but it kind of blew up on me. Trask and his boss said I was not to talk to her ever again unless I had every word cleared with him first, which was difficult because Gloria and I were involved at the time. So that kind of ended things there."

"You were waylaid with her?"

"For a time." Doc was admiring the view of Gloria as she leaned into the van about three car lengths ahead of him, remembering being waylaid, when she turned and peered in his direction. She leaned forward, staring, and then took a tentative step in his direction. Doc said, "Gotta go," and did a quick

U-turn.

* * *

Doc found the picnic table on the side of the Scheeler's building and parked. An compact woman with a hairnet was sitting at the table smoking a cigarette when they pulled up. Nelson was nowhere to be seen, so Doc sent LeBlanc into the store to get a couple of Cokes and then called Palmer. Palmer didn't pick up, so Doc left a message and then sent a text to be sure. By the time LeBlanc returned, the woman with the hairnet had left, and Doc was sitting at the table, back to the wall. It was easily over eighty degrees, but the table was in the shade, and with the light breeze blowing along the wall it wasn't uncomfortable. There was a slight odor from the dumpster in back of the building, but nothing terrible, and it was relaxing to just watch the traffic move by.

A slight boy with thick-framed brown glasses poked his head around the corner of the building and walked up to the table. He wore blue jeans and white tennis shoes and a red polo that said "Scheeler's" on the right breast. "Um, are you the BCA agent?"

"I'm Agent Hunter," said Doc as he showed his ID, "and this is Agent LeBlanc. Why don't you sit down, Paul?"

Nelson hesitated a moment before deciding to sit on the same bench as LeBlanc. He perched on the end, one cheek hanging over the edge. His glasses had slid down his nose, and he pushed them up with a finger.

"So, Paul," said LeBlanc, "we're investigating the death of Blake Rose."

"And all the rest?"

LeBlanc glanced at Doc. "And all the rest. We understand you had some trouble with Blake at school last year."

Nelson used a fingernail on his right hand to clean the nails on his left. "Yeah, I guess."

"So, what happened?"

Nelson didn't look up. "I stayed late after school last fall and was getting some things from my locker. I guess football practice was done because a bunch of players came walking by. Blake was one of them. I was getting some books out of my locker and Blake slammed the door on me. Blake was trying to push the door closed and my wrist was caught in the door, and I yelled for Blake to stop. He just started laughing and said I needed to say please, and I did, but he didn't stop. Finally, one of the other players told Blake to stop, but he just kept pushing, and my wrist was starting to bleed. Then the other player pulled the locker open enough for me to get my hand out. Blake yelled at him and kicked me before they all walked away."

Nelson had started to rub his wrist while he talked, and LeBlanc said, "Your wrist OK?"

"Yeah. It still hurts sometimes, but it's a lot better."

"You made a complaint about the incident with the principal?" said LeBlanc.

"I didn't want to make things worse, so my mother did. I had to go with her to the principal's office."

"And what did the principal do?"

"She told my mom she'd looked into it but Blake denied it, and no one else would say they saw anything."

"Who was the player that helped you?"

"I don't know," said Nelson. "I had my eyes closed. I was crying."

"You like to shoot things, Paul?" said Doc.

Nelson swiveled his head to look at Doc. His blond

hair was shaggy on the top and shaved close on the sides, and it flopped in his face when he moved his head. "No."

"Someone told us that you and some other boys like to go down to the dump and shoot. Is that true?"

Nelson was looking at his hands again. "I guess. I've done it a few times."

"Are you a good shot, Paul?" said Doc.

"Pretty good."

"And where did you get the pistol you use?"

"My mom."

"Your mother?"

"Yeah," said Nelson. "She has a conceal-and-carry permit. She made me learn to shoot after my dad left."

"Where did your dad go?" said Doc.

"I don't know. He used to hit my mom, and she got a gun and made him leave. That was like five years ago, maybe more."

"Your mother have more than one pistol?" said Doc.

"She's got a couple," said Nelson, his eyes fixed on his hands.

Doc said, "Where were you Sunday morning, Paul?"

"Church."

"With your mother?"

"Yeah." Nelson's head was trying to duck into his shoulders like he was a turtle.

"Paul, if you know anything about the murders of the Roses or the others, and you're not telling us, you will go to jail. You know that, don't you?" Nelson wouldn't look at him, and Doc thought the kid was maybe going to cry.

"I don't know anything!" His voice came out high and squeaky.

Doc glanced at LeBlanc and then waited a moment before telling Nelson he could go. They watched the boy leave, walk to a line of cars at the back of the building, get into an old silver Sonata, and drive away.

"We need to check some alibis, LeBlanc." Doc was about to say something more when his phone buzzed. "Sheriff."

"Where the hell are you, Hunter?"

"Um, well . . ."

"You need to get down here."

"Down where?"

"The police station. The media wants a statement, and we figured you should be the one to give it."

"We being you and Palmer?" said Doc.

"Yeah. So, when can you get here?"

Doc blew out a breath. "Boy, LeBlanc and I are way out in the boonies interviewing kids. You and Palmer are probably going to have to handle that yourselves."

"What are we supposed to say?"

"I'm sure you'll think of something, Sheriff," said Doc. "You find anybody near the county attorney's house who saw or heard anything?"

"The shots woke the neighbors on either side. The woman to the west, Mathers, said she got up and looked and saw a vehicle drive away. Couldn't tell what kind but it sounded kind of loud. Both neighbors said it was about a quarter past eleven when they heard the shots."

"OK. You know anything else?"

"Only that this whole thing is blowing up now."

"Well, just don't call it a rampage when you talk to the media, and you'll be fine. I got to go."

Doc disconnected and looked at LeBlanc. "We need to

get out of town for a bit. Any of those kids we need to see live on a farm or out in the country?"

CHAPTER 19

The killer was watching the early evening news on television. He didn't usually do that, but he'd seen the media in town and someone had told him that the sheriff was going to make a statement. He picked Channel Five out of the Twin Cities, the ABC affiliate, because he'd seen it before and the weather girl was a cute blonde.

The killings in Morris was the lead story for the male anchor. "The town of Morris has been rocked by a series of brutal murders, including the killing of the county attorney, Lee Feller, and his wife, Cindy, just last night. Gloria Beaman is on the scene in Morris."

Beaman came on-screen, standing in the street in front of police tape strung across the road. "I'm standing outside the home of the Stevens county attorney, Lee Feller, just outside of Morris." She turned slightly, but there was really nothing to see except a police car parked inside the tape blocking the driveway.

The yard was heavily wooded and the house was well back from the road. It could not be seen. "Mr. Feller and his wife, Cynthia, were shot to death late last night in the most recent of a series of murders here that have the people of Morris behind locked doors. These two murders are what we believe to be the latest in a series that started with the murder of three people on a farm just outside of town on Sunday and then the dean of the college being found dead in his home yesterday. The Stevens County sheriff, Larry Pickus, gave a brief statement from the Morris police station earlier."

The screen showed Pickus standing at a makeshift podium in the lobby of the police station with Bill Palmer just behind him and to his right. Pickus was wearing his uniform but had opted not to wear a hat. He'd seen other law-enforcement officers give announcements inside with their hats on, and he thought it looked silly. He didn't want to look silly with just over a year until he was up for reelection.

Pickus leaned toward the microphones and cleared his throat. "Um, thank you all for coming." The lights of the cameras were shining on him, and he felt like the proverbial deer in the headlights, only these lights were more like the warming lights over a food cart. There were a couple of chuckles after his greeting and he figured he'd made a mistake by opening things that way. He hadn't talked that part over with Palmer, assuming it would just be friendly to thank people.

"I'm Sheriff Larry Pickus, and this is Morris police chief Bill Palmer next to me." Pickus looked to his left for Palmer, couldn't see him, and then to his right. Palmer gave him a sideways glance and then nodded as there were more laughs from the media. Pickus wiped his forehead with the back of his hand. "OK, it's pretty warm in here, so I'll make this brief. Um, last night the county attorney and his wife, Lee and Cindy Feller, were shot in their home. These killings may or may not be related to a couple of other killings we had in the last week, but the sheriff's department is investigating that with the help of the Morris police. We urge anyone with any information on these killings to contact my office or the office of the Morris police. Thank you."

Pickus's statement had taken all of ten seconds. In that time his tan sheriff's shirt had begun to turn noticeably darker around his collar and along his sides. A reporter shouted, "Sheriff Pickus. How many killings have there been this week?"

Pickus added them up in his head. "Six. Well, four if you don't include the Fellers."

"Why wouldn't you include the Fellers?"

"Well, I would, but there were four before them." Pickus ran his hand across the top of his head and looked at his palm. It was shiny with sweat.

"And who else has been killed?"

"That would have been the Roses on Sunday, Don and Sharon and their boy, Blake, and Dean Alcott."

"How were they all killed?" A different voice.

Pickus blew out a breath. "They had been shot."

"All of them?"

"Yes, all of them." There was a visible dark stripe running down the front of Pickus's shirt now.

"That's a lot of killings in just a few days. Should people be concerned?"

"Well, of course they should. There's a killer out there. It's not a rampage yet, but it's getting close."

A woman right in front said, "You just said there's a killer out there, inferring it's a single killer and these killings are related. Is that correct?"

Pickus looked for Palmer, but the chief had backed away. Both of Pickus's hands went to his scalp. It felt like his head had been under the shower. "We got the BCA working on that."

"Why isn't the BCA here?" said the same woman.

"That's a damn good question." A drop of sweat cascaded down the sheriff's nose and into his open mouth. He was about to say something else when he felt someone pulling on the belt at the back of his trousers and turned to see Palmer there. He thought maybe Palmer wanted to say something for a minute until he realized the chief was trying to get him to end the conference. Pickus turned back to the audience, said, "Thanks again, but I got to go," and left.

Beaman came back on camera saying she would continue to follow the story and sent it back to the studio. The killer thought the sheriff looked like an idiot, and that the news girl was hot, and that he might drive around to see if he could get a look at her. He wondered where she might be staying, but then decided it might be best if he was careful and didn't go snooping. Still, she looked even better than the weather girl. He was happy not to hear any mention of the killing in Wahpeton. Apparently, they hadn't figured that out yet, or they were playing dumb on that so people didn't get any more riled up than they already were. He wondered about the BCA, though. Perhaps they weren't there because they had some information that they were investigating. Something that might lead them to him.

He thought about that for a while, wondering if he had done anything that might give him away at any of the shootings, but couldn't think of a thing. As far as he knew, he'd been quick with them all, in and out. No one had seen him, and he hadn't left any fingerprints or DNA or other evidence that the police all look for on those TV shows. He'd been careful.

The killer watched the rest of the news but didn't pay attention, going over what he still had to do. He'd have to kill at least two more, and maybe others. They all deserved to die for what they had done. Others should probably die as well, but two for sure. Two of them who let Blake Rose do what he did and get away with it. They could have stepped up and put an end to it, but that would have meant no more Blake Rose at quarterback, and they couldn't jeopardize their precious football, could they? The weather girl came on. She usually went outside to do her segment, and the killer was hoping she'd be dressed in something that would let her stay cool, but she didn't go outside this time. She told the camera that there was a front coming in from the Dakotas with the potential for some storms. The reporter woman in red was even hotter than the weather girl, the killer thought, and switched off the news. He knew where the county attorney lived, or, had lived. Maybe he'd drive by.

* * *

Doc talked to Miranda, who didn't tell him much he didn't already know about the Feller murders. It appeared to be the same person. Killer could have gotten in through the garage or the front door but did not leave any prints. Nothing in the home appeared to be disturbed. Miranda said he was planning to stay the night as he still had a few things to finish, and there was supposed to be a storm on the way. Doc thanked him and wished him good luck in finding a room.

Judy Salo picked up Doc's call after the first ring and said that she and her brother would be there for about an hour and that their father was not home. Doc told her that he and

Agent LeBlanc would like to stop by and ask a few more questions, and she said that would be fine. When Doc stopped where he had been the previous night, the two Salo children were sitting on the front step.

Doc and LeBlanc got out of the car and walked up to the Salos. Judy Salo sat with her thin arms crossed across her chest. Her hair was dark, cut short and brushed back. She wore a pink polo and washed-out jeans with rips in the thighs and above the knees. Tom was leaning back on his elbows. The boy looked nothing like his father. He had blond hair, blue eyes, and long legs sliding down the steps. Doc and LeBlanc held out their IDs to the pair, but neither bothered with much more than a glance.

"When we were here last night, your father said that Blake Rose tried to grab you and drove off without you when you got out of his car," said Doc.

"He didn't *try* to grab me," said Judy. Her delicate face flushed with anger. "He *did* grab me. And yeah, he drove off. What a creep."

"How'd you get home?" asked LeBlanc.

"Tom came and got me."

LeBlanc's eyes shifted to the boy. "How did you feel about Blake going after your sister?"

"I didn't like it, and I let him know it," said Tom. He was as tall as Doc, with a similar build. A big kid. "I dropped Judy at home and then drove out to the Rose farm. Blake wasn't home so I waited. When he drove in I let him know what I thought."

LeBlanc glanced at Doc. "And how did you do that?"

Tom sat up. "I grabbed him by the front of his shirt and pushed him up against the side of his precious car. I told him that if he ever tried anything with my sister again he'd regret it."

"And did he try anything again?"

"He gave me a dirty look when I saw him downtown the next day," said Judy. "But that was it."

"Do either of you hunt?" said Doc.

"I think Dad took Tom deer hunting when he was younger," said Judy, looking at her brother, who nodded. "Dad's a big hunter so he made us learn to shoot but neither one of us are into hunting or anything."

"Shooting? With pistols?" asked Doc.

They both shook their heads. "We didn't have anything to do with what happened to Blake, but neither one of us is too sad about it, Agent," said the girl.

"Anyone else you know who might want to see Blake dead?"

The brother and sister looked at each other for a moment, a silent pact being made. "No," said Tom.

There was a rumble of thunder. Far off, but coming their way. Doc thanked them for their time, and he and LeBlanc went back to the car. The air had turned heavy while they were talking to the Salos, the clouds now a solid blanket. A drop fell on the windshield as Doc started the motor to get the air going.

"What do you think?" asked LeBlanc.

"I think that the boy could have taken care of Blake with his fists if he'd wanted to hurt him. He wouldn't need a gun, and it would be a lot more satisfying."

"And the girl?" said LeBlanc as he watched the siblings get off the steps and walk into the house.

"I don't think so. I can't see her doing it when she had her brother to take care of things."

"Maybe they did it as a team."

Doc looked across at LeBlanc. "Hmm. That's something to think about." There was another rumble, and Doc said,

"You need to make a phone call?" LeBlanc pretended not to know what he was talking about and Doc played along. "The girl from the diner?"

Doc drove LeBlanc back to his car. There was diagonal parking on the street in front of The Windmill and a parking lot across the street. Every space was filled. Doc guessed that the media had gotten word of the restaurant. He pulled up behind LeBlanc's car on the street, told him he'd see him in the lobby in the morning, and LeBlanc dashed through the increasing rain to his car.

The lot of the Ramada was full, too. Doc found a spot on the north end of the lot and pulled in. He could see the lightning to the west now, close, reaching toward the ground like someone was lighting up the cracks under black ice. The thunder was a constant rumble, the volume increasing with each new flash. There was little wind, and he was glad of that. As a child he had seen a tornado rip through the neighborhood, watching out his window as it took the roof and half the house of a friend who lived across the street. The boy had been all right, but the sight had left a mark somewhere deep in Doc, and he was wary of any conditions that looked like they might spawn a tornado.

He called Palmer again about the information on the other girls, leaving a second message. Thought about calling Pickus to see if he knew about the Churches and Wyman and the football player owning pistols, but decided he'd had enough of the sheriff for the day. Someone parked two cars away from him, the raindrops like silver bullets in the headlights. The driver, a man in a suit, ran for the building with a briefcase held over his head. Doc thought about going in, ordering a pizza, and putting for a while, but for some reason that just seemed too lonely for a night like this.

"You want some company?" said Doc when Hailey Draper answered.

"Where are you?"

"I'm still in Morris, so over an hour away in this rain for sure."

"That should work. The baby will be down by then," she said. "Have you eaten?"

"Not yet. How about you?"

"No."

"What if I get something on the way?"

"Like?"

Doc realized he didn't really know what there was between Morris and Spicer. "Um, I'm open for suggestions."

"There's a good Chinese place in Willmar. It's a little farther for you, but not much. Get me shrimp broccoli and an egg roll. I have wine."

Doc found the Chinese place—he remembered seeing it when he had been to the Knudson's—and made it by eight. She opened the door for him, wearing a ruffled sleeveless top with three buttons undone, nothing underneath, and a short white skirt. She'd put on lipstick, pink, and wrapped her hair up in a bun. He stood on the step with a brown bag in his hand, staring.

"You going to come in?"

Doc stepped past her, slipped out of his loafers, and said, "Where do you want this?" as he held out the bag.

"I'll take it. Why don't you pour the wine?"

Hailey had opened a nice bottle of chardonnay that sat on the table with plates and silverware. A candle burned in the center of the table. Doc poured while she brought over the open white containers, each with a spoon inserted. They sat on opposite sides of the table, serving themselves.

"This smells good," said Hailey. "But I don't know why they give you so much white rice?"

"We've assigned a task force to figure that out but so far all they've done is gain weight."

Draper laughed. "So, where'd you get the name Doc, Doc?"

Doc gave her a quick reply, his standard response without too much detail when people asked.

"Wow, so you really are a doctor? Should we have said grace?"

"Maybe next time." Hailey gave him what he thought was maybe a little too serious of a look and he knew right then he shouldn't have said that. "So, tell me about your family."

She told him about her parents and her two brothers and asked about his family. He said his sister was three years older and lived in Wisconsin, his dad a doctor, his mother doing a lot of charity stuff, and that they lived in the Minneapolis area. They chatted comfortably while they finished eating, the scent of pine mixing with the odor of the food and the candle, the temperature in the cabin cooling with approaching storm. The dishes were carried to the counter, Hailey saying she'd take care of them in the morning. Doc pushed two chairs up to the picture window facing the lake and then poured the remainder of the wine. They sat, sipping, quiet, watching the storm move across the lake, the lightening putting on a show.

"Will the thunder wake the baby?"

"Not that one," said Hailey. "When he is out, he's out."

Draper was looking at him, and Doc caught her doing it. "What?"

"You like to ask questions but you don't seem big on answering them," said Draper.

"I'm a cop. It's what I do."

She looked at him with searching eyes, a look he'd seen before, and he wanted to look away but her eyes held him. "You catch your killer yet?"

"You want to confess?"

"I don't think so."

"Then I haven't. I've got some ideas, but not just yet."

She finished her wine. "You have any other ideas?"

CHAPTER 20

The baby was up early, which was fine with Doc, because he didn't want any more questions from LeBlanc. He was back at the Ramada by quarter to seven, showered, shaved, and changed into a green polo from Interlachen Country Club. Interlachen was the site of the 1930 U.S. Open victory by Bobby Jones, when he won the grand slam. Doc's father was a member, and he had played many rounds there growing up.

Doc was in the lobby a few minutes after seven but there was no sign of LeBlanc. He waited until seven fifteen, and was about to call LeBlanc when the elevator popped open and the agent stepped out. LeBlanc was in his usual dress shirt, khakis, and sport coat, but he didn't seem quite so chipper. He had a tired and relaxed look that Doc recognized.

"Sorry I'm late," said LeBlanc. "Wake-up call never came."

"Hmm. Alarm clock didn't work either?"

"No."

"Should we wait for anyone else to come down?" said Doc.

LeBlanc took a worried look over his shoulder at the elevator. "Nope. Let's get going."

The sidewalks and roads were still damp from last night's rain, steam rising in spots. The Windmill was full, with a short line of people waiting for tables just inside the door. Doc and LeBlanc had to park two blocks east, and when he saw the line LeBlanc suggested they go somewhere else, but Doc said it would be OK, and they squeezed inside. The elderly crowd in the waiting line gave Doc a dirty look as he and LeBlanc passed. Doc looked over the silver heads and saw the person he was looking for, the waitress from the first day, and waved. She smiled and motioned with menus she held in her hand. Doc and LeBlanc followed her to the only open booth in the place. She set coffee in front of each of them, leaving the carafe, smiled at Doc, and said she'd be right back for their order.

"How'd you do that?" said LeBlanc.

"What?"

"Get a table. It said no reservations on the door."

"I called early this morning and mentioned I knew you and that you were a close friend of Tina's."

LeBlanc's face flushed.

They ordered, LeBlanc getting the French toast and Doc the "country breakfast"—pancakes, eggs, bacon, toast, and hash browns. As they ate, they went over what they knew and didn't know and what the next steps would be. They decided that the priority would be talking to the other girls who had been assaulted by Blake Rose, as well as the football player Pickus mentioned, and then they'd move on to the two other boys who were shooters, Larry Evers and Randy Estes. When they finished eating, the waitress came and cleared the dishes, asking if they wanted any pie. Doc smiled and looked at LeBlanc, who flushed again, and Doc asked for the check. He looked out the window, watching the traffic in front of the restaurant, and sipped his coffee.

"You don't look happy," said LeBlanc.

"I'm not. We should have someone, or a couple of someones, in our sights by now, but it just seems like our list of possibles is expanding. Every day we don't catch this guy is one less day I'm playing golf."

"It's going to be too hot and steamy to play today anyway," said LeBlanc as he sipped.

The waitress dropped off the bill with a big smile, and Doc paid in cash. They squeezed by the seniors waiting at the entrance and walked back to the car.

"Let's go over to the police station. I still haven't heard from Palmer."

The police station was a mistake. It wasn't as busy as the day before, but there were plenty of media people milling around. Doc pulled to the curb a block away and dialed Palmer, who still didn't answer. He tried the police station then, identifying himself, and saying he would like a way into the building that did not involve going through the front door. The person on the phone told him about a door in back, which should be locked but probably wouldn't be, but he could call again if it was when he got there.

The door was unlocked. The agents found themselves in a T-shaped hallway, one leg running against the back of the building, the other to the front lobby, which was full of the media. Doc grabbed a cop walking by, identified himself, and said he had an appointment with the chief. "Is there a way to get to his office without going through the lobby?" said Doc.

The cop pointed to stairs to their right. They found the office, with "Police Chief William Palmer" on the nameplate to the side of the smoked-glass door, and walked in. Doc, expecting to be in an outer office, was surprised to find himself facing Palmer, who was sitting behind his oak desk.

"Sorry to barge in on you, Chief," said Doc. "You have a second?"

Palmer leaned back in his chair and pulled the cheaters off his nose. "What can I do for you?" he said in a tired voice that matched his face.

"You haven't returned my calls, Chief."

"I've been a little busy."

"I caught a replay of the press conference. Smart idea to stay out of it. Must have been pretty hot under those lights."

"That wasn't any fun, Hunter. You should have been there."

Doc wasn't quite sure why it wasn't fun for Palmer, who hadn't done anything. "So, you have those names I wanted?"

Palmer pushed a piece of paper across his desk and said, "I was about to call, but like I said, I've been busy."

Doc looked at the paper. There was only one name. "I thought there were two?"

"No, just one."

Doc leaned forward. "Pickus distinctly said *two*. Now, I want the other name or I will have you up on charges of withholding information in a murder investigation."

Palmer leaned forward as well, hands on the edge of his desk. "You think you're so damn smart, don't you? You run all over the damn state, sticking your nose in where it doesn't belong, riling everyone up, and then riding out of town again without a care. Well, you have no idea what it's like to run a town like this day after day and deal with all the assholes telling you how to do your job and making sure you know that your precious job depends on what they say." Palmer was red in the face now.

"You're right, Palmer, I don't care. All I care about is catching a killer, and I'd like you to help with that but if you prefer to be on the six o'clock news when they march you into your own jail, then that's fine, too."

Doc had mirrored Palmer's position on the other side of the desk, their faces inches apart, LeBlanc wondering how he would ever stop the two big men if they got into it. Palmer finally backed off, falling back in his chair.

He closed his eyes for a moment, and then opened them and said wearily, "Jess. Jessica Palmer. She's my daughter."

Doc looked at Palmer for a moment and then dropped his head. "Jesus. Your own daughter? You protected Blake Rose and the damn football team even though it was your daughter?"

Palmer looked to his right, out his window. "I'm not proud of it."

"Ah, jeez," said Doc. He looked down at the name on the paper again and then back to Palmer. "You get any calls after the news conference?"

"About a thousand. Nothing to go after yet."

Doc held up the paper. "Is this the girl from the college or the high school?"

"The college."

As they were heading out, Doc looked into the lobby. He locked eyes with Gloria Beaman. "Agent Hunter?" shouted Beaman, raising a hand. "Doc?" Doc turned and bolted out the back door, practically running to his car, LeBlanc hurrying to keep up. Both men were sticky from the humid air by the time they were in the car. Doc started his car, made the same U-turn as he had done before, and drove away.

"Kind of avoiding the blonde, huh?" said LeBlanc as he buckled himself in.

"Yeah. Kind of."

"She looks pretty hot."

"Oh, she's hot all right. Touch her and you get burned."

LeBlanc grinned. "So, where to now?"

Doc handed LeBlanc the paper Palmer had given him. "See if you can get hold of her."

CHAPTER 21

The girl's name was Shelly Olson. Olson worked in the college library and said she could talk to them there. Doc and LeBlanc found the library and walked up to the information desk, asking for Olson. A woman there told them to wait a moment, stepped into a glassed room behind the desk, and talked to a girl inside. The girl pulled her long hair to the side, looked through the glass at the agents, and nodded. The woman came out and said, "She'll be right with you."

Shelly Olson came up to the agents, introduced herself and looked at their IDs, and said they could use the small conference room. The agents followed her to a heavy blond-wood door next to the room she had been in, and she opened the door with a key. The room had a small round Formica table of speckled tan surrounded by five uncomfortable plastic chairs with chrome frames. One wall had a large dry-erase board; the others held landscapes from around the area, each labeled with the date and the name of the student who had taken the photograph.

Olson was a pretty girl. Average height, with round green eyes and full lips. A nice figure was evident under her yellow blouse and tan skirt. She sat and said, "What can I do for you?"

"We're investigating the death of Blake Rose, Miss Olson," said LeBlanc. "We understand you had an altercation with him last year."

"Yes. Blake was in English class with me. He asked me out, and I said yes. Blake picked me up—"

"Where was this?" LeBlanc broke in.

"At the dorm. Anyway, he picked me up about six thirty. I thought we were going to a movie, but he said right away that he'd left his wallet at home, and we could stop by and get it and still make the show. It was dark by then. He drove us out of town about a mile and then turned down this gravel road. That didn't feel right to me, and I asked him where we were going. He said to his parents' place to get his wallet, but then he pulled off the gravel road and stopped under this big oak. That was when he reached over and grabbed my breast."

"And what did you do?"

"I pulled his hand away and slapped him. He just smiled, and then he put his hand on my thigh. I pulled it off, and he grabbed me by the wrist, leaning over, trying to kiss me." As the girl told her story, she stared at the blank dry-erase board. "I turned away, and he laughed as I tried to get my arms free. Somehow, I managed to get away and out the car door. He rolled down the window, called me a bitch, said I didn't know what I was missing, and drove off."

"You walked back?"

"No, I called a girlfriend who came and got me."

"You reported this to the college?" asked Doc.

"Yes, and the police. But they both said it would be just my word against his, and since there hadn't been any sexual contact there was nothing they could do."

"You still had Blake in your class after that?"

"He only showed up twice more before the semester ended. He gave me a dirty look but never said anything."

"Who else knows about this, Miss Olson?" said LeBlanc.

"My dad, my roommate—she's the one who picked me up—and that's about it."

"No other boyfriends you might have mentioned it to?"

"No. I'd just as soon forget it and no one else know." Olson sat back and stared at LeBlanc, arms across her chest, holding her anger inside.

"Where are you from?" said Doc.

"Just north of Benson."

"And you live with your parents?"

"I'm staying in the dorm and working on campus," she said.

"But you lived in Benson until you came to the college?"

"Yes, with my father. My mother doesn't live with us."

Doc leaned back, legs stretched in front of him, chin dropping nearly to his chest. "How did your father react to what you told him?"

"He wasn't happy, if that's what you mean. But I convinced him I was fine and would be OK."

"What's his name?"

"Gerry, with a 'G.'"

"Is your father an outdoorsman, Miss Olson?" said Doc. "Does he hunt and shoot?"

"Yes, birds and deer. He fishes too."

"So, he has guns?"

Olson's eyes grew noticeably larger. "Yes."

* * *

Doc and LeBlanc walked back to the entryway.

"We'd better check out the dad," said LeBlanc.

"Yeah. You want to see if you can find anything on him? Why don't you wait for me in the car?"

LeBlanc looked out the doors at the red-brick college buildings shimmering in the heat, remembering how his shirt stuck to his back after just the short walk from the parking lot. "You know it's illegal to leave kids in a car on days like today? I think I'll wait here."

"I'll be back in a minute." Doc walked into the administration area to find the same girl who had greeted him there on Sunday.

"Oh, Mr. Hunter," she said as she stood. "Thank you so much. I mean, Mrs. Lester has been so nice to me. And she gave me a raise."

"Glad to hear it," said Doc. "How are you doing, Tracy?"

"Just fine, thanks."

The girl was staring at him like she had more than a major crush on him. "Is Mrs. Lester here?"

"I'm sorry, you just missed her. She's gone to lunch. Can I leave her a message?"

Doc thought about what he'd like to say to the woman for not telling him about the Olson assault, but just told the girl he would come back another time.

"No problem, Mr. Hunter. If you want to call me and

let me know when that might be, I can make sure she's here." The girl scribbled something on a sticky note and handed it to Doc. "This is my number. You can call anytime."

Doc looked at the slip to see her name, phone number, and a heart drawn around them. "Thanks."

LeBlanc was on his phone when Doc returned. Doc eavesdropped for a minute and then walked outside. The sun was high, the clouds of the morning melted away, a slight breeze from the northwest easing the humidity. Doc stood on the sidewalk in front of the school and flipped down his sunglasses. Across the parking lot and the street next to it there was a football field used for practice by the college team. A blocking sled was sitting idle beyond the far end zone.

Doc hated the blocking sled and blocking practice in general. As far as he was concerned, all it did was make you sore and tired, and then you weren't able to practice the things you really needed to practice. He dogged it in practice, and the coaches gave him hell about it, but he didn't really care. They'd make him run laps and do push-ups to punish him, but he saw those things as important for his conditioning as a receiver, so he didn't mind. But then, in his last year at the U, a new receivers coach had made Doc stay after practice and hit the sled for an hour by himself.

On the following Saturday, in the first offensive series against Illinois, Doc hand-checked the safety who got by and took down the Minnesota runner for a loss on third down. The receivers coach was all over Doc on the sidelines after the play, and Doc let the coach know what he thought of him. On the next series, Doc was again called on to block. As he walked out to his position, he looked to the sidelines, spotted the coach, and pointed his finger at him. The ball was snapped, and Hunter drove off the line. The safety was looking into the backfield and had taken the fake, thinking the play was going away from him, and taking his eyes off Doc. Doc hit him at full speed, driving his helmet into his midsection. Doc stood over the unconscious kid for a moment before turning to find the smiling face of his coach on the sidelines.

Doc switched his attention from the blocking sled to the other side of the field, where eight small children were lined up along the sidelines. An adult stood behind the one closest to Doc, arms wrapped around the child, teaching him how to swing a golf club. The other children stood with irons in their hands, watching, until the adult backed away, and then they all started hitting balls across the field. Doc glanced back up at the cloudless sky. It would be a good day to be on the course.

LeBlanc came out of the building and stood next to Doc and saw the kids by the field. "Must be a golf lesson."

"Got to start young," said Doc.

"How often do you golf, Doc?"

"Not often enough." He stepped off the curb, and LeBlanc followed. They got in the car and rolled down the windows until the air-conditioning kicked in. "What did you find out?"

"Gerry-with-a-G Olson seems to have some issues. He has a DWI and was arrested for shooting a neighbor's dog. His ex has a restraining order against him. He's spent a couple of nights in jail after altercations in a Benson bar."

"Should probably have a visit with the Benson cops about him and then go talk to Gerry." LeBlanc's stomach grumbled loudly enough for Doc to hear. "Hungry?"

"I could eat."

"There's a little place down by Hancock on 9. Shouldn't be full of media types. Why don't I drop you off at the hotel, and you can get your car and we'll meet there. Then you can go on to Benson and talk to the cops and Gerry Olson."

"What are you going to do?"

"I'm going back to Willmar to see Linda Knudson again. I've got a few more questions."

They rendezvoused at the Northwoods Café, which Doc thought was kind of an odd name for the place considering it wasn't anywhere near the north and there was only a lone oak next to the parking lot of the building, with flat farmland all around. The only patrons were two balding men in coveralls nursing Millers at the bar. Someone had tried to give the place a cheery look with white wainscoting along with red-and-white checkered curtains and tablecloths. But much of the white paint on the wooden floor had been worn off years ago and the heavy oak bar, stained nearly black, just didn't seem to fit. The agents both had salads and turkey clubs.

As they came out of the café, Doc stopped and looked at LeBlanc. "Be careful with Gerry with a 'G'. I have a not-good feeling about him. See what the Benson cops think about talking to him on your own. You may want one of them with you." LeBlanc said he would do that and walked to his car. Doc flipped down his sunglasses and watched him go.

CHAPTER 22

Rusty Knudson was driving a tractor through the yard when Doc pulled in. He turned off the tractor and jumped down, wiping dirt from his hands with a rag that hung from his back pocket. "Didn't expect to see you again, Agent. Has something happened?"

"No, afraid not. I was wondering if I could ask your daughter a few more questions?"

"This isn't about the rape, is it? 'Cause if it is, you can turn right around and leave."

"No," said Doc. "Nothing about that."

Knudson looked suspiciously at Doc and said, "I think she's inside. She's supposed to work tonight."

Linda was sitting at the table, eating a cookie and looking at her phone. She looked up when the men walked in.

"Agent Hunter."

"Linda. I have a few more questions for you."

The girl immediately had an apprehensive look on her face. Her father pulled out a chair and sat next to her and said, "It's OK."

Doc sat opposite the girl and said, "Did you know Jenny Wyman?"

"Not well. I know she left Morris during her senior year."

"Because of Blake."

"Yeah, because of Blake."

"I know you said you didn't have any other boyfriends besides Mark Church, but I'm wondering if you can give me the names of the boys you did date."

The girl sighed. "OK. There was David Morton, Charlie Rayes, and John McDonald."

Doc was making notes and looked up at the mention of McDonald. "That's it?"

"Um, I guess."

"Anybody you turned down?"

"Luke Ritter. He was a friend of Blake's, so I just said no."

"This was after your incident with Blake?"

"No. The summer before college."

"But you went out with Blake?"

Linda looked at her phone lying on the table. "I know. But he was the quarterback, and . . . I was stupid."

Her father put his tanned and dirty hand over his daughter's, giving Doc a look of warning.

Doc stood. "OK. Thanks, Linda. Um, I'm wondering if I could borrow your high school yearbook from your senior year."

"I guess so." She went to her room and returned with

the book.

"Thanks. I'll get this back to you."

Doc was just back in his car, opening the book, when his phone buzzed. "Pickus. What's going on?"

"We got him."

"What do you mean?"

"We got the killer!" he practically shouted. "Well, not yet, but we will."

"Slow down," said Doc. "What are you talking about?"

"I asked Kuck to stop by the co-op to ask Salo just to confirm where he had been on Tuesday night. When he got there the gal that works for him said he was gone. Cleaned out his office and took off. Kuck went to his house and his kids ain't seen him either. Most of his clothes were missing."

"Hold on, Sheriff. I—"

"He did it, Hunter. Bastard killed the Roses, the dean, and the Fellers. He's got a pistol missing. We're going to get him."

"Sheriff." But Pickus had disconnected. Doc immediately called Trask.

"Did you put the fraud guys on Ed Salo?"

"And how are you today, Agent Hunter?" said Trask.

"Not very damn good. Ed Salo just took off running and now every cop in the county is after him. They're going to kill him."

"Aw, shit. Let me make a call, and I'll call you back."

Doc waited a minute, watching Rusty Knudson walk out of the house and pass in front of his car, giving him a look that said Doc was not welcome to stay. His phone buzzed.

"The fraud guys contacted Salo yesterday and said they would like to talk to him. Apparently, it only took a quick look at his accounts to see there are some major problems."

"Crap. OK, they must have scared him. I don't think he's the killer but I have to see if I can find him before the sheriff does," said Doc. "LeBlanc and I will get on it."

"What are you going to do?"

Doc watched Knudson climb onto his tractor. "I don't know."

Doc's tires were spinning in the gravel when he popped out on 9 going north. He called LeBlanc. "Ed Salo is running, and Pickus thinks he's the killer. We got to find Salo before they do or it's likely they'll kill him, and we'll never know if he is or not. You got any ideas how we can do that?"

"They have an APB on Salo's vehicle?"

"I didn't look, but I suppose so," said Doc. "Where are you?"

"At the Benson police station."

"You haven't been out to see Gerry Olson yet?" said Doc.

"No. I—"

"All right. Tell the Benson cops you're sorry, but you have to go. Meet me at the Salo place. I want to talk to the kids. You'll probably be there before me, so just hang for a second, and make sure one or both of the kids are there."

Doc turned on his lights and siren and made it to the Salos only a couple of minutes after LeBlanc. There was a Morris cop car at the end of the driveway, and Doc waved as he went past. He pulled in behind LeBlanc's car, LeBlanc leaning on the side. Doc jumped out, running for the door. "Are they here?"

"The girl is, just inside."

Doc knocked once, but didn't wait for an answer and stepped into the house. Judy Salo was sitting on the steps with her mother, who had her arm around her. "Mrs. Salo?" said Doc. "I'm Agent Hunter of the Bureau of Criminal Apprehension and this is Agent LeBlanc. Do you have any idea where your husband might be?"

The woman looked up at Doc and then over at LeBlanc. She had the blonde hair of her son and it was evident where the children got their blue eyes. Both she and Judy's eyes were bloodshot from weeping. She was thin, with legs that looked too long for her torso.

"The police have already asked. I don't know. I gave them the address of his brother, but I don't think he'd go there. They aren't that close."

"Where is that?" said Doc.

"Albert Lea."

"And where's your son?"

"Ed got him a summer job at the co-op in Ortonville. He should be coming."

"OK. It's very important that we find your husband," said Doc. "And by 'we' I don't mean the Morris Police or the sheriff. I mean Agent LeBlanc and myself. The police think your husband may have killed the Roses and the others."

"He would never do that," said Mrs. Salo. "He just wouldn't."

"Right. Well, that will be for the courts to decide, but right now—"

The phone in Ruth Salo's hand buzzed. It was a number she didn't recognize. "Hello?" Then: "Tom! Where are you?" Doc stepped forward and reached out his hand. Ruth laid the phone in his palm. "Mr. Salo, this is Agent Hunter. Are you somewhere safe?"

"I'm coming back. I need to make things right."

"Where are you now?" Salo gave Doc his location. "Is your vehicle out of sight?" Salo said it was. "All right, Mr. Salo. Whose phone are you calling from?" Salo said it was the phone of a friend. "OK. Do not turn your phone on. I will have a BCA agent come and get you and drive you to the BCA headquarters in St. Paul in his car. Do not go anywhere in your vehicle. Is that clear?"

"I'm coming back to Morris."

"Not a good idea. The police here think that by running you declared yourself to be a murderer," said Doc. "They are out after you in full force, Mr. Salo, and I don't think they want to play nice." Salo was silent. "Mr. Salo?"

"I want my lawyer with me."

"That's fine. Who is your lawyer, and where is he located? If you give me his number, I'll call him and tell him to meet you in St. Paul."

"I can call him."

"I'd rather you didn't, Mr. Salo," said Doc. "I don't know who is tied to who in this thing, and it would be better if he didn't know how to find you." Salo was quiet again. "Mr. Salo?"

"Yeah, I'm here. Let me talk to my wife."

"I'll call you back to give you the name of the agent who will be driving you to St. Paul." Doc handed the phone back to Ruth Salo and listened.

"What's going on, Ed? What have you done?" She was silent for a few moments before saying she understood and hung up. "He's going to do what you said."

"Good." Doc took out his card and handed it to the woman. "If you have any questions, or if he calls again and says he's changed his mind, call me immediately." Ruth looked at the card and then up at Doc, nodding once. "I'm going to leave Agent LeBlanc here until we know your husband is safe at BCA headquarters. He can reach me for you if you prefer." She looked at LeBlanc and gave another nod. "I need to borrow your phone for a moment to get the number your husband is using." She thought about it for a moment, and then unlocked her phone and handed it to Doc. Doc held the phone out to LeBlanc and had him jot down the number before returning it to Ruth Salo. Doc turned to LeBlanc. "Gary, let's talk outside for a minute."

They got to Doc's car, and he told LeBlanc to hang on a minute, he had to call Trask.

"I found Salo," said Doc to Trask. He told Trask where Salo was located, the phone he was using, and what he had told Salo to do. "I'm afraid he'll do something stupid, like try to come back here. How soon can you get someone over there?"

"Moody isn't far, in Mankato," said Trask. "He should be able to get there in about twenty minutes."

"OK, tell him to step on it, and then tell him to call me when he has Salo, and they're on their way to St. Paul. I'll call Salo's lawyer then."

Doc disconnected and turned to LeBlanc. "Stay close to them, Gary, like a second skin. If you get any inkling that Salo has changed his mind and might be headed back, call me. And don't let them talk to the sheriff and his men or the Morris cops. Pickus will be back. Tell the Salos to say that their lawyer told them not to say anything."

"No problem. Where are you going?"

Doc looked up at the blue sky, a canvas painted with God's whiskers here and there—a sky he would like to be under holding a driver on the first tee. "I'm going to call Salo and then go read a book. Watch them."

CHAPTER 23

The killer had gone out looking for Beaman the previous night, but it had turned into a total bust. There was a major traffic jam on 59, something that never happened in Morris. Everybody and their uncle wanted to see the Feller home and maybe get on television, but it wasn't going to happen. The police had blocked the turnoff from 59, waving people by. Everyone was still slowing to a crawl, hoping they could see something, which was silly because the Feller home was nearly half a mile from 59. Finally, the wind and rain did what the police couldn't, and the stream of vehicles disappeared.

The killer was waiting in line on 59 until he was close enough to see the flashing lights of the squad car and decided it would be best not to try to get closer. For all he knew the cops might be checking licenses and vehicles. He waited until the car ahead of him had moved a car-length closer to the turnoff, checked his side-view mirror, and did a U-turn.

In five minutes, he was back in town, cruising. The killer had his list with him, but he didn't need to look at it. He took a right on Fifth, a left on Montana, and a right on Sixth, pulling to a stop across from a redwood-sided split-level. There was a small red hatchback in the driveway, but that wasn't the vehicle the killer wanted to see. He was looking for Bill Palmer's truck.

The killer stared at the house. A dim light in the picture window was changing in intensity and color. Someone was watching television. It would be much more difficult to kill the chief. More difficult than the others, certainly. They had been almost too easy. Walk in, bang you're dead, walk out. Well, Blake's parents had been a bit of a surprise, but they just stood there like they wanted to be shot. Easy.

The chief wouldn't be so easy. Obviously, he'd have guns, and he'd likely have a security system. Probably locked his doors, but maybe not. The guy was a conceited prick and thought he could take anyone. Palmer was married and had two kids, one a junior and the other in middle school, maybe seventh grade. That would make things more difficult. And then there was the fact that Palmer was a cop. From what he'd seen on television shows, it seemed like anytime someone killed a cop the rest of the cops got angry, and the killer almost always ended up dead.

As the killer sat thinking about how he would kill Bill Palmer, the sky darkened and the wind began to pick up. A small branch from the oak tree above the killer's vehicle bounced off the hood, startling him. There was a flash of lightning with thunder not far behind. Big drops of rain were bouncing off the hood and pounding the roof. Through the waterfall running down his side window, he saw a light across the street. The garage door of the Palmer house went up, and a dark figure scurried out. Palmer's wife. She ran to the red hatchback, jumped in, and pulled the car into the garage. The killer watched her exit the car inside the garage and then reach for the garage door opener control on the wall by the door. The door slowly closed. As the light disappeared under it, there was a bright flash of lightning and the quick boom of thunder. The killer started his truck and drove home.

CHAPTER 24

Doc left town, going south, stopping at the Northwoods Café. Two farmers at the bar glanced at Doc when he stepped in and then went back to watching the news on the television behind the bar. Suddenly, Salo's picture was on the screen, and Doc walked up to the bar to listen. It was a picture of Salo kneeling with a rifle next to a lion, and the graphic below was flashing information with the number of the Stevens County sheriff's office and the Morris police. Then Pickus was on. It looked like he was at the Morris police station again. "Mr. Salo should be considered armed and extremely dangerous. Call the Stevens County sheriff's office immediately if you see him." A reporter asked if Salo was the killer he was looking for, and Pickus said, "That could be. It's highly likely."

"Aw, shit," said Doc. The farmers drinking their beers looked at him, and Doc said, "Sorry," and then walked to a table and sat. He checked his phone to see if he had missed a call from

Moody or Trask, which he hadn't, and then leaned back in his chair. As he finished looking at his phone, there was a shadow over him. He looked up, expecting the waitress, and then said, "Aw, shit" again.

"And it's nice to see you too, Agent Hunter," said Gloria Beaman. "Mind if I sit down?" She didn't wait for an answer, pulling out a chair.

Beaman's hair and makeup were perfect, and so was the rest of her as far as Doc remembered. "Gloria, you know I'm not supposed to be talking to you. If Trask knew, he'd shoot me himself."

She leaned forward on the table, her breasts stretching the fabric of her blouse to the point where Doc thought she might pop a button. "I just wanted to say hi and see how you were doing." She gave him a big fake TV smile.

"And I'm just here on vacation."

"You trying to find a new girlfriend?" she asked, glancing at the yearbooks in front of Doc. He pushed them to the side.

"No. I think I have enough."

"You think one of the kids is the killer?"

He shook his head. "I told you, I'm just here on vacation."

"Then you won't mind if I buy you a beer?"

Just then, his phone buzzed. He looked at the screen. Moody. "I need to take this." He swiped the answer icon, and said, "Hunter."

"Moody. I have Salo and we're on our way to St. Paul. Thanks for ruining my night."

"Not a problem," said Doc. "And thank you for calling, sir." Doc heard a swear word as he disconnected. He looked at

Beaman.

"Good news?"

"Aw, jeez Gloria. You go get us some beers. I need to make a call." Doc stood and went outside as Beaman walked to the bar. He called Salo's lawyer and told him about Salo. The man said he would leave for St. Paul shortly. Doc thought maybe he should call Pickus to tell him what was happening, so he did, only to get the sheriff's voice mail. He left a message. Finally, he called LeBlanc to tell him, and told him to let the Salos know and then he could take off himself. Doc came back in to find Beaman at his table with the beers, nibbling on popcorn from a machine in the corner. "Still here, huh?"

"You're welcome."

Doc sat down, took a sip of beer, and shoved a few kernels of corn in his mouth. "Thanks. I don't think this popcorn is going to be enough. Have you eaten?"

They ended up having steaks that were just a little too done, but not bad, and a bottle of cabernet that went really well with the meal. Gloria tried a few more questions about the case but Doc stonewalled her so she gave up and they talked golf. Beaman was a golfer, a ten handicap, and she and Doc had played a few rounds. They'd gone to the nineteenth hole after their rounds and then to other places to get more comfortable. Doc complained about not getting enough time on the course and she did the same, telling him her job was getting to be more work and less fun.

"You think you'll get an anchor job?" said Doc.

"I'm doing more studio pieces, subbing a bit, but I don't see it right now. I'm going to send out some tapes."

"Network or station?"

"Both, I guess. I'm not getting any younger."

"Ah, you still look good."

Beaman didn't know whether he was bullshitting her or not and then decided it didn't really matter. "Thanks, Doc. What about you?"

"I think I'm pretty good at what I'm doing but I really want to give the golf thing a try, you know? Like you said, I'm not getting any younger."

As they worked on a second bottle, Doc remembered their golf rounds, especially afterwards, Gloria getting more attractive as they drank. Before long, the bottle was empty, Doc asking if she wanted to get a nightcap somewhere. They headed south, nearly all the way to Benson, and ended up at the Motel 6.

Doc was sitting in bed with his back to the headboard when Beaman came out of the shower in the morning with a towel wrapped around her.

"You still got it, Doc."

Doc wasn't so sure. He was feeling a bit tired after the week so far, and there were still a couple of days to go. "Thanks. I was worried I might have forgotten it somewhere."

Beaman smiled as she started to dress. "Oh, I don't think so."

She was trying to be playful, but Doc could pick up the serious tone underneath. "Um, Gloria, you know—"

"Don't say any more, Doc. I know what you're going to say. Just promise me you'll give me a heads-up when something is breaking."

"Yeah, well, we have Ed Salo in custody."

"What? When?"

"Last night. That call I took at dinner."

Her face turned dark, a look Doc remembered. "You

bastard! Why didn't you say something?"

Doc shrugged. "We kind of got busy."

Her head tilted, and she stared at him. "But you don't think he did it, do you? That's why you have the yearbooks."

"Gloria, you know I can't say . . ."

"I'm probably in trouble for not being on the Salo capture. You damn well better let me know when something else is breaking. You owe me, Hunter."

* * *

Pickus had called the previous night and left an irate message. Doc had turned off his phone, so he didn't get it until just after Gloria left. Doc hoped he had cooled down a bit overnight.

"Pickus."

"This is Hunter."

Pickus started up right away. "Hunter, you bastard—"

Doc momentarily tuned Pickus out, wondering if he'd ever been called a bastard twice in such a short period of time. "Listen, my phone has been on the fritz, and I didn't get your message. Did you get my message last night about catching Salo?"

That set Pickus off again. Doc listened as long as he could stand it, and then cut in: "Tell me about the gun that's missing."

"It was missing from Salo's gun case in his trophy room in the bottom drawer."

"You think it's the weapon?"

"It's a Beretta nine millimeter. We'll know when we find it."

Doc was silent for a moment. "You check out where

Salo was when the shootings happened?"

"Kuck is on it. I got him, Hunter, and I want him back here."

"Well, you may have to wait on that."

"Why?"

"It seems Mr. Salo has been ripping off the co-op to finance his hunting trips. He's likely going to be charged with fraud and a whole bunch of other stuff."

"Damn it, Hunter! This is your doing. I want him back in Morris!"

Pickus was gone. Doc set his phone on the nightstand and thought about things. If Salo's gun was used, then possibly Salo was their killer. But it just didn't seem right to Doc. For one thing, it seemed to him that a big-game hunter like Salo would have used a rifle. It was what he was comfortable with. The second thing was that Salo never confirmed he had killed anyone when Doc had talked to him. He hadn't denied it either. Still, when Salo talked to his wife, it seemed to Doc that she should have been a lot more upset by what he said than she was. Unless he didn't tell her.

Doc pondered that for a moment more before he realized he had a bigger problem now. Pickus and Palmer would pull their men from the hunt. Their killer was in custody. The real killer was now free to roam and start up again.

He called LeBlanc. "We have a problem."

"That I've been calling your room and your cell phone, and you're not answering?"

Doc looked at his phone log. "Sorry. I got—"

"Waylaid. I know."

"Anyway, our problem is that Pickus thinks the killer is in custody so he's going to call off his men. Palmer too, I suppose."

"You don't think it's Salo?"

"No. Doesn't feel right," said Doc. "Are you at the hotel?"

"The Windmill."

"Hold me a seat. I'll be there as soon as I can."

CHAPTER 25

The morning news carried the story of Ed Salo being held in St. Paul. Some news outlets suggested that Salo had turned himself in; others didn't mention how he had been apprehended. All of them went through the killings in Morris.

The killer had seen the press conference with the sheriff the evening before. He was considering going out to eliminate another name on his list, but figured with the police out searching for Salo, that would not be a good idea.

There was no mention of the gun. He didn't really want to stop using it, but after the Fellers, he just didn't want to take the chance of being caught with the gun. Needed to get rid of it. He had access to other guns, like the one he'd used to kill the druggie, or maybe he'd try something new. That might be fun.

He spent the evening planning how the next two names on his list would be killed. If he could make it look like an accident with the cops thinking Salo did it, especially for Palmer, then maybe he wouldn't have to worry. And then he would be done.

And that seemed a little sad. Others were responsible for what had happened, at least partly, and they needed to suffer. They weren't as directly involved as Palmer, but they had a part. It didn't seem right that they would get off. It wasn't fair. And, as he thought about it, he knew he didn't really want to stop. It would bother him to see those people walking around, thinking the rapes weren't their fault. Thinking Jenny's death wasn't their fault. No, it wasn't right. They all needed to pay.

But there was more to it. Shooting the druggie in Wahpeton had been hard. The guy was a scumbag, a killer himself really, and he needed to die. But shooting someone, well, it wasn't like shooting a squirrel or a deer. This was a person. Somebody his parents would say was created by God in God's image. He didn't really believe that, but it made him stop and think. It was a person, after all, and unless you were a cop or a soldier, killing somebody was against the law. Like about the worst law you could break.

And maybe that was what made it such a rush. Breaking the law. Being an outlaw. But he wasn't just doing this to kill someone; he had a purpose. He was making things right. He was kind of like the law when he thought about it, making sure that the people responsible for Jenny's death were brought to justice. The avenger. And damnit if it wasn't exciting, too. Shooting the gun and popping that druggie, seeing the look on his face in that instant, watching him drop and the life just trickle away. Man, he knew he'd have to do it again. Tonight.

* * *

Doc slid into the booth opposite LeBlanc. He had taken a quick shower at the motel but was in the same shirt as yesterday, deciding he was too hungry to stop at the Ramada to change. His hair was still damp, and his eyes were a little droopy. LeBlanc looked at him and shook his head.

"It's a good thing you finally showed. Some of the blue-hairs waiting for a table were looking at me like they wanted to string me up. Even the waitress stopped asking if I wanted more coffee."

"You already eat?"

"A while ago."

"Sorry."

Doc was looking at the menu when the waitress—the same one he'd on the first morning—came by and said, "Good morning." She flipped over the coffee cup in front of Doc and started pouring.

"Good morning to you," said Doc with a big smile. "Is the French toast still good?"

"Best this side of the street."

"What's on the other side of the street?"

"My apartment," she said, winking.

"OK. Bring me the French toast and sausages, and I'd better have some orange juice too just so I'm a little healthy."

She said, "You look plenty healthy to me," winked again, and left.

"Jesus, Doc. Don't you think you better slow down a bit?" said LeBlanc after the waitress left.

Doc watched her walk away, a nice view from his perspective, and said, "What?"

"Women," said LeBlanc. "Maybe take a day off?"

Doc looked at him and said, "Yeah, you might be right."

The coffee tasted the same, strong and bitter. "So, Pickus, and I'm guessing the majority of the cops in the area, are not too happy that we snuck Salo out from under their noses, and their disposition will likely get worse if Pickus does find the gun that did the shooting. Meaning we are pretty much on our own on this thing."

"What about the murder weapon? If it is the murder weapon, you really think we should keep looking for someone else?"

Doc looked at the coffee cup between his hands. "We almost got to hope they don't find the gun for a while. I'm guessing we're not going to be given too much more time as it is. Trask will pull us."

"So, you have a plan?"

There was no plan. Doc was waiting for the 'click' that came when things fell into place, but that hadn't happened. He decided to send LeBlanc back to Benson to finish with the police there and talk to Gerry Olson. In the few minutes he had spent there, LeBlanc had looked at a couple of reports in Olson's record and decided he was not the most levelheaded or hospitable person. That base needed to be covered. Doc wanted more time to go over the yearbooks since that hadn't happened the night before. LeBlanc was to call him when he was done with Olson, and they would decide what the next step was at that time.

Doc went back to the Ramada, took another shower, brushed his teeth, and changed into a T-shirt from Superior National along the north shore of Lake Superior. Doc considered the course a moderate challenge, but the views of the lake and the forest were peerless. He also put on clean shorts before opening the two yearbooks side by side on the bed. After flipping through a dozen pages, he pushed the books to the side, lay on his back, and fell asleep.

* * *

The Benson police department was housed in an unremarkable concrete-block building that had been painted a two-tone beige and was directly across the street from the Dollar Store. There were other city offices in the building, which took up a good half block. LeBlanc walked up to the duty officer inside the office, the same one who had been there the day before, and told her he'd like to talk to whoever it was on the staff who could tell him about Gerry Olson.

"That would probably be the chief," she said. She made a quick call and pointed to an office behind her. "Just go right in, Agent."

LeBlanc knocked on the open door of the small office anyway, and a man with flat brown hair sitting behind an industrial-sized metal desk looked up at him over half-moon reading glasses. Chief Taggert stood, invited the agent in, and shook LeBlanc's hand over his desk before sitting again.

"So, you want to know about Gerry Olson?" said Taggert in a deep voice that reminded LeBlanc of an actor he couldn't quite place. Guy with a big mustache. Sam someone.

"If you wouldn't mind," said LeBlanc. "His name has come up as a person of interest in our investigation of the murders up by Morris."

"I thought they had the guy. Salo, right?"

"Mr. Salo has been detained but not charged. We're trying to cover all bases."

Taggert leaned back and took off his glasses. "OK, well, it may be in your best interest to pin it on Salo and skip talking to Olson if you can."

"Why's that?"

"As you saw in the records, the guy has been a pain, but he is more than that. He's just plain mean. I tell my officers and anyone who asks to steer clear. I'm not saying Gerry Olson wouldn't kill anyone—he may have, for all I know—but if you have any reason not to try to talk to him, then don't. I think his wife was lucky to make it out alive, and I'm not sure why, or how, his daughter continues to live with him. When you hear someone described as 'he'd just as soon kill you as look at you,' that's Gerry Olson."

"So, not Mr. Congeniality?"

"Not even close."

"OK, Chief," said LeBlanc. "I appreciate the advice, but I need to talk to him."

Chief Taggert shook his head and then stood. "Well, we don't need any more killings around here, so I guess I'd better take you out there." Taggert pulled his holster from the coatrack next to his desk and began to strap it on.

"I'm OK doing this on my own," said LeBlanc. "Really."

"No, you're not, Agent. You have a weapon?" LeBlanc said he did, and Taggert said, "Let's go."

They went three miles south on Highway 12, took a left on Twentieth, went half a mile, and then took another left on Fiftieth. LeBlanc looked out at acres of beans and corn, the only trees huddled around the farm sites they passed. As they drove, Taggert told LeBlanc to let him do the talking when they got there. Taggert slowed, turning off Fiftieth and coming to a stop at a gate across a gravel drive.

The gate was a big X made of treated one-by-six boards

with studs on either side and barbed wire strung across the boards. Hung on the barbed wire were several signs. The "No Deliveries" sign was probably the nicest of the bunch, with the "No Trespassing" sign a close second. The others were "Trespassers Will Be Shot," "Attack Dogs on Premises," "Private Property Protected by Armed Guards," and "I Shoot First—I Do Not Ask Questions."

Taggert looked at LeBlanc. "You still want to go in?"

"Are there dogs?" asked LeBlanc. Taggert said he didn't know, and LeBlanc said, "Yeah, let's go in. It's my job."

"I'll call," Taggert said. He took out his phone. "Gerry, this is Chief Taggert. I'm at your gate and need to talk to you." Taggert listened for a minute and said, "I'm with an agent from the Minnesota Bureau of Criminal Apprehension. He has a few questions for you about your daughter." Taggert pulled the phone from his ear and looked at the screen. Olson had disconnected. "Um . . ." The gate swung open in front of them. "I guess we're going in."

Taggert moved his cruiser slowly down the quarter-mile gravel drive, barbed-wire fencing on either side. Painted planks nailed to fence posts said "Go Back," "Stop," "Leave Now," and "You Will Be Shot." LeBlanc was starting to wonder if this wasn't a loose end that could be tied up at a later date if need be. He unsnapped his holster and checked his weapon. They pulled into a cluster of worn-down buildings, Taggert stopping in front of a house that LeBlanc guessed had not seen a drop of paint since well into the last century.

A big, barefoot man in dirty striped coveralls and a muscle shirt stood on the covered porch of the house, a shotgun in his large hands. He was bald on top, his blond hair cut short on the sides. There was a noticeable scar on the man's right cheek, and his nose had a knob where it had been broken.

Taggert looked at LeBlanc and said, "Ready?" LeBlanc nodded. They got out of the vehicle at the same time, both watching Olson, who raised his shotgun. Before they could take a step, Olson said, "Far enough."

Taggert and LeBlanc stood partially behind their open doors, Taggert on the same side as the porch. "Put the gun down, Gerry. We just want to talk," said the chief.

"I'll put it down when I damn well feel like it. Now say what you've come to say and get out."

"Mr. Olson, I am BCA agent LeBlanc. I want to ask you a few questions about your daughter."

"What about my daughter?"

"We understand that your daughter made a complaint against Blake Rose."

At the sound of the name, Olson swung his shotgun in LeBlanc's direction, causing LeBlanc to duck. Olson was unshaven, a week or more, and had a tattoo of what LeBlanc thought was a pitchfork running down the right side of his neck. The man had a belly, but his arms looked powerful, like those of a lineman in the NFL. "That piece of shit is in the ground where he should be."

LeBlanc rose slowly, looking over the hood of the car at Taggert and then back to Olson. "Where were you last Sunday morning and Sunday evening, Mr. Olson?"

"Here. I'm always fuckin' here," he replied. "You piece of shit. You think I killed him?"

"We're just trying to—"

"You goddamned piece of shit! You're trying to set me up with this and take my land aren't you, you fucker? I ought to—"

"Listen, Gerry," said Taggert. "There's no need to—"

"You're behind this aren't you, Taggert?" Olson swung his gun back to the right and fired.

LeBlanc watched Taggert fall backward. By the time he turned back to Olson, the man was swinging his gun back in LeBlanc's direction. LeBlanc started to duck behind his door but was too slow. He felt a searing pain in his shoulder and the side of his neck as he hit the ground. The noise from the blasts was loud, but LeBlanc picked up the click of Olson opening the chamber of his gun. LeBlanc reached up through the shattered window of the car door, cringing in pain as he pulled himself up, and then reached for his gun.

Olson had reloaded and was snapping the gun shut when LeBlanc fired.

CHAPTER 26

The sound of a vacuum in the hall bumping against the door woke Doc. He stared at the ceiling for a moment and then turned to look at the clock. He'd been out for nearly two hours. "Jesus, Hunter. You need to get a little more sleep." He sat up in bed, cross-legged, and looked at the yearbooks next to him. There was something there, he was sure—he just needed to find it.

Doc went to the bathroom, got a glass of water, and sat back on the edge of the bed. He made it through two more pages before his phone buzzed.

"I want him, Hunter," said Pickus in a fuck-you tone. "Salo's the killer and I want him back here."

"Wait a minute. You got a weapon yet?"

"Not yet, but I will. Our new county attorney is on the way to St. Paul right now to charge Salo with murder and get his ass back here."

"Listen, Pickus, maybe we need to slow down on this a bit. I mean, there's a lot we don't know."

"We know enough. I got my killer and I'm making sure everyone knows. There'll be a news conference at noon. See you."

"Pickus—" said Doc, but the sheriff was gone. "Damn." Things that would start moving fast now. Once Trask heard about the murder charge, he'd likely pull him from the case. Doc stared down at the yearbooks and thought whoever had taken the gun in Salo's drawer had to have done so before the Roses had been murdered. He needed to find out who had access to the trophy room during that time. But first, he needed to make a call.

"Hello," said the voice of Gloria Beaman.

"It's Doc."

"Why, hello. Are you lonely again?"

Doc thought about the night before, which had been nice, but he didn't think he needed to be that lonely again for a while. "The murder weapon is likely Salo's. The sheriff will have a press conference about it at noon. They're going to charge Salo with the murders."

"You don't sound too convinced of Mr. Salo's involvement, Pete. Something else you want to tell me?"

"This is it, Gloria. You didn't get it from me. We're even now."

"But, Pete. I thought after last night—"

"Sorry, Gloria. I have to go." Doc disconnected and looked at his phone screen. There had been a call from a number he didn't recognize and a message. He pushed the playback icon.

"Agent Hunter. This is Sergeant Mills of the Benson police. I'm afraid there has been a shooting."

* * *

LeBlanc was at the Stevens Community Medical Center, a few blocks south of the college. Doc parked in a handicapped spot in front and rushed in. The person at the information desk directed him to the second floor. Doc found the elevator, pushed the "up" button, found he couldn't wait, and took the stairs, two at a time. He rushed to his right down the beige hall to a nurses' station.

"I need to see Gary LeBlanc." The nurse looked up from her computer screen. "Agent Gary LeBlanc. I need to see him. I'm Agent Pete Hunter."

"Oh, Agent Hunter. The Benson police said you would be coming. You'll need to have a seat in the waiting room."

"But I need to see him now!"

"I'm sorry, but Agent LeBlanc is in surgery. The doctor will speak to you as soon as he is out."

Doc had never been good at waiting. He cried and threw a fit when his mother said he had to wait for Santa. He yelled at his first cop partner when he was told he'd have to wait on a stakeout. He'd lost more than one girlfriend because of his impatience. He picked up a magazine in the waiting area but retained nothing he read. Dropping it on the chair, he stood and began to pace. He walked the hall, back and forth in front of the nurses' station to make sure they knew he was waiting. After an hour, a doctor in scrubs walked up to the station, pulling off his surgical cap, and the nurse pointed him in Doc's direction.

"Agent Hunter?"

"Yeah."

"I'm Doctor Adams. I operated on Agent LeBlanc."

"Yes?"

"Mr. LeBlanc has lost a lot of blood. I removed a large number of shotgun pellets from him, and he is resting now."

"He'll be OK," said Doc, more as a statement than a question.

"He should be. We'll watch him, check for infection. There are so many wounds with something like this, but yes, I think he will recover."

Doc blew a breath out through his mouth. "Thanks, Doctor. When can I see him?"

"It's going to be at least three or four hours. He's heavily sedated. If you want to leave your number with the nurses, I'm sure they will be happy to call you."

"Did he say anything?"

"Sorry, no." The doctor patted Doc on the shoulder. He turned, took two steps, and then turned back. "Say, aren't you the Pete Hunter who played at the U?"

Doc said he was, and they ended up talking football for a few minutes before he went back to the waiting area and sat, pulling out his phone.

"Doc," said Trask. "I hear Pickus caught your killer for you."

"I don't think so."

"What do you mean?"

"Listen, Don," said Doc. "LeBlanc has been shot."

"Oh, Jesus. Is he OK?"

"Don't know. I talked to the doctor, and he said things look good, but no guarantees."

"What happened?"

"I sent him to talk to the hothead father of a girl Blake Rose had assaulted. According to what the Benson police said, it looks like the father shot both LeBlanc and their chief, and

LeBlanc shot the father. They've flown the chief to Minneapolis. The father is dead."

"Oh, man."

"Yeah."

"OK, I should come out there," said Trask. "Has anyone notified LeBlanc's parents?"

"I don't know."

"I'll call them. Keep me notified on his condition," said Trask, and then paused. "What did you mean when you said you didn't think Pickus has the killer?"

"I need more time on this, Don. I need to look at a few things just to rule them out. Salo could be the guy, but it just doesn't feel right to me."

Trask was quiet again. "You'd better do what you need to do in a hurry. The superintendent won't be happy if he finds out you're still poking around."

CHAPTER 27

It was early afternoon when Doc stepped out of the medical center. The sun had just ducked under a cloud. Doc reached up to move his sunglasses down, but they weren't on their usual perch. He found them on the passenger seat as he got into his car. There was a rumble from his stomach as he put his sunglasses on, and he remembered the Dairy Queen only three blocks west.

Doc brought the yearbooks in with him, glancing at them as he ate. He found it difficult to focus, thinking about LeBlanc and what he had sent him to do. Something that probably hadn't been necessary, and now he might die. Doc was trying to talk himself out of it, but the guilt weighed on him every time he tried to look at the yearbooks or think about the case. Maybe Pickus was right. Maybe Salo had done it. Doc just wanted to forget the entire investigation. Move on to something else.

Doc was crunching a cone when he saw something. A

comment by the photo of a boy in Jenny Wyman's yearbook. There was no comment by the same picture in Linda Knudson's yearbook, but he remembered something similar by another photo much earlier in Knudson's book. It was a group photo, and Doc was sure the same boy had been in the photo as the one making the comment in Wyman's book. He was flipping back, looking for the photo, when his phone buzzed.

"Agent Hunter?"

"Yes?"

"This is nurse Megan Alford from the ER at the clinic. Agent LeBlanc is awake."

LeBlanc had no color. Doc had seen it before, but it just gave him the creeps. Too close to a place he didn't want to go. The surrounding machines were beeping, and there seemed to be tubes everywhere. Doc was too hyped to sit so he stood by the side of LeBlanc's bed. LeBlanc's eyes cracked open and his head moved slightly toward Doc.

"You could have told me that you needed a break," said Doc.

LeBlanc gave a pinched smile, which turned into a grimace.

"Listen, Gary. Geez, I'm sorry. I should never had sent you in there."

"Not your fault," said LeBlanc in a raspy voice. "It needed to be checked out, and I made the decision to go see Olson. It was my choice."

Doc wasn't sure that he really believed him, and then felt bad that someone who was hurting as much as LeBlanc was trying to make him feel better. "Yeah, well, we can argue about it when you get out of here." Doc tried on a smile, then abandoned it. "Can you talk enough to tell me what happened?"

LeBlanc looked at the ceiling. "Olson just flipped out. He thought he was getting set up by Taggert for the murders and turned his gun on him before he fired at me. I managed to get a shot off before he could reload. I walked up to Olson, who looked down. I picked up his gun and then went to check on Taggert. He was hit pretty bad. I called nine-one-one, and that was about it for me." LeBlanc tilted his head back in Doc's direction. "Water," he said in a harsh whisper.

Doc brought the straw up to LeBlanc's mouth as he leaned forward, helping him get it in, holding the glass. LeBlanc took a long sip, and then another, and dropped his head back on the pillow. Doc put the glass back on the tray.

"How's Taggert?" LeBlanc asked.

"Don't know. They flew him to Abbott."

"And Olson?"

"Dead."

LeBlanc looked at the ceiling for a moment, and then closed his eyes. Doc watched him for a minute, not knowing if he was awake. Not knowing if LeBlanc had ever killed a man before and afraid to ask.

"Trask is coming to see you. You should ask him for a medal and a big raise. If I were you, I'd ask for the raise first."

LeBlanc gave a weak smile and cracked his eyes open again. "You need to get whoever is responsible, Doc. You can do it."

Doc wasn't so sure. LeBlanc closed his eyes again, and his breathing slowed. Doc stayed for fifteen minutes more, not saying anything, waiting until the nurse came and told him he needed to leave. A doctor walked in after the nurse, not the same one who had done the surgery, and Doc asked her how LeBlanc was doing. She said he was stable and his vital signs were good, but that he would likely be in intensive care until at least tomorrow.

Doc walked back outside. The clouds had cleared, the sun now well on its way down. A large crabapple tree dominated the center of the turnaround in front of the clinic. Its blossoms were mostly gone, the small green pods that would be apples starting to appear. A few bees were working on the last flowers. Doc watched them numbly, feeling like he did after he had visited the Illinois safety in the hospital. The kid who would never walk again. The media department at the university had played it up as a feel-good story, but Doc had not felt good about it, and he still didn't.

LeBlanc was right. If anything good was going to come from all of this killing, then Doc needed to find out who had pulled the trigger on the Roses, the Fellers, and Dean Alcott. If it was Salo, that would be fine, as long as he was sure. But right now, he wasn't sure of anything, except that he needed to keep looking. He called Trask to let him know that he had talked to LeBlanc, and the doctor said things looked good. Trask said he should be there in about an hour, and after he saw LeBlanc they could have dinner.

Doc wanted to stay close to the hospital, in case something happened, so he went back to the Dairy Queen. He got his table in the corner, and another cone, and sat down with the yearbooks again. He made notes in a small pad as he worked, flipping pages back and forth, looking at the index to find where students were identified in photos.

At six o'clock his eyes were tired, and he took a break to watch the news. The capture of the Morris killer was the lead story again. The picture of Salo and the lion was back up and then a quick snip of the latest news conference by Pickus. The sheriff said they were still looking for the murder weapon but the citizens of Morris could again be secure in knowing their town was safe. Questions followed, and from the responses Pickus gave, one might have imagined that Salo had already been convicted and would soon be hanged in the Morris town square.

"Jesus." Doc watched the news through the weather. No rain was expected through the coming weekend, and the temperatures would be steady in the low eighties. Golf weather. Doc thought about what he needed to do to wrap up the investigation, assuming Salo was the killer. There would be no time for golf for at least a few days. "Shit."

* * *

Trask called Doc at seven thirty. "You ready for dinner?"

Doc pulled the cleaned stick of a Dilly Bar from his mouth. "I could eat," he said.

"Where are you?" said Trask.

"The DQ. It's close to the hospital."

"I'm not eating at the DQ."

"Meet me at The Windmill." Doc gave Trask directions.

The Windmill was about two-thirds full. A girl walked up, someone Doc hadn't seen before, and said, "One?" Doc said there would be two. She pulled a couple of menus from a slot by the front counter and said, "This way," leading Doc to a booth. She asked if Doc wanted coffee, and he said he did, and then he said, "Kind of empty in here from the other times I've been here." The girl took a glance around, said, "A little late for most folks," and walked away.

Trask came through the door, and Doc waved him over. He slid in across from Doc. The waitress returned and filled their coffee cups.

"How's LeBlanc doing?"

"About like you told me," said Trask. "I talked to the doctor who operated on him and he said he pulled a lot of BBs out, but none of them had hit anything vital. His parents showed when I was there, and they'll be staying with him tonight. He's going to be OK, Doc. Not your fault."

Doc was looking down into his coffee.

"What's good here?" said Trask as he picked up the menu.

"Everything I've had. They serve breakfast all day if you want that."

Trask ordered a patty melt and fries, and Doc did the same.

"I saw the sheriff's latest grab at fame," Trask said. "Sounds like he's a super-cop. Practically figured out the whole thing on his own. Didn't hear him mention you at all."

"Naw. I've pretty much been playing golf and taking it easy with Pickus running things. He should probably have your job."

"I'm about ready to give it to him," said Trask.

"Why's that?"

Trask stared at Doc. "Never mind. Not your problem. You're still looking at this thing?"

The food came, and they ate while they talked, Doc saying he wasn't too sure about anything, that maybe Salo did it or maybe he didn't, but he was still looking. Trask told him that Salo would be charged with murder in the morning. He could leave Doc here to poke around as long as LeBlanc was still in the hospital, but after that he'd have to pull him in. Doc said he understood.

The waitress came back when they were finished and picked up their plates, asking if they would like pie. Trask looked at Doc and said, "Do I?" and Doc nodded. They both ordered the cherry because the waitress said it was good, especially with some ice cream. Doc was hesitant to have any more ice cream, having gone way over his limit for the month in just the last few hours, but he did anyway and was glad he did. As he was finishing, he spotted another waitress across the room, excused himself, and walked over and talked to her. Trask watched as the woman listened, put her hand on Doc's bicep, and then he gave her a hug before walking away.

Trask looked at Doc. "How many waitresses in here have already seen your putter this week?"

Doc looked at the waitress he'd been talking to and said, "None."

"What about that one?" Trask said. "Is she a second dessert for later?"

"Naw. She and LeBlanc have gotten a little friendly. I just let her know he was over in the clinic."

Trask looked over at the waitress. "LeBlanc? You let LeBlanc beat you out?"

"What can I say?" said Doc with a small smile. "The guy has moves."

Trask looked at Doc again, but he wasn't returning the smile. "It's really not your fault, Hunter. You do what you need to do to satisfy yourself that Salo is or isn't the killer. I can't give you any more manpower now with Salo in custody, but you call me if you need help."

* * *

CHAPTER 28

Doc went back to his room and sat on the edge of the bed. He clicked through the channels until he couldn't stand it anymore, and went back out, ending up in a country bar downtown called the Golden Saddle. There was a good crowd inside, listening to a live band. Doc found a stool at the bar and asked the bartender if they had any IPAs on tap, thinking he might get a dirty look for not ordering a Miller or a Budweiser, but the woman said they had five, and a new one from a brewery in Marshall was really good. Doc ordered that, and it was good. He swiveled on his stool to watch the band.

   The Golden Saddle was standing-room only after the band started the second set. The temperature and noise in the bar increased with the crowd, and Doc felt like he was about to fall asleep as he finished his second beer. He threw down the last of it, put a twenty under his glass, and left. In ten minutes, he was back in his room. He sat on the end of the bed, kicked off his shoes, and flopped on his back. Doc closed his eyes, thinking he'd probably fall asleep with his clothes on, but his mind wasn't ready for a break.

He got up, and padded over to the desk, where the yearbooks lay open, side by side. His notepad was there too, and he picked it up, looking at the three names he had jotted down. John McDonald, Paul Nelson, and Randy Estes. All of them had made notes in both yearbooks, all saying something a little more than "Have a nice summer." Doc pulled his putter from his bag and dropped two balls at his feet. He thought about LeBlanc, the three boys, Ed Salo, and Hailey Draper.

* * *

He was in LeBlanc's room at the hospital just before nine. LeBlanc was sitting up, a tray with what the clinic must have considered breakfast in front of him: lime Jell-O and orange juice.

"Getting room service now?" said Doc as he pulled up a chair.

"Yeah. The chef went all out, I see." LeBlanc took a sip of juice through a straw, made a sour face, and pushed it away along with the Jell-O.

"How you feeling?"

"Kind of like someone shot me, I guess. Just tired. Not much energy."

Doc looked at LeBlanc. "That's good. You need to stay that way for at least a few days."

"What?"

Doc picked up the Jell-O and the plastic spoon. "You going to eat this?"

"Umm, no," said LeBlanc. "So, I need to stay near death

because . . . ?"

"Not near death," said Doc with a mouth full of Jell-O. "Just feeling bad enough so you stay in the hospital. Trask said I can stay here and poke around as long as you're still laid up."

"You still don't think Salo did it?"

Doc finished the Jell-O and put the container back on the tray. He took the top off of the orange juice and drank that too. "I want to talk to John McDonald, Paul Nelson, and Randy Estes. They all made notes in the two yearbooks that said they had more than just a passing interest in the girls."

A nurse stopped in and looked at the tray. "Good job, Mr. LeBlanc. Would you like anything else?"

LeBlanc looked at Doc, who said, "His throat is a little sore, so he asked if I would see if he could get something a little more substantial, like pancakes and sausage, and maybe some coffee."

The nurse shook her head, and then picked up the tray and said, "I'll see what we have."

"I'm sure I'll be in here at least another day. You should be able to get that done in a day."

"Yeah, well, I've got a few other things I want to check, and, as it's Saturday, I was thinking I could use a little time off."

"Doing what? Getting waylaid?"

"No. I don't think so," Doc said. "Maybe just go out to the range for a bit and get loose. It helps me to think." Doc smiled at LeBlanc, but thought the man still looked only a shade better than death.

LeBanc yawned and said, "Thanks, by the way."

"For what?"

"Tina. She came and visited me last night."

"Oh, so that's why you look so tired." Doc grinned. "Listen, I'll let you rest. Take it easy, but don't get better too fast." Doc lightly touched LeBlanc's shoulder, stood, and walked out. As he exited the room, the nurse was coming with the tray for LeBlanc. "Say, he just went to sleep, so he won't be needing that." The nurse looked up at Doc, shook her head again, and handed him the tray, saying, "Eat it over there and bring the tray back to the nurses' station when you're done."

* * *

CHAPTER 29

Doc was spinning his wheels and he knew it. He went back to his room, putting for a while, hoping something would click. That didn't work, so he found a course with a driving range, Wildwoods Golf Club, and hit a large bucket of balls. He saw a T-shirt he liked in the pro shop when he was through, bought that, and then stopped by the hospital again. Tina was with LeBlanc, so he just stuck his head in the room for a minute to see how LeBlanc was doing and left.

After hitting balls in the hot sun he decided he'd better change his shirt before finding some dinner. He went back to the Ramada, was drawn to his bed like a man to a hardware store, and passed out. A little over an hour later he woke, took a shower, and tried to get dressed. Getting dressed in clean clothes was a problem as he had none. Well, not exactly. He had his new Wildwoods Golf Club T-shirt, but that was it. No clean shorts or boxers. Doc walked up to the front desk.

"Can I help you, sir?" said the brunette with bright blue eyes and a big smile who appeared to be about his mother's age.

"Yeah. I'm Pete Hunter. I'm staying in 108. I don't suppose you have a laundry service here?" Hunter lifted his duffel bag.

"I'm sorry, we don't. But the Suds and Duds is just off of Fifty-Nine on Fourth. They should be open."

Doc thanked her and walked out to his car, put the duffel bag in the back seat, and drove to the Suds and Duds. It was just past six. There were only two others in the laundromat, both men slightly older than Doc, both looking like the clothes they were wearing were the end of their wardrobe. Apparently, the Suds and Duds was the place to be when you were a single man on a Saturday night in Morris, thought Doc. He fiddled with the detergent dispenser and the machine until he got it going and sat on an uncomfortable plastic chair with his notebook.

He was looking at the list he had made when he thought about something LeBlanc had said about the Salo kids possibly teaming up to do the killings. He didn't think that felt right, not after he had seen the girl crying after the arrest of her father. But there was something there. He pulled out his phone.

"Hello?"

"This is Agent Hunter. Is this Judy?" Salo said it was and Doc said, "Are you home? I was wondering if I might stop by your house for a few moments. I have a couple more questions."

"Um, I guess so. It's just me. Mom went to St. Paul, and Tom is out for a while but said he would be back later."

"All right. I have a few things to finish up. How about eight?"

Doc finished his laundry, bought a sub sandwich and a

Coke, and went back to his room. He ate his sandwich watching the end of *Die Hard*, the first one, which was by far the best as far as Doc was concerned. Doc turned off the television as the movie ended and sat staring at the blank screen. That was about as much as he felt like he knew about who was doing the killing. His mind drifted back to his theology classes where he had studied and tried to understand God's will. He wondered now how it could be God's will that so many people had been killed, and there would likely be more if God didn't hit him in the head pretty soon. It made no sense. "Oh, hell." Doc got up and changed his shorts and boxers. It was getting close to eight.

Doc knocked at the front door of the Salo house. Judy Salo, in white shorts and a dark-red blouse, her hair pulled back with a headband, opened the door and invited him in.

"Your brother back yet?" asked Doc.

"Not yet."

"Does he go out at night a lot?"

"He's in college," she replied. "Are you checking on him?"

"No." Doc looked around the entryway and then back at Salo. "I'm wondering if I can take a look at your father's trophy room again."

The girl turned and started walking toward the stairs to the lower level. Doc followed. In the basement, Salo flipped on the light switch by the door and leaned against the wall there, like she was afraid the animals might come to life and she'd need to run. Doc surveyed the room. It looked much the same as it had, except that the gun cabinet was open and the guns were gone. He walked over, pulled the doors all the way open, and opened the drawers. They were empty too.

"The police took all the guns."

Doc ignored her comment. "Do you ever have kids over here?"

"Umm, sure. Why?"

"How about week before last? Maybe Friday or Saturday?"

"We had a party on Friday."

Doc was looking at the tiger again. Big teeth. "Inside? Anyone come down here?"

"The boys like to come down here, look at the animals and the guns." Salo held her position by the door.

"Do you remember what boys might have been in here that Friday?"

"I don't know," she said. "People were in and out."

"OK, do you remember what boys were here?"

Salo leaned against the wall. "I don't know." Doc looked at her, and she folded her arms across her chest. She named four boys he had not heard of before, and then said, "John McDonald, Larry Devers, Rickie Kern . . . um, Randy Estes, and a bunch of football players."

"Not Paul Nelson?"

"I don't think so."

"OK, good. And who were the football players?"

"I don't know," she said. "There were a bunch of them. They kind of travel in packs."

Doc remembered party-hopping in college with teammates. "Was Blake Rose here?"

"God, no. My brother would have killed him."

"Luke Ritter and Zean Thomas?"

"I'm pretty sure they were here."

There was an opportunity for any of those boys to take the gun, including Tom Salo who could have done it at any time.

"How do you and your brother get along with your father?"

The girl tilted her head as she looked at him. "Fine, I guess."

"Do you know when he's coming home?"

"My mom hasn't called yet."

Doc thanked her for her time and left, walking quickly to his car and ducking in, trying not to feed the mosquitoes. The sun was an orange glow on the horizon, and the humidity was creeping up. It was still, not a breeze. Doc figured Sunday was going to be a steamer. He wondered if the killer was done, but decided he didn't think so. He just didn't know who would be next.

CHAPTER 30

Zean Thomas was north of town about five miles. He'd taken 9 to 61 and then followed that north to the gravel turnoff for the dump. The entrance to the dump was a quarter mile down, beyond a chain-link gate. The gate was connected to a steel pole on one side. There was a loop of chain around the end of the gate and another steel pole on the other side, a combination padlock holding the loop closed. Sunset had passed, the sky losing its light in a hurry. Thomas stopped in front of the gate, his headlights on, and got out of his pickup. He walked to the gate, held the lock up so his headlights were shining on it, and spun the dial.

Nearly every kid in school knew the combination, as did most people in town. Kids worked at the dump during the summer, some getting there early to make sure it was open. The city council had considered getting a lock with a key, but had decided that there was really nothing in the dump worth stealing. Besides, most of them had been at the dump shooting after hours when they were kids. There was nothing really wrong with it, and it kept their kids out of trouble.

Thomas drove past the gatehouse, an old double-wide, where you had to report what you were dumping and pay a fee, and then down a slight incline. The bulk of the dump was in a low area of a hundred acres or so, with a spot to the right and behind the gatehouse where people put their used appliances. The dump was shaped like a tilted bowl, with the higher rim closest to the gatehouse.

Years ago, someone in town had read that pieces of meteorites were extremely valuable, and then thought that the dump might actually be the site of a meteor strike since the surrounding ridge was about the only piece of land for miles that wasn't flat. Word got out and soon every farmer in the county was searching the dump with shovels and picks, looking for meteorites, although most of them had no idea what one would look like. People started coming from miles away, and soon there were so many vehicles and people looking for meteorites that it was impossible for the dump trucks to get in there. Finally, the mayor called a meeting of the city council to discuss the problem. Two council members, Lane Chase and Bubba Decker, who owned the big motel downtown and the Happy Hunter Restaurant, respectively, wanted to turn the dump into a tourist attraction and start a new dump somewhere else.

The mayor, who owned the hardware store at the time, was inclined to go along with the idea but decided to contact the college to see if they could send someone out to the dump to see if it was in fact a meteor crater. The professor said the indentation was not from a meteor but was the work of the glaciers thousands of years ago. Decker and Chase still wanted to make the dump a tourist attraction, and the mayor did too, but the mayor's brother-in-law was a lawyer, who advised the mayor he might be opening himself up for a charge of fraud, especially since he now knew for sure that the dump was not a meteor site. And so the dump stayed the dump. A sign was posted saying that the dump was not the site of a meteor, and that anyone caught trespassing would be fined, but some still went out there for a month or two afterward.

The road circled the dump to the west, with ramps at intervals, where dump trucks and vehicles could back in and drop their loads. Thomas drove as far as the second ramp, and turned so he was facing the center of the dump, stopping just at the beginning of the incline. His headlights shone on the piled refuse below.

Thomas, like a good portion of the town, had been to the Roses' funeral earlier in the day. His family had come too, but his sister had thrown a fit as they were about to go and so they were some of the last to get to the church. The football players from the team had decided to sit together, taking up nearly three pews in the front. When Thomas entered, Ritter had looked back and waved him forward. Thomas looked at his father, who nodded, and Thomas slipped up the aisle, squeezing in next to Ritter. Thomas was dressed in a suit, as were most of his teammates. As he stepped into the pew, he nodded to the head coach in the pew behind, the coach's sport coat looking like it was two sizes too small.

The church was hot, Thomas perspiring before the service had started. The ladies were all using their programs to fan themselves. Thomas wanted to take off his suit coat but no one else had, so he left it on, wiping perspiration from his brow with his palm. The organ started to play, and everyone stood. The minister walked down the aisle first, followed by the three caskets. There were people Thomas didn't know following the caskets, some weeping, and he assumed they were related to Blake and his parents. The caskets were lined up in front, the family members moved into the front pews, and the minister began the service.

Thomas finally did take off his suit coat during a hymn, as did Ritter and several others, thankful when the procession of caskets and the family moved down the aisle and out of the church. The cemetery for First Methodist was directly behind the church, bordering a cornfield that was looking perky after the rain. The procession went directly to the graveyard. A good portion of the congregation followed, but a number got into their cars and left, including many of the players. They had paid their respects, but they did not respect their dead quarterback. Thomas and Ritter and their families stayed, and then went downstairs for lunch after the graveside service.

Thomas picked at his food, eating three cookies and not much else. He felt restless, like he needed to do something, and wished there was football practice in the afternoon. He asked Ritter and a couple of other classmates if they wanted to go out to the dump to shoot in the evening, but all had turned him down. Thomas was sitting next to Ritter at a long table with a fold-up bench, the kind you find in every school cafeteria across the country, when he heard his sister yelling behind him. He turned to see his father standing, waving at him that they were leaving.

The restlessness had remained with Thomas for the rest of the day. His parents were watching *Doc Martin* on PBS when he walked by on his way out, his mother asking him where he was going. He said he didn't know, walked to his pickup, and drove away.

* * *

What was left of the day was fading over the rise behind Thomas as he sat in his truck watching the piles of rubbish. The creatures would soon make their appearance, hunting for treasure. Thomas reached into the rear of the cab and pulled the old Marlin 60 into his lap. The rifle was a .22, not much good for anything but shooting cans and rats and squirrels. Just right for the dump.

Thomas had learned to shoot with the rifle when he was barely ten. His mother's brother had a farm north of Marshall, and they had gone for a visit one summer. His uncle claimed the squirrels were getting into his corn bin, and he wanted Thomas to dispose of them. He showed him how to shoot, despite the protests of his sister. Thomas had parked himself behind the chicken coop next to the grain bin, waiting for the squirrels. Two gray squirrels appeared, squeezing under the wire mesh. Thomas raised the rifle and pulled the trigger. His shot pinged off the mesh and the squirrels ran, climbing a nearby oak and chirping at the boy below. That was their mistake. Without the cover of the mesh, Thomas had a clear shot.

Thomas stroked the smooth, stained stock, looking through his windshield, thinking about Blake Rose. He wasn't that sad that Blake was dead. The guy was a friend when it was convenient, and he let you know that the only reason the team was any good was because of him. Unfortunately, Thomas thought the part about the team was true. They had a real chance at a national championship with Blake, but without him, they would have trouble in their conference. Football was a big part of Thomas's life. It made him feel special, important, when he walked around town or on campus, especially when the team was winning. But now . . .

Thomas loaded the rifle and stepped out of the truck. The sky was clear and stars were now visible to the east. He was looking up, feeling sorry for himself, when he heard a sound. He moved around to the front of the truck, just to the side of the left headlight, to get a better look. There was the sound again, ahead of him and to the right, and he caught movement. A dark shadow. Thomas raised his rifle.

* * *

The killer was watching Thomas from a berm on the ridge behind where Thomas had parked, and about ten yards to the east. The city let an acre-wide strip of land around the dump grow wild as a buffer. On the northern edge a rutted road ran between the buffer and the field next to it. The killer had taken that road. He had pulled off into the brush and walked to his position overlooking the dump nearly an hour earlier.

Lying on his chest like a military sniper, the killer looked through binoculars at Thomas, and then set them to the side. Thomas was only thirty yards away, and the binoculars were too much—they made Thomas appear too close. The guy was not the jerk that Blake Rose was, but he hadn't done anything to stop what Blake did. He was responsible, and he needed to be punished.

Thomas got out of his truck, and the killer reached for his Weatherby. The killer had taken a nice buck with the rifle last fall, and he had no doubt it would handle this assignment. He balanced the end of the stock below the barrel on a bare tuft of sandy soil and peered through his scope. Thomas was looking up into the sky, like he was pondering his place in the universe. The killer moved his eye away from the scope and watched Thomas, wondering what he was thinking. Thomas had a rifle in his hand, but the killer did not feel threatened. The .22 wasn't much more than a BB gun, a toy.

There was a noise, and the killer heard it at the same time Thomas did. Thomas moved toward the front of his truck. The killer trained his rifle on Thomas as he moved, the boy now perfectly silhouetted against the headlights. He was bringing the barrel up for a head shot when he heard the sound again, louder this time, swiveling his rifle in that direction. It was a raccoon on its haunches, a big one, holding something to its mouth. It would be an easy shot, but he wasn't here for raccoons. The killer pulled his eye away from the scope and rotated back to Thomas to see him raising his rifle. Lowering his eye to the scope, the killer brought Thomas's head into view and squeezed the trigger.

For a minute, the killer watched from his position for any sign of movement, but there was none. He slid and jogged down the rise, rifle in hand, finding Thomas on his stomach, blood pooling below his skull. He stood for a moment, staring, remembering. And then a thought popped into his head. He felt in Thomas's pockets, found nothing, and then moved to the driver's door and opened it. Thomas's phone lay on the console.

CHAPTER 31

Bill Palmer was next. But he would not be so easy. Besides the fact that the man was a cop and armed all the time, finding a good location was an issue. The killer didn't think he could park on the street like he had done before—there were too many people and too many lights at night. Parking somewhere close and walking was a possibility, but going into the house was not an option. Palmer would have guns, and he'd probably keep them close. And there would be no way to get to him at work.

The killer thought about this for most of Sunday, and finally decided the only way to get a shot at Palmer and have a chance of getting away unseen was to get him away from town. The killer considered kidnapping one of Palmer's kids or his wife and then calling Palmer, telling him he would have to meet him by himself if he wanted his kid back alive. It was why he had taken Thomas's phone, so his number could not be identified. That might work, but it would mean he'd have to kidnap someone without being seen, and then likely kill the kid after he killed the chief. He wasn't sure he wanted to kill a kid.

But now, holding Thomas's phone, he'd thought of something that might work. Tell Palmer he knew something about the killer, and he'd meet him to talk to him about it. Tell him he had to come alone and outside of town because he was afraid and didn't trust anyone. As long as no one had found Thomas's body, there was a chance it would work. A good chance. And he knew the place. The picnic area out by the airport. Plenty of trees to hide behind, and he could park on the north side opposite the main entrance and come through the woods. It would be a risk, but if it didn't go like he thought, he could just ditch the phone.

It would have to be tonight. The dump would open Monday morning, and someone was sure to find Thomas's body then. The killer pulled out Thomas's phone and dialed the police station.

* * *

"Chief!" yelled the officer at the front desk. "Call for you."

Palmer looked at the clock. He was off in ten minutes. With a deep sigh, Palmer picked up the phone. "Hello. Chief Palmer."

"Chief, this is Zean Thomas," said the killer.

"Zean. Where the hell are you? Your mother has been worried sick about you."

"I need to talk to you, Chief. Talk to you alone. About the killer."

The boy sounded scared, nervous. Not the voice Palmer remembered. "Now, Zean. Why don't you just tell me now, and then you can go home."

"No. Someone might be listening. I don't trust anybody but you. Come out to Miller's Park by the airport. But you need to come alone. I'll be by the picnic tables."

"Zean, listen—" But the boy was gone. "Shit." He hit the redial button but there was no answer. Palmer grabbed his keys and walked up to the policewoman at the front desk. "Tammy. Call Mrs. Thomas and tell her Zean is OK. I just talked to him. I'm going to go meet him, and then I'll send him home, and I'll head home after."

"You want me to go with?"

"Naw. I'll see you on Tuesday."

Palmer went out to his cruiser. It was ten o'clock, and he just wanted to be home. He'd made a big deal about how he would work Sundays when he became chief, to show the mayor and the council that he was willing to do whatever he had his officers do, but it was wearing on him. He was missing too many of his kids' activities, and his wife was angry that he was never at church. He kind of liked having Mondays off, nobody home but him, but it might be time to make a schedule change.

Palmer took 28 west out of town. A mile past the airport he took a right into Miller's Park. The park had been the site of numerous keggers over the years, several of which Palmer had busted, only to let the kids go once he figured he'd scared the shit out of them. Most of his officers had participated in keg parties here, and he guessed his kids probably would, too. He just hoped they'd wait until they were in college, and that they didn't drive.

Palmer moved slowly down the gravel driveway that led to the picnic area; he didn't want to hit a deer. He was a little surprised by how dark it was in the park. The oaks and poplars created a dense canopy that blocked out nearly all the light from the stars and the half moon. He went slower, watching the woods on either side. He thought he saw something peek out at him from behind a tree on the right and was focused on the spot, barely turning his head in time to see a deer standing in the road in front of him. Palmer slammed on his brakes, skidding a short distance in the gravel, the deer taking off. "Shit!"

The drive angled to the left, and Palmer picked up a light ahead. The parking area for the picnic tables had a single yard light. Bugs were swarming the light, an occasional bat zipping through for a quick meal. Palmer pulled in next to the cement slab with the picnic tables and turned off his motor, leaving his lights on. The picnic tables were under a roof, the tables chained and padlocked to U-hooks in the cement. Light from the parking area did not reach far under the roof. Palmer leaned forward, peering at the tables under the pavilion, but could see no one. He got out and then reached back into the car to get his holster, strapping on his gun.

* * *

The killer was ecstatic. His plan had worked. So far, anyway. It was like God was paving the way for him. Like he was a holy avenger. He watched the chief get out of his car, hitch up his pants, and walk to the front of his cruiser, standing in the headlights. Heard him call for Thomas. Only Thomas wasn't coming. Ever. Thomas had gotten what was coming to him, and now it was time for Palmer. Only, he wanted Palmer to know why he was going to die.

The killer had been behind a tree on the far side of the pavilion. He wanted to be sure Palmer had come alone. He watched him for a moment more after the chief had called for Thomas, and then, seeing no one else exit the cruiser, walked between the tables, out of the darkness. He bumped a table as he came, and Palmer turned his way, raising a hand to his brow to shield his eyes from the overhead light.

"Zean?" said Palmer.

The killer walked past the last table with his rifle pointed at Palmer's chest. "No."

"What is this?"

The killer moved closer, backing Palmer up against his front grill. "This is justice. This is because Jenny Wyman is dead, and you killed her."

"I didn't—"

"That's right. You didn't do a damn thing about Blake, and Jenny Wyman and Linda Knudson and those other girls all paid the price. Just so this piece-of-shit town could have a championship football team."

Palmer raised his left hand. "Listen to me. We can figure this out." As he talked, he reached for the gun on his right hip, moving his hand slowly, keeping his eyes locked on the killer. "Why don't you just put the gun down, and we can talk?" Palmer wrapped his hand around his gun and eased it from the holster.

The killer hadn't seen Palmer go for his gun, but the light behind Palmer shifted as the chief lifted his arm, spooking the killer. He fired, the shot catching Palmer in the chest, knocking him back onto the hood of his car. As the chief went down, his hand came up, and he fired.

The killer felt a blow that spun him sideways, and then searing pain in his left shoulder, and he cried out. The blood was already staining his shirt when he turned back to Palmer and fired again. The killer's second shot went through the bottom of Palmer's jaw as he lay on the hood, shattering the skull and the windshield behind. Palmer's body slid slowly off the hood.

He could see Palmer's lower legs stretched out on the ground, but the chief's upper body was shielded by the glow of the headlight. The killer poked Palmer's leg with the barrel of his rifle before moving through the light, now getting a look at the man's head. Immediately the killer's stomach lurched, and he turned away, bending at the waist and vomiting on the ground. The killer wiped his mouth with the back of his hand, leaning forward, trying to catch his breath.

* * *

Palmer's wife called the station at midnight. "Tammy, is Bill still there?"

"No, he left almost two hours ago."

"Is he out on a call or something?"

"He said he was going to talk to Zean Thomas," said the policewoman.

"Zean Thomas? What about?" said Mrs. Palmer.

"I don't know, but Zean's mother called the station a couple of times looking for him. Said he didn't come home Saturday night."

"Hmm. Wasn't Zean a friend of Blake Rose?"

"Yes, you're right," said Tammy.

"The boy is probably just upset," said Palmer's wife. "And the funeral was just yesterday, too. Bill is probably just talking him into going home."

"I'm sure you're right, Mrs. Palmer."

"Please call me Jane, Tammy. Well, I guess I'll just wait

to hear from him."

"Should I call you if he calls in?" said Tammy.

"No. I think I'm going to bed. Good night."

CHAPTER 32

The killer stumbled through the maze of picnic tables, rifle in his left hand, his right hand clutching his throbbing shoulder. He winced each time he bumped a table, finally stumbling off the concrete pad and nearly falling. Stopping for a moment, he stared into the black woods ahead.

There was a footpath through the woods to where the killer had parked, used by hikers and deer and others who wanted to use the picnic area at night but not have their vehicle blocked in by police. It was fairly easy to follow during the day, difficult at night even with a good light. The killer retrieved his phone from his pocket, trying to get the phone to unlock with his finger, but it wouldn't recognize his print, his finger too smeared with blood. He tucked the phone under his chin while he wiped his hand on his pants, and then tried again. The screen would not open. "Damn." Using his thumb, he pushed the power button, icons becoming visible in the upper right corner. He pulled down the settings screen and found the light icon. Tilting the light down to his feet, he lifted it slowly, trying to determine which direction he should go. This would not be easy. The pain in his shoulder was increasing, coming in waves, making it hard to focus. And he needed to hurry—the police would soon be on their way.

The trail was dirt and moss and decaying leaves and pine needles, easy to see for a few steps, and then becoming indistinguishable from the surrounding area for several yards. The killer moved slowly, panning the light up and down, side to side, looking for signs of the direction he should move, trying to ignore the pain. This was too slow. He knew the general direction; he just needed to get out of the woods. Shining the light as far ahead as it would penetrate, the killer picked up his pace. He wandered off the trail, hitting a thick blockade of thornbushes, backtracking, moving slowly again. There was a shiny spot on the ground, and then another, and then a third, this one on a yellowed birch leaf. Blood. He shone his light on his left arm, seeing the trail of blood from his shoulder running down his arm and off the back of his hand. "Damn." He moved forward again.

After twenty yards, the killer tripped on a root. He fell on his left shoulder, screaming in anguish, losing hold of his rifle and phone. Rolling on his back, holding his shoulder again, the killer swore. He rolled to his right side and pushed himself to a sitting position, rocking forward and back, the pain excruciating. His eyes were shut tight, teeth clenched, his breathing rapid. Finally, gaining control, he opened his eyes, seeing only the faint outline of a black shape. A tree, perhaps. There was no light.

The killer sat, legs outstretched, holding his left shoulder again and hugging himself tight. A mosquito found the back of the killer's neck, and he released his hold on his shoulder to slap it. He swore again. The killer drew his feet under him to his left, leaned to his right, and pushed himself to his knees before standing. Bent at the waist, he surveyed the ground in front of him looking for his phone, turning slowly to his right. Panic increased as he continued to turn, seeing nothing. The realization that he would now have to wait for morning becoming clear, not knowing if he would live that long, sure the police would come before then. There was a noise to his right, a strange high sound, and then another. He jerked his head in that direction, straining to see and hear. Coyotes. Hunting a wounded animal. The killer held his breath, his heart trying to jump from his chest. Then, he felt a lump in his pocket. Zean's phone.

The killer found his rifle and made it out of the woods, emerging thirty yards south of his truck, the vehicle outlined in the moonlight. After opening the door, he pulled himself in by the grab handle. The rifle was in his left hand, across his lap, and he used his right hand to set the stock on the floor of the passenger seat, resting the barrel against the seat. He leaned back. His shoulder burned like it was on fire. He needed to clean out the wound and look at it, but he couldn't go home. The killer had packed a bag before he came to meet Palmer, assuming he would have to run after shooting a cop, but he had not included any first-aid supplies. He needed to go somewhere close; his arm was sticky with blood.

The killer didn't think he would make it out of the field where he had parked, the pain shooting through him with each bump, but eventually he got back to the asphalt of 65. He crossed 28 and headed south on 63. He started to push the Ford faster on the tar, but slowed again after a pothole nearly caused him to lose control. He found County 7 about six miles southwest of town and turned east. He turned off the tar after a couple of miles, moving south and east on the gravel, until he spotted the yard light he was looking for. He turned into the driveway of the Rose farm.

The killer turned off his lights as he turned into the driveway. Ten yards in, he saw a large black shape in the driveway, shiny, illuminated by the yard light, and he stopped. A truck. Someone was here. About to back out, he realized the shape was the Roses' Silverado, still parked where he had shot them. Thinking he shouldn't leave his truck in the open, in case he stayed a bit, the killer looked to his left and could make out that the door to the Quonset hut was open. He pulled in behind a red Farmall 560 and parked. Picking up his bag off the passenger seat, the killer pulled on his door handle and pushed the door open with his leg. He climbed out, closed the truck door with his hip, and pushed the door of the shed closed. The killer went to the house.

The front door was locked, but the killer had been here before and knew there was a key under the old milk can on the steps. He put his bag on the step and moved the can to the side, crouching, feeling for the key. His fingertips felt the dirt that had been around the base of the can and under it, but there was no key. The killer groaned as he stood, fetching his phone from his pocket again, turning on the light and finding the key.

The killer held the screen door open with his thigh and fumbled with the lock as he held the light on it with his right hand, his shaky left hand working the key. His left arm ached with each movement, but he finally got the key in and turned the handle. He picked up his bag and stepped inside, flicking on the light, not thinking about what he had done there a week earlier until he saw the dark splotches on the floor and the side of the stove. The killer paused, staring, thinking about shooting Blake Rose and driving the knife into his groin. Then the pain rose back to his consciousness, and he winced.

The main bathroom in the farmhouse was through the kitchen. The killer set his bag and phone on the kitchen table and walked through the doorway opposite. Stairs to his right led to the basement, the bathroom to his left. He stepped into the bathroom and found the light. A bloody ghost he didn't recognize stared back at him from the mirror over the sink.

He pulled open the mirror, finding a half-empty tube of antiseptic cream. The killer leaned forward. His face was streaked with reddish-brown mud, dirt from bloody hands that he had rubbed across his sweaty face. His skin was pale, almost yellow, his eyes bloodshot. "Jesus." The burning pain of his shoulder seemed to be reaching down his arm, and he looked that way. "Jesus." His T-shirt was sopping with blood. The wound itself was nearly black, small pieces of leaves and other debris stuck to it.

The killer reached behind his head with his right hand, grabbed the collar of his shirt and said, "This is going to hurt." He screamed as he pulled on the shirt, lifting his left arm and then ripping the shirt off, the dried blood tearing away. He sat on the toilet, head down, tears running down his cheeks, energy nearly gone. Reaching behind the shower curtain, he found the knob for the water and turned it on, holding his hand under the stream, waiting for it to warm.

The water ran over his head, and he rubbed his face with his right hand, before turning to let the stream hit the wound. His legs buckled at the pain, and he grabbed the showerhead to hold himself upright. Slowly, he moved side to side, the stream rinsing away the debris and much of the dried blood. But it wasn't enough. He knew from health class that a wound needed to be clean to avoid infection. There was a washcloth draped over the side of the tub, and he picked it up, soaked it under the showerhead, and began to gingerly dab the wound. He needed to do more. Folding the cloth, he dragged it across the wound. Daggers of pain shot up his neck and his eyelids squeezed together, the howl of a wounded animal escaping his lips. The killer bent over, right hand on his thigh, the water hitting his back as he struggled to catch his breath. After a minute, he stood erect, moved the wound under the stream, and dragged the cloth over it again.

The wound was ugly, the skin jagged, the bullet having dug a trough as it moved across his shoulder. It was bleeding freely again as the killer stepped out of the shower. He pressed a towel to it to stop the flow, holding it in place for almost a minute before lifting it away. The blood began to fill the low areas in the wound as he watched. He squeezed the antibiotic cream into the wound, where it mingled with his blood. The killer pushed the towel back on the wound. Then he wrapped the towel in first-aid tape from the cabinet.

Taking a bottle of ibuprofen from the cabinet, the killer walked naked into the kitchen and went to the cupboard by the sink. He filled a glass with water, poured the pills on the counter, put five in his mouth, and washed them down. Pulling boxers and shorts from his bag and stepping into them took all of his remaining strength, and he dropped into a chair by the kitchen table. Trying to keep his eyes open, he realized now that he needed to turn off the light in case someone drove by. The killer stood shakily, went to the light switch, and flicked it off. With his right hand, he felt for the doorframe to the sitting room. His hand touched a desk and then found the arm of the couch next to it. The killer sat on the couch, lowered himself slowly so that he was lying on his back, and shut his eyes.

CHAPTER 33

Jane Palmer woke at two and reached her arm across the bed. Her husband was still not home. It wasn't usual, but it wasn't something he hadn't done before. She just wished he would call when he was going to be late. She didn't sleep well when she didn't know. Jane lay there for a moment, thought about calling the station again, then closed her eyes, rolled over, and went back to sleep.

At five thirty, light was creeping around the edges of the shades. Jane rolled over to see her husband's side of the bed still empty. During the school year she had to be up in half an hour to get ready for school, but in the summer she could sleep in. She closed her eyes and tried to go back to sleep, but eventually sat up. Picked up her phone and called her husband's number, but went to voicemail. Odd.

"Morris Police Station."

"Tammy? This is Jane Palmer. Are you still working?"

"Double shift, Mrs. Palmer."

"Huh. Well, I was wondering if you had heard from my husband."

"Um, no ma'am. He didn't come home last night?"

"No," said Palmer. "And he doesn't answer his phone."

"OK. Well, we have GPS on all the squads. Why don't I see if I can track him down and then give you a call back?" Tammy did not want to know where the chief's car was. If the man was meeting some woman somewhere, that was his business, and she did not want to get in the middle of it. Still, she was curious. She clicked on the icon for the tracking app on her desktop and watched as the map opened. Each squad was identified with a number on the map, the chief's car number one. Number one seemed to be in Miller's Park. Could be a rendezvous. There had been more than a few couples parked there that had been chased away. Tammy blew out a breath and picked up the microphone on her desk.

"Jack. This is Tammy. Where are you?" She knew he was sitting in front of the bakery but she wanted to hear what he said.

"Um, just cruising north on Nine through town," came the reply. "What's up?"

"I need you to drive out to Miller's Park."

"Why?"

"The chief is having trouble with his car."

Tammy sat back, smirking. She'd hear about it from him, but for now it seemed pretty funny. Especially if the windows on the chief's car were all steamed up.

Fifteen minutes later a scream made her jerk in her seat. "Tammy!"

"What?"

"Oh God, Tammy. Oh God. He's dead. The chief is dead."

The woman sat stunned. Her phone rang. "Morris Police."

"Tammy, it's me. Jane Palmer. Did you find him?"

* * *

By six thirty, Sheriff Pickus, two deputies, an ambulance, the medical examiner, and just about every cop in town was at the park. Pickus took charge, getting all the cop cars out of the parking lot and out on 28 before taping off the entrance to the park. He knew about the back way in and sent Kuck and another Morris squad to secure that area just in case. The medical examiner arrived shortly after the lot had cleared, Pickus letting the vehicle onto the lot.

Pickus couldn't take his eyes off of Palmer. The sight was revolting but held him like a magnet. He'd seen him just the day before. What the hell had happened? Pickus walked around the pavilion, noting the bloodstains here and there and starting to wonder if Palmer had shot his assailant. He finally walked back to his car and picked his phone.

* * *

Buzzing. Doc looked at the clock. Not even seven. "Yeah?"

"Hunter. This is Pickus. Are you still in Morris?"

"The scenery makes it hard to leave."

"Get out to Miller's Park. Now. Palmer's dead. Somebody shot him."

Ten minutes later, Doc was showered, dressed, and in

his car with a cup of coffee from the lobby. He put on the lights and watched his GPS as he drove to Miller's Park.

The sheriff's deputy at the entrance to the park pulled the tape for him, and he drove to the lot. Pickus was leaning against his car, the medical examiner kneeling in front of Palmer's squad. His assistant was standing next to him. Doc popped out, leaving his sunglasses on his head, and Pickus waddled over.

"Someone ambushed him. Blew a hole in his chest and nearly blew his head off. We think it was Zean Thomas."

"Zean Thomas? How do you know?"

"He called the station last night. Said he needed to talk to Palmer."

"And we know this because . . . ?"

"Palmer told his dispatcher as he was leaving. Said he was meeting Thomas, and that she should call Thomas's mother and tell her they had found him."

"The kid was missing?"

"Yeah. Guess his mother called the station a couple of times yesterday. Said he went out and didn't come home on Saturday night."

Doc looked at the back of the medical examiner. "So, it could have been anybody that called?"

"Palmer said it was Thomas," said Pickus. "I got men on the way over there now."

Doc's eyes got big. "What do you mean? You've got people on the way to Thomas's house to kill the kid?"

Pickus looked at Doc and then away. "I got to go. I need to get over there."

Doc opened his mouth, ready to yell at the sheriff, to tell him he could not take down the kid. He was thinking he needed to get over there as soon as he could when Pickus stopped and answered his phone.

Pickus spoke for a moment, disconnected, and then turned to Doc. "That was my dispatcher. Milly Larsen called. She runs the dump. A garbage hauler was going to drop a load this morning, but there was a pickup blocking his way. They found a body beside the truck. They think it's Zean Thomas."

* * *

Doc called Carl Miranda as he followed Pickus to the dump. They drove around three dump trucks and a pickup full of junk at the entry and down the gravel road. The dump truck was still there. The driver, a large man of about forty with dirty jeans and an orange fluorescent vest over a green T-shirt was leaning on his door as they walked up.

"I'm Sheriff Pickus, and this is BCA agent Hunter. Your name is?"

"Darrin Stuhl."

"OK, Mr. Stuhl. Please tell us what you know."

"Um, so I drove down here to dump my load. There was a truck on the ramp. I got out, looked at the pickup, and couldn't see anyone. I yelled but nobody answered so I went back to get Milly. She walked back with me, and we found the guy in front of the truck."

Doc looked past Stuhl to the pickup. "OK, Mr. Stuhl. I'm sure you've got places to be but if you could just hang here for a bit we'd appreciate it."

Doc moved past them. Pickus didn't like the fact that the agent had taken over. He gave Stuhl a quick grin and went after Doc.

Doc walked down the ramp, looking in the pickup as he

went, and then moving to the front of the vehicle. Thomas was on the ground, his face nearly gone. His arms had been chewed and pulled, making him look like he was stretching.

Pickus came up to Doc's shoulder. "Oh, Jesus."

"Yeah. Is that Thomas?"

Pickus looked again. "I think so."

"You better call off your men at the Thomas house now," Doc said. "Hopefully they haven't killed anybody."

Pickus scowled at Doc, then turned and walked back up the ramp. Doc could hear him on the phone. He walked back and stood next to Doc.

"Coyotes. Lots of them around. Damn things are even in town now. The truck is Zean's, or his parents' anyway." Pickus was still looking at the body. "What do you think happened? You think he shot Palmer and then came over here and shot himself?"

"No."

"How can you be so sure?"

"I'm just guessing at this point, but it's nearly impossible, and pretty stupid, even for a kid, to try to kill themselves with a twenty-two." Doc nodded at the rifle a foot down the ramp from where Thomas lay. "No way a twenty-two would do that. And I'm no ME, but I'm guessing that if this body has been here long enough to get chewed up like this, then it's been here longer than the chief's."

"Hmm. So, where the hell does that leave us?"

Doc wasn't sure. These weren't the up-close-and-personal killings of last week. What had changed? "Get the dump truck out of here after you get pictures, then close the dump."

"Close the dump? What are they going to do with all of that garbage?"

"I don't know. Call the mayor to find an alternative site or tell them just to hang on for a day."

"Oh, shit." Pickus kicked at the ground. "Well, this still doesn't get Salo off the hook."

Doc looked over at Pickus and then walked up closer to the body. Stooped and peered at the head. Stood and walked back to Pickus but looked over him at the ridge around the dump. "I'm going for a walk and then I'm going back over to look at the Palmer scene. If I were you I'd keep my head down, Pickus. He's using a rifle now."

Pickus's ducked his head and scanned the ridge behind him. "I got to tell Milly to close the dump." He took off for his vehicle in a hurry, leaving Doc standing.

Doc found what he was looking for twenty minutes later. Footprints and matted grass. He looked down at the dump where Thomas's body lay and lifted his hands like he was holding a rifle, pointing. Looked down at the ground again and decided the killer had probably been lying down when he shot, using the ridge as a rest. Smart. He took out his phone.

"You on your way?"

"Yeah. I can't wait to get there," said Miranda.

"It is scenic here, I have to admit," said Doc. "Listen, I got another one."

"You are kidding me this time, right?"

"Naw, I'm past the kidding stage. This one is out at the town dump, north of Morris. I think this guy was killed before the chief, so why don't you come and do this one first and then go do the chief."

"Unbelievable. You ever going to catch this guy or should I rent a townhouse out there?"

"I wish I knew what to tell you. I'm at the dump right

now. I think the killer used a rifle from the ridge northeast of the body. You should be able to find the spot pretty easy. I'm going back out to the park where the chief was killed, so call me when you get to the dump."

"You need to catch him, Doc."

CHAPTER 34

Doc called Trask as he drove, giving him an update. Trask cursed when he heard about Palmer, knowing what kind of reaction that would bring from law enforcement, the media, and his boss. He asked about LeBlanc and Doc told him he hadn't seen him today but that he looked better yesterday. Trask said he would call the hospital and was sending another agent to help. He didn't know who yet, but he would call Doc back when he did.

Doc made it back to the park just as the ME was finishing up. He was standing by his van as Doc approached.

"I suppose you'd like me to leave the body where it is until your technicians are done."

"I'd appreciate that, yeah," said Doc. "Anything you'd like to share?"

"Chief Palmer was shot twice, both times from close range with a large-caliber weapon. I'm guessing he was shot in the chest first and then in the head." The man pushed his glasses back up his nose, and Doc said, "Why's that?"

"The shot that hit him in the head entered through the bottom of the jaw and exited through the top of his skull. It would be hard to make that shot without the man's head leaning back, most likely from the force of the shot to the chest."

"How long ago?"

"Between ten and midnight, I'd guess."

"OK, thanks," said Doc. "The BCA technicians should be out at the dump soon. You headed that way?"

"Afraid so," said the doctor, but he made no move to get in his van. "One more thing. Whoever shot Palmer didn't have much of a stomach for it."

"How's that?"

"He threw up next to the body. You'll need to watch where you step." He looked past Doc to where Palmer's body remained. "This is way out of hand now, Agent."

Doc knew it. He was letting people down. He watched the van disappear down the road and then looked up as a crow squawked overhead. The sky was clear, another nice day coming, though a number of people in Morris wouldn't be able to enjoy it. There would be no nice days for many here for a long time.

The sun was low enough that much of the lot and pavilion area was still in the shade, so Doc moved his sunglasses to the top of his head. He walked over to Palmer's body. Much of the man's head was missing. After closing his eyes and taking a deep breath, he opened his eyes again, catching the smell. Looking immediately to his left, he saw where the killer had likely gotten sick. Someone not used to seeing a death like this. But who would ever get used to something like this?

Doc moved to Palmer's vehicle. Gloves on, he looked inside to see the car's light switch was in the on position. Thought about that for a minute before he stepped back over to the body, looking at the belt. Now he noticed the empty holster. His eyes worked the ground around the body, and then he went on his knees to look under the car. He walked around the back of the car and then toward the front. The gun was there by the tire. Doc wondered if the weapon had been fired, but he guessed it would have been too long ago to smell anything if it had. Still, the chief had apparently had his weapon out. Possibly because the killer had told him to toss it away. But that didn't seem right. He would have tossed the gun toward the killer or to the side in front of the car. Not here.

He walked back to look at the body and then at the car, noting the blood on the hood and the windshield. Doc closed his eyes, trying to imagine the scene, the shooting, as if he were Palmer. Moving slowly, he stepped past the vomit to where he thought the killer had stood when he fired. Palmer had pulled his car up to the landscape timber edging that separated the gravel parking lot from the mowed area around the pavilion. The ground cover was a mixture of grass and clover, recently mowed, and fairly thick. Doc moved slowly, hands on his thighs, eyes to the ground, but saw nothing.

That changed when he reached the cement slab. The slab was a dirty gray but the dark drops were easy to spot. He glanced at the first table. Another dark blotch. The killer was bleeding. Doc looked back at Palmer. The chief had shot him.

Doc called Pickus. "Where are you?"

"Just leaving the Thomas place."

"Are they OK?"

"No," Pickus said. "Their kid is dead."

"You know what I mean," said Doc.

"They aren't hurt."

"Probably scared shitless."

Pickus was silent.

"OK," Doc said. "Listen. You have dogs?"

"Yeah, two canine units."

"Get them out to the park. I think the killer is hit."

* * *

Pickus roared into the lot with two other squads from the city. They all had on vests and tactical gear, carrying every weapon they had been able to buy with the funding received after 9/11. They were out for blood. As they pulled more weapons from the trunks of their vehicles, Doc hurried up to Pickus.

"Jesus, Pickus. What are you doing?"

"I've got men coming in from the perimeter of the park. If he's in there, we're going to get him."

"You're going to end up shooting each other, that's what you're going to do," said Doc. "We need to tread carefully and preserve the scene. Where are the dogs?"

Just then the van with the canine units drove in, skidding to a stop. The handlers were out in seconds, dressed like the other cops, getting the animals from the back of the van.

Pickus looked at Doc. "Where's the blood?"

"Jeez, Pickus. You're really going to do this, aren't you?" Doc shook his head and started to walk toward his car.

"Where do you think you're going, Hunter?" shouted Pickus.

Doc flipped down his glasses, looked over his roof, and said, "I need some breakfast."

CHAPTER 35

Doc was back at The Windmill. He had the farmer's breakfast, which seemed to have all the same things as the country breakfast, with the addition of a bagel. Doc didn't know a lot of farmers, but the ones he did know didn't eat bagels, so he thought that was a little strange. Miranda called him while he ate, to tell Doc he had arrived, and would call again before he moved on to the park. Doc warned him about the army going through the woods there and said he might want to put on his siren and lights on the way in.

Doc finished breakfast, looking at his list, wondering about the killer while he worked on his third cup of coffee. He thought about pie for a minute, but then thought he wasn't really getting any exercise, and then he thought about Hailey Draper. He was thinking he should maybe call her later when something that had been below the surface popped up, triggered by thinking about a phone call. It also reminded him he had not checked in on LeBlanc, so he called the clinic.

"How you doing?"

"Very sore, but they tell me it means I'm healing. How much longer do you want me to stay in here?"

"You don't need to worry about that anymore."

"Why's that?"

"The killer took out Zean Thomas and Chief Palmer."

LeBlanc was silent for a moment and then said, "Wow. The guy has gone off the reservation."

"It looks to officially be a rampage now. He ambushed Palmer at a park west of town. I think Palmer got a shot off and hit the shooter before he died. Pickus and his posse are combing the woods as we speak."

"Anything I can do?"

"Nah. Trask is sending reinforcements. You just get better," said Doc. And then he added, "Wait a second, can you transfer me to admitting?"

"I'll get a nurse. Hang on."

Doc was finally connected with a guy in admitting, identified himself, and asked if anyone had stopped in to be treated for a wound this morning. It was a long shot, and the guy said no one had been admitted with anything like that. Doc thanked the man, paid his bill, and walked to his car. He hoped his next long shot would pay off.

The Morris police station was nearly empty except for the officer at the front desk. "Can I help you?"

Doc said, "I hope so," and showed her his ID.

"OK, the chief mentioned you," said Tammy. "What can I do for you?"

"Um, do you know who answered the phone when the chief got the call before he left last night? Was it on his cell?"

"No, Agent. It came through the desk here. I was on duty."

Doc leaned on the counter. "Can you tell me what number the caller used?"

She scratched her right eyebrow lightly. "Yeah, it'll be in the log. Hang on." She hit some keys on her computer and put her finger to the screen. "Here it is." She recited the number.

"OK. Now can you look that number up and tell me who owns it?"

She typed some more, watched her screen for a second, and said, "Looks like it's a phone for Rod Thomas."

"For his phone plan?"

"Yeah. I can't actually see what phone is used by what member of the family. There are three numbers listed."

Doc thought for second and said, "OK. Can you please write down the number for me?"

Tammy jotted the number on a sticky note and handed it to Doc. "God, this has been an awful day." A tear sparkled in her eye.

"Yes. I'm very sorry about Chief Palmer."

"Thanks. He was a really good man." She looked past Doc and then up at him. "Say, um, Agent Hunter, I normally wouldn't say anything, but, after yesterday, I think I need to say something to someone."

"What's that?"

"Well, Mrs. Thomas called in a few times saying her son was missing. And we don't do anything unless it's forty-eight hours, but, now that he turned up dead, I thought I should mention something to someone about Luke Ritter."

Doc stood. "What about Luke Ritter?"

"His mother, Barbara, called this morning to say he was

missing. That he didn't come home last night," said Tammy. "I mean, with what's been going on, I just thought I should say something. I did put out an ATL on his truck."

Doc thought about what she said, told her it was good she had mentioned it, and he would look into it. Tammy said, "Thanks," looking relieved, and gave Doc a weak smile. Doc hustled back to his car and raced to the hotel. He found the yearbooks on the desk where he had left them and flipped through. Luke Ritter had written in Linda Knudson's book by his picture, saying he was going to miss her and hoped they would be able to get together in the summer. There was nothing by his picture in Jenny Wyman's book, but he remembered a note by a group picture near the front of the book.

He found the picture. It was a group of students who had participated in a field trip to Minneapolis. Only some of the students were identified, including Wyman. But behind Wyman there was a boy, Luke Ritter. There was a heart drawn including Wyman and Ritter, with an arrow through it. Doc stared at the picture for a moment, thinking about how Ritter had been at the Salos. It could be. Doc pulled out the note Tammy had given him and dialed the number.

A sleepy voice answered. "Hello?"
"Luke?"

CHAPTER 36

Luke Ritter had been up several times during the night. He had tried to sleep on his right side or back but every time he moved, even a little, he woke in pain. After taking more ibuprofen he'd try to sleep again but deep sleep was thwarted by images of headless men coming for him. Sometime close to morning, he woke to find himself shivering, the quilt he had pulled off the back of the couch unable to keep him warm. Ritter stumbled into Blake's parents' bedroom and climbed under the covers and curled into a ball. Less than an hour later he woke, soaked in perspiration. Ritter took off the covers and sat on the edge of the bed. Light streamed into the room and hurt his eyes so he shut them tight, his chin resting on his chest.

Ritter felt more tired than he could ever remember, and his head was pounding. It was an effort just to open his eyes a crack. He stumbled into the kitchen, plucked more pills off the counter, and washed them down. Through the window over the sink he looked out at the garden where he and Blake had eaten strawberries and had a raspberry fight. A long time ago. Ritter went back to the bed, and was about to lie down again when he noticed the sheets stained with blood. He glanced over at his left arm to see that the towel was dark. Blood had run down his arm, and he poked at it, surprised to find his arm was nearly numb. He guessed this was maybe a bad thing, that he should clean out his wound again, but the bed looked too inviting, and he lay down once more.

This time he woke on his back. There was music. A song he recognized and a buzzing on his right hip. His hand felt the shape in his pocket and reached inside to remove the phone.

***

Burt Ingvie lived alone. He'd been in a few relationships, but they ended up being too much work, and he had enough to do with the farm to run. To entertain himself, he had purchased a big-screen television and a police band radio. He'd sometimes just have the radio on in the background when he was in the house. What was broadcast had never been exciting, until the Rose killings. The chatter had picked up considerably since then, especially with the other killings. And it had sounded to him this morning like the chief of police had maybe been killed out by Miller's Park. Ingvie listened as long as he could, finally deciding he needed to get to work after hearing an "attempt to locate" announcement for a truck.

Ingvie had the farm to the south of the Roses'. Ingvie's farm was small, only 360 acres. He had a herd of dairy cows, so a good piece of his land was devoted to pasture. The remainder was planted with feed corn, alfalfa, and wheat, but it wasn't enough for him to make a living. As a result, he rented 160 acres from John Rose.

Rose was an asshole as far as Ingvie was concerned. He charged too much for the property and bitched at Ingvie if he was a day late with his rent. But Rose did let him store his tractor in the Quonset hut and park his attachments behind the building, and Ingvie liked that because he didn't have to run a tractor over a mile down the road.

Ingvie pulled his pickup into the Roses' driveway Monday morning. He saw John Rose's black truck sitting in the yard, and that gave him kind of a creepy feeling. He had heard that the Roses had been shot in the truck, before they even had a chance to get out. Ingvie slowed to nearly a stop, looking at the truck, wondering if there would still be blood in it where they had been shot. He heard John Rose had nearly had his head shot off so there would likely have been a real bloody mess. Before seeing the truck, on his way over, Ingvie had thought about taking a look around the place at the buildings and maybe the house where the kid had been killed. He assumed that the place would go up for sale soon, and maybe he could buy it. It sure would be nice.

But now, seeing the truck, Ingvie got a little spooked. Maybe he would look another day. He pulled his pickup next to the Quonset hut, got out, and walked to the big hanging doors. There was something on the edge of the door, dark, like dried blood. Ingvie looked at the door edge, couldn't figure out what it could possibly be, and decided he didn't really care. He wanted his tractor. After pushing the doors open, he stood looking into the dark building, letting his eyes adjust.

There was a pickup parked right behind his tractor. "What the hell?" How was he supposed to get his tractor out? He walked around the truck to the driver's door, looking in the driver's window. About to reach for the door handle to open the truck to see if the keys were in it, he noticed that the handle and the surrounding area was smeared dark red. Ingvie backed away, looking at the truck, wondering if this was the vehicle where the Roses had been shot, and not the black truck. But that didn't seem right. He'd never seen this truck here before, and he knew the kid didn't drive a truck. He looked back at the big hanging door.

And now the memory of the announcement on his radio surfaced. Ingvie moved around behind the truck and squatted, looking at the license plate, trying to remember the numbers and letters they'd broadcast. He stood and looked at the truck again, deciding it certainly could be the truck on the alert. Ingvie walked to his truck and drove home to call.

* * *

"Luke. This is Agent Hunter. Do you remember me?"

"Yeah. What do you want?"

"I want to save your life, Luke."

"What? What are you talking about?"

"Luke, if they haven't already, very soon the Morris police department and the Stevens County sheriff's department will be sending every officer they have to capture you. And they won't be worried about capturing you alive." Ritter didn't respond, but Doc could hear him breathing. "I can get you in safely, but you need to tell me where you are." Nothing. "Luke, did you hear me? Are you OK?"

"I don't feel good."

"You've been shot, Luke. You need a doctor to look at your wound right away."

"That bastard Palmer shot me. Why did he have to shoot me?"

"Luke, you need to give yourself up. Tell me where you are."

"Yeah, I don't think I can do that," said Ritter. "I need to get away."

"There will be no getting away, Luke," Doc said. "You shot a police officer. They will hunt you down and kill you. I guarantee it."

"I don't know. I think I just need to get going."

Ritter disconnected. Doc tried again, but there was no answer. "Shit!"

* * *

Ritter looked at the phone in his hand, watched the call from the agent come up, and then slid the phone back in his pocket. He was thirsty—middle of the summer picking rocks in a field thirsty. Needed water, and more pills. Ritter rolled to his left and screamed, rocketing to a sitting position. His movement had caused the blood-caked towel to rip from his wound. His head went back, eyes closed but tears leaking.

Blood was beginning to flow again from under his makeshift bandage, and he watched the bright threads creep down his arm. He cried out again. Ritter looked at the doorway to the bedroom and knew getting to the kitchen would be a mammoth effort. His first attempt to stand failed. He leaned forward on his second attempt, torso over his knees, and pushed himself up with his right arm. Going forward too quickly, he took a step to catch himself, reaching for the door frame at the same time. With his left arm. He knew as soon as he started to lift the arm that it was a mistake, but he couldn't stop himself. The room seemed to wobble as he yelled.

Ritter switched hands, pushing against the door frame to stay upright. He looked up, past the couch and the door frame into the kitchen. It seemed a mile away. But he worked his way along the couch and into the kitchen, moving to the kitchen chairs for balance, and then to the counter, resting after each step. By the time he was at the sink, he was working hard for each breath, like he had been running sprints at practice for an hour, sweating like it too. He poured a glass of water down his throat. His stomach lurched, but there was nothing to come up. Ritter filled the glass again and then looked at the sink for the ibuprofen he had spilled. The pills were gone. He picked up the bottle and tipped it. Nothing. Ritter looked in the direction of the bathroom. Were there more pills above the sink? He didn't remember.

There was no choice. He had to have more pain pills. Ritter moved his hand to the front of the sink, took a step, and felt something under his bare foot. Looking down, he moved his foot back. A pill. And two others nearby. Ritter picked up the glass of water, turned his back to the counter, and slid down to the floor. He scooted along the cabinet until he could reach the pills, gathered them up, and put them in his mouth. He washed them down with a large sip and then finished the glass, more slowly this time. The water helped, but he held little hope that the pills would have any effect on the blinding pain. He had to get help.

Ritter reached for the phone in his pocket, then stopped. He'd heard something, a noise outside. He crawled across the floor to the kitchen table, pulled himself up to a chair, and stood, leaning on the table. There was a small window facing the driveway. Ritter looked out the window and then turned to look out the screen door. He reached into his pocket, pulled out the phone, and hit the button for the last number.

"Luke?"

"OK, come and get me. I'm at the Roses'. But you better hurry. The cops are already here."

CHAPTER 37

Doc burned it down the highway and over the gravel roads. There was a cop car halfway across the road, a cop leaning against it, just as there had been when he showed up a week earlier. The cop pushed himself into a standing position and raised his arm, but Doc did not slow, swerving around the front of the squad, missing it by inches. He fishtailed dangerously close to the ditch but regained control and gunned it to the Roses' driveway, which was completely blocked by a cop car. Doc slammed on his brakes and leaned out his window, yelling at the cop to move, but the cop shook his head.

Doc jumped out of his car and ran. The cop at the end of the driveway tried to grab him as he went by, but Doc slapped the man's hand away and kept going. The cop took off after him but the man was short, fifteen years older than Doc, and overweight. He was never going to catch Doc. The cop yelled for Doc to stop or he would shoot, but Doc kept running.

Pickus was standing by the Roses' truck with a Morris cop—a sergeant. He ran toward them.

Pickus looked back at the sound of the shouting. "What the hell are you doing here, Hunter?" Pickus asked.

"I'm not here to kill someone like you are, Pickus," said Doc as he caught his breath. He looked at the house and then the yard. There were cops ringing the house, all in combat gear and heavily armed.

"I got a cop killer in there, and I'm going to take him as I see fit. Now you get your ass out of here."

"There's been enough killing, Pickus. He's just a kid," said Doc. "I can talk him out of there."

"How are you going to do that?"

"I told him I'd come and get him out."

Pickus's face went red. "You *what?* You've been in contact with this killer, and you didn't inform me? I ought to shoot you right along with him."

"He trusts me, Pickus. You don't want any more of your people to get hurt, do you? Let me talk to him."

Pickus turned to the cop next to him and then back to Doc. "Fuck you, Hunter. This is my rodeo. Get your ass out of here."

Doc looked at the smaller man and said, "Really? You're really going to make me do it?"

"Do what?"

"For one thing, this is not your rodeo. This became a BCA investigation when I showed up, and as the ranking BCA agent here, I am in charge." Pickus opened his mouth to protest, but Doc held up his hand. "If you don't do as I say, then I will call my boss and let him know that you're impeding my operation. He will then call the governor to let him know, and

I assume you will lose your job and be brought up on charges." Doc thought the little man was about to explode. "What's it going to be, Sheriff?"

Pickus looked down at the ground and then back up at Doc. "You've got ten minutes."

"Good choice, Sheriff," said Doc. "Now, I'm going to walk out in the yard in front of the house and talk Ritter outside. I do not want to be shot, so you will call your army and tell them to stand down. Is that clear?"

Doc was sure Pickus was going to tell him to fuck off again, but the sheriff said, "Fine." He grabbed the Morris cop by the upper arm and led him away toward the Quonset hut. They talked for a second and then both were on their radios. They walked back to Doc.

"Ten minutes, and you are on the clock," Pickus said.

Doc was about to say he'd take all the time he wanted, but he hoped that would be enough and started walking toward the house. He also hoped all the armed men he saw positioned around the house were not going to shoot him. About halfway to the front door, Doc stopped and pulled out his phone.

"Hello," said Ritter.

"I'm here," said Doc. "I'm in the front yard. Can you see me?"

Ritter had been sitting in a kitchen chair, his head seeming to get heavier each minute, now nearly impossible to hold up. He looked through the small window and could only see the cops behind the black truck, but then he looked out the window on the screen door and saw Doc waving. "I see you."

"OK. Now just do what I say. Can you walk?"

"I think so."

"All right. I need you to come out of the house and put

your hands in the air. Come out slowly. Don't have anything in your hands. Have you got that? You need to go slow."

"I have to go slow. It's all I can do. I'm hurt bad."

"OK, we'll get you some help, but you need to come out now."

Ritter looked at Doc in the yard and said, "I'm coming." He disconnected, slid the phone into his pocket, and stepped toward the door.

Doc turned and yelled to Pickus, "He's coming out. Hold your fire." Doc turned back to the house and saw the screen door start to open.

* * *

After every step, Ritter bowed his head and blew out a breath. It took him a long time to reach the screen door. He looked out. The tall BCA agent was there, but he could also see at least three cops, all dressed in black and holding what looked like HK MP5s.

Ritter was having second thoughts. He looked back at the rifle he had brought with him. It was leaning against the stove where he had shot Blake. If he was going to die, maybe he could take out that fat sheriff before he did. The man was just as responsible as Palmer was. Maybe he could just get off one more shot? But as Ritter looked at the rifle, he knew that wasn't going to happen. He didn't have the strength. The agent yelled his name, and he turned to see the man had moved a little closer. He should have made sure that the agent wasn't armed, but maybe it just didn't matter. Ritter leaned on the handle of the door and pushed it open.

***

The screen door banged against the railing on the steps as Ritter practically fell out, grabbing the railing on the opposite side to stop his fall. Doc ducked at the noise and sudden movement, afraid someone would start shooting. Ritter worked his way slowly down the steps. It was evident he was in pain, weak. His left arm and side were bloody. At the bottom of the stairs, Ritter held on to the railing, bent over like an old man who should be using a walker. Finally, he stood upright and looked at Doc with dead eyes.

***

Barbara Ritter was tired of the police refusing to do anything to find her son. She had called his phone a dozen times the day before with no answer, as well as talking to every friend of his she could remember. She called the Thomases, surprised to hear that Zean was also missing. The mothers wondered if the boys hadn't gone off somewhere together. Each promised to call the other if they heard anything.

But Barbara Ritter was not one who could sit. She needed to act. It made no sense to her that her son would leave home without saying anything. She'd checked his room, and as far as she could tell, all of his clothes were still there, along with his video games. Something had happened, she was sure of it. And then a thought hit her. If Luke and Zean had gone off together, Zean would know where Luke was. And even if they weren't together, there was a good chance Zean would know something. She picked up her phone from the kitchen counter and went through her contact list. She had called Zean more than once, looking for Luke. She pressed the icon by Zean Thomas's name. The call went to voicemail, and she left a message. Where could they be? Barbara Ritter decided to try her son one more time.

* * *

Ritter had taken two wobbly steps. He was trying to hold his arms up, but could only get his right hand about up to his shoulder and his left wouldn't go up at all. It was all he could do. The agent was telling him to keep coming, but Ritter didn't think he could go any farther. He was perspiring heavily again and shaking, his head feeling like it would explode at any second. His chin dropped to his chest, too heavy to hold up, and he closed his eyes. He didn't think he could do it.

Ritter had lifted his head again, willing himself to take another step, when he heard the song of his ringtone and felt the buzzing of the phone in his pocket. He dropped his arm and reached into his pocket, pulling it out to see his mother's name on the screen.

* * *

Doc wanted Ritter another few steps from the house. He didn't want him to get spooked, turn, and try to run back inside, sure the cops would open fire on him if he did. He had yelled at Ritter to get both hands up, but the boy either didn't understand or was unable to raise his arms. Based on what Doc could see of him, and his bloody arm and shoulder, he guessed Ritter could no longer move his left arm. Doc looked at the cops on the perimeter with their rifles at their shoulders and considered moving up to Ritter, but that might scare the boy, and it could get

ANGRY SINS

Doc shot.

He had just called again for Ritter to keep coming, when he heard music. What the hell? The sound was coming from Ritter. Time stopped as Ritter dropped his arm and Doc realized what he was doing. The boy's hand slid into his pocket and pulled something out. Doc dropped to the ground, screaming, "No!"

CHAPTER 38

Doc was back at the hospital. He had packed up his room at the Ramada and checked out, stopping at The Windmill on the way and ordering two chocolate shakes to go.

"Thanks, Doc," LeBlanc said. "How'd you know I liked chocolate shakes?"

"I'm a detective."

LeBlanc looked at him. "Ah."

"So, you out of here soon?'

"Tomorrow," said LeBlanc. "And then I go into rehab."

"Rehab? For a little thing like getting shot?"

"Not my idea. It's company policy."

"No shit," Doc said. "For how long?"

"A couple of weeks."

"Nice. Maybe *I* should get shot." Doc grinned.

"You may want to try something else," said LeBlanc. "Trask got you on another case, or is he giving you a few days off?"

"He owes me for this. I believe I might be heading up to Brainerd. There's a golf course that has my name on it."

"Not getting waylaid? What about that reporter, G-L-O-R-I-A?"

Doc had seen the news vans lined up in front of the police station on his way over. He guessed Gloria would be there, but he didn't stop. He also guessed Pickus was giving another press conference about how the town was again safe thanks to him, and he didn't think he could handle listening, especially when he thought about all the people who were dead and all the people left behind with crushed lives that would never be the same. All for a damn football team.

"No. I think I'll pass on that." Doc finished his shake and tossed the cup in the trashcan as Tina popped her head in. Doc smiled at her and turned back to LeBlanc. "Easy on the rehab."

Clouds had moved in from the west, nothing dark or threatening yet, but the sun was gone and there was that feeling in the air like there might be a few drips later on. Doc popped his sunglasses down anyway and walked to his car. He sat with his legs outside while the engine ran, thinking he was tired of living in a hotel, that he wanted to be home. It was nearly two hours to get there, nothing much to see on the way and nothing much to do when he got there. Except golf. As long as the rain held off.

Doc headed north, the clouds thickening, a light sprinkle on his windshield when he pulled into the Wymans' yard. He walked up to the door and knocked. There was no sound, so he knocked again. Doc was reaching for the screen door handle when Eloise Wyman opened the door.

"Mrs. Wyman?" The woman stared up at Doc in a haze,

a cigarette between her fingers. Her eyes were bloodshot, and he could smell the alcohol.

"Yes?"

"Mrs. Wyman, I'm Agent Hunter. I visited you last week and borrowed this book. I wanted to return it."

Wyman leaned forward and stared at the yearbook through the screen before opening the door and taking it from him. She ran her hands over the cover, caressing it. A tear formed on her eyelid as she looked up at Doc. "Did it help?"

"Yes ma'am. Thank you."

"Good." Wyman turned away and shut the door.

Doc headed back south. The clouds got thicker, and there were a few more drops, but the rain seemed reluctant. He drove into the Knudson farm as Rusty Knudson was walking out of the machine shed, wiping his hands on a rag he stuffed into his back pocket.

"Agent Hunter. What can I help you with now?"

"I just came to return your daughter's yearbook," said Doc, holding out the book.

"I can take that. Linda's not here right now. She's working."

"OK. Well, please tell her thanks for me."

Knudson was looking at Doc. He had something to say, but it took a minute to work out how to say it. "So, it was Luke Ritter?"

"Yeah. He's dead, so we'll really never know, but yeah, it was him."

"God. He was just a kid."

"Yeah, just a kid." A large drop of rain hit Knudson on the head and then one hit Doc, and they looked up at the sky. "I better get going."

Doc sat in his car for a moment listening to the increasing rain hit his roof while he watched it run down his windshield. The sound echoed in the car, a hollow, lonely sound. Doc reached for the start button but then stopped and picked up the phone from the passenger seat. He checked the weather radar to see most of the state was going to be wet for a good portion of what remained of the day and then tapped another icon.

"It's me. Doc. It's raining here and it's making me sad. Do you mind if I stop by?"

"Why does it make you sad?" said Hailey Draper.

"I've got the rest of the day off and I can't go golfing."

"Well, I guess it would be cruel of me to say no, so you'd better come on over."

Thanks for reading ANGRY SINS, the first book in the Doc Hunter Murder Mystery series. You can find links to my other books and a little about me at www.cenelsonbooks.com. If you'd like to join my mailing list just put your email in the pop-up. (I will never share your email with anyone.) You'll get a ***FREE STORY*** and be first to know about new releases, special offers, and an occasional tidbit beyond what's on the web site. And if you enjoyed this book, please leave a brief review on Amazon. Just click on the link http://www.amazon.com/revire/create-review?&asin= B083F5CBY6. (You will need to log in.)

    Thanks!
    C.E. Nelson

Made in United States
North Haven, CT
20 September 2024